Ans	_____	M.L.	_____
ASH	_____	MLW	_____
Bev	_____	Mt.Pl	_____
C.C.	_____	NLM	_____
C.P.	_____	Ott	_____
Dick	_____	PC	2/08 _____
DRZ	_____	PH	_____
ECH	_____	P.P.	_____
ECS	_____	Pion.P.	_____
Gar	2/08 (Funk)	Q.A.	_____
GRM	_____	Riv	_____
GSP	_____	RPP	_____
G.V.	_____	Ross	_____
Har	_____	S.C.	_____
JPCP	_____	St.A.	_____
KEN	_____	St.J	_____
K.L.	_____	St.Joa	_____
K.M.	_____	St.M.	_____
L.H.	5/09	Sgt	_____
LO	_____	T.H.	4/08 _____
Lyn	_____	TLLO	_____
L.V.	_____	T.M.	_____
McC	_____	T.T.	12/08
McG	_____	Ven	_____
McQ	12/07 (Fleming)	Vets	_____
MIL	_____	VP	_____
	_____	Wat	_____
	_____	Wed	_____
	_____	WIL	_____
	_____	W.L.	_____

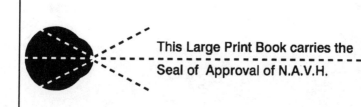

This Large Print Book carries the
Seal of Approval of N.A.V.H.

GOURDFELLAS

MAGGIE BRUCE

WHEELER PUBLISHING

An imprint of Thomson Gale, a part of The Thomson Corporation

Detroit • New York • San Francisco • New Haven, Conn. • Waterville, Maine • London

LIBRARY OF CONGRESS CATALOGING-IN-PUBLICATION DATA

Bruce, Maggie.
   Gourdfellas / by Maggie Bruce.
       p. cm. — (A gourd craft mystery) (Wheeler Publishing large print cozy mystery)
   ISBN-13: 978-1-59722-562-5 (pbk. : alk. paper)
   ISBN-10: 1-59722-562-2 (pbk. : alk. paper)
       1. Gourd craft — Fiction. 2. Handicraft — Fiction. 3. Artisans — Fiction.
   4. Casinos — Fiction. 5. New York (State) — Fiction. 6. Large type books.
   I. Title.
PS3602.R8325G679 2007
813'.6—dc22   2007014650

Published in 2007 by arrangement with The Berkley Publishing Group, a member of Penguin Group (USA) Inc.

Printed in the United States of America on permanent paper
10 9 8 7 6 5 4 3 2 1

For Bruce and Mark and Jeremy,
forever my guys.

ACKNOWLEDGMENTS

My writing life wouldn't be the same without the feedback I get from Judy Greber, Triss Stein, Jane Olsen, and Meredith Cole. I'm grateful for their perceptive comments, the kindness with which they were delivered, and the camaraderie of sharing manuscripts and laughter, with some good political rants thrown in for good measure.

My gourding life has blossomed thanks to Dyan Mai Peterson, Bob and Kathy James, Joy Jackson, and all the dedicated gourders I've met at shows and festivals and online. What a great and generous community you all make up!

My life has been enriched by so many wonderful, loving people that I can't even start to name each of them, or these acknowledgments would become a novella. Still, I need to thank Irving Weiss, Karen Bozdech, Steven and Debra Weiss, Ken Wallace, Ben Davis, Anita and David Orlow,

Lynn and Michael Hassan, Maria Nardone, Jan Roth, Nancy Gallagher, my friends at Gilda's, and the Gogs — Judy, Margaret, Sue, Lia, Linda, and Nancy — for the love and support that has helped get me through some interesting (as the Chinese saying goes) times.

Most of all, even though the book is dedicated to them, I thank my guys — Bruce, Mark, and Jeremy — for all the ways you've shown your love, and for letting me love you with all my heart and soul.

CHAPTER 1

Sometimes you get an early warning signal. You sense that the placid surface of your life is about to be disturbed by a storm. Maybe it takes a while for the pressure to build enough for you to recognize that you'll have to spend enormous time and energy to return things to their proper places. I knew something was wrong as soon as my friend Nora got into my car.

She didn't look at me, didn't start chattering about her son Scooter, didn't kiss my cheek in a spontaneous burst of affection. Maybe she was simply distracted, but I had the sense that something was bothering her in a deeper place. I offered a silent prayer that whatever it was could be chalked up to a bad day. My already overloaded life — clients with freelance writing work they wanted done yesterday; a juried art show for which I needed to have twelve new pieces ready next week; once a week sessions as a volunteer mediator — had me scheduled to the nanosecond. Good, bad, or neutral, I couldn't cram another thing into my life.

Except, here I was on my way to a town meeting to hear arguments for and against allowing a casino to be built outside of Walden Corners, New York, population 3,245.

"Where's Susan?" I asked. Susan Clemants, who got up at five and then taught sixteen-year-olds about the industrial age all day, hated driving after dark. "I thought she was coming with us."

Nora buckled her seatbelt and turned to me, her light brown skin glistening with a sheen from the mist that had turned the April evening diaphanous with fog. I switched to low beams as I backed my blue Subaru out of her driveway.

"She's driving herself to the meeting." Nora sounded troubled, her voice tentative. "Said she felt as though she needed to be on her own. That she was tired of arguing with the rest of us and upset because we didn't get it. I don't like this whole casino question, Lili. Who ever thought it would cause so much trouble?"

Susan had been adamant. A casino would provide reparations to Native Americans for centuries of injustice. She didn't want to hear about how much it would change everyday life — which was exactly what concerned many of us.

"I know. But she's entitled to her own opinion, right?" I groaned and glanced at the clock on the dash. We would just about make it in time for the town council meeting, scheduled to start promptly at seven. "I hope she's not really serious about not coming with us. I disagree with her but so what? We're friends. We're grown-ups. Don't you think she's overreacting?"

"Elizabeth phoned her." This time, Nora's voice was barely audible. "She stomped up one side and down the other of poor Susan. Said Susan would be singing a different tune when some lowlife ended up peeing in her front yard at three in the morning after the casino plied him with drinks to keep him at the tables. Said that if Susan wanted to save the world that was her business but a lot of other people had worked too hard all their lives to build a community here. And they weren't ready to give it up to satisfy either greed or guilt."

"Sometimes, Elizabeth just likes to push people's buttons. I mean, she's an attorney. She loves arguing." I still had moments of wariness around Elizabeth, whose sharp tongue and quick mind served her better in

11

court than it did around a dinner table.

"So does Susan. At least about this casino thing. I still can't believe what she said to me."

I glanced away from the road to see whether Nora's face was as troubled as her voice. She bit her lower lip and shook her head, her gaze fixed on her knees.

"Nora?" I said as gently as I could.

She lifted her head. "Susan said, 'Of all people, you should be thinking about justice. I'm sure your daddy would have been on the side of the oppressed.' Can you believe it? Now all black people have to support the casino. We've been friends since third grade, but that's the first time Susan ever told me I wasn't black enough for her white liberal self."

Maybe it *was* possible for friendships to get lost in a swirl of politics and misunderstanding, but I didn't want to believe that about this group. Nora Johnson, Elizabeth Conklin, Susan Clemants, and Melissa Paul had been sharing the triumphs and challenges of their lives since grade school. Allowing me into their circle six months after I moved to Walden Corners from Brooklyn was one of the things that made my life full and rich. I didn't want an argument about a casino to jeopardize the monthly poker games that I'd come to count on for good company and the occasional ten dollar win.

"I don't know what to say, Nora. Isn't Susan allowed to have a difference of opinion without being judged by her friends? She wasn't being intentionally mean and she sure wasn't being selfish. She's not the only who feels that the casino is a pretty good way to make up for social and economic injustice. Nathaniel Bartle said it loud and clear at the very first meeting."

Nathaniel and Susan *did* have a point, as did the people touting the economic advantages of bringing in the casino. But that was one side. The arguments on the other side, about safety and preserving the nature of the community, made a lot of sense, too. I'd begun to feel like a shuttlecock in a game of opinion-badminton. This casino business had turned the political into something personal.

In a few weeks, the community would vote on the issue — but meanwhile the rationality factor seemed to drop as the emotional factor went way up. Homeowners put up signs supporting the casino, and those signs disappeared in the middle of the night. Graffiti, not quite nasty but still unsettling, was scrawled across the wall of a store whose owner opposed the casino. Discussions in the diner and in shops all over town started at a decibel level usually reserved for talking back to the television news or scolding misbehaving dogs.

I flipped my directional signal and turned into town, joining the line of cars that snaked their way up the hill toward the Walden High School parking lot. From the look of things, everyone within twenty miles of town had something to say about this casino.

I didn't know the man standing at the front of the stage, but I feared for his health.

His face, pale when he'd started to address the noisy crowd, had grown so red that I worried about burst blood vessels. His eyes bulged, and a geyser of fury erupted in a sibilant explosion from his thin mouth.

"Sin and salaciousness! Steal your money, sure, but casinos steal the soul of a place. Sorrow and sickness, that's what's in store!" A thick fist pounded the podium, rattling the microphone. His entire body trembled with righteous fury as his exhortation spilled over the packed auditorium of Walden High School.

I ducked, not wanting to get splattered with all that anger and alliteration. Melissa

Paul, owner of the Taconic Inn, rubbed her toes and suppressed a giggle.

"A little over the top, but he's right," Nora whispered into my left ear. "You want to lose your money, go to Atlantic City. Don't mess with my town."

Elizabeth Conklin, seated on the other side of Nora, clenched her jaw. "And definitely don't preach at me as though you've heard The Word," she said.

Ira Jackson, a small, pinched man with a small, pinched mind, who just happened to own the land on which the casino was to be built, sprang from his seat two rows in front of us. "That's a pile of horse manure. You all have any better idea how to pay for the roads and the schools around here? You done something lately to make jobs for the farmers run off their land by the corporations? You gonna donate a new wing for the county hospital? We need that damn casino, that's all!"

Heads turned toward his reedy voice, and a tornado of shouts swirled through the room.

"It's someone else's time to speak. Sit down, Mr. Jackson!" Joseph Trent, the town council member who was chairing the meeting, tapped on the microphone.

"No casino in my town!" another voice

15

shouted.

A compact, open-faced woman whose pixie haircut made her blue eyes seem huge, took the microphone from Trent's hand and said, "Would you all calm down? This meeting is for the council to find out what the citizens of our town think about this damn casino. I want my voice to be heard. I'll do whatever I can to keep Walden Corners just as it is, but we have to follow procedure. If you have something to say, sign up to speak, don't —"

"We need jobs!" someone shouted from the back.

"Who was that?" I asked. "I thought she was going to turn things around for a second there."

Nora said, "Trisha Stern. She's lived up here for about three years. A physical therapist. This is getting way out of hand."

"Order! Order!" Joseph Trent yelled into the mike, pounding a gavel on the table in front of him and glaring over the top of his glasses. "The chair recognizes Marjorie Mellon."

The scheduled speakers, lined up in the center aisle, shifted forward as Marjorie headed to the stage. A stubby man in a denim jacket and battered John Deere cap moved to the front of the line. Susan Clemants and her red tresses followed right behind him. I glanced over at Elizabeth, who appeared to be looking at everything in the auditorium except Susan.

The crowd continued to hurl shouts as a string bean of a woman jogged to the microphone, her gray curls bobbing and her dark eyes focused straight ahead. Where was the civility, the due process, the tolerance for other points of view? This roomful of ordinarily respectable — and respectful — citizens was behaving like a mob driven by bloodlust. I half expected to see Sydney Carton kneeling in front of the guillotine as the crowd cheered.

"When other people spoke, I was quiet. Now I want you to give me my two minutes." Marjorie's back was erect and her face stern. "I may be a cleaning woman, but I know a thing or two about business around here."

As she paused and scanned the crowd, I looked around too. Marjorie ran the only commercial cleaning service in town, which meant that the business climate in Walden Corners was of great importance to her.

"I know we need to build a new wing on the elementary school and buy two new snowplows. We need some kind of recreation center so that our children have something to do besides playing around with drugs and each other. Our police force has three computers that break down every other day and two cruisers with over one hundred thousand miles on them. The tax base of Walden Corners won't even support those crucial things. Plus, with the cost of natural gas going out of sight, you all are going to have to send your kids to school in their parkas and mittens because where we'll find the money to cover the heating bills is a big mystery. So one alternative for paying for these essentials is to raise the taxes of every single citizen in this town."

Now Marjorie was the one who sounded like a preacher, but a call of yeses and a reply of hisses were the only responses to her sermon. I'd just paid the second installment of my annual property tax, and it shocked me to realize that it had taken me three weeks of hard work to earn that money. I was one of the lucky ones, with training and skills and enough energy to scramble for work that allowed me to make more than the minimum wage — usually.

"Nope, didn't think you'd like that. So the other way is to let this one casino come in, and bring jobs and tourist money and new revenues. We can put clauses in the agreement to make sure it stays respectable and we can solve our money problems for years to come. Or we can raise property taxes. Pretty simple decision, I'd say." Marjorie straightened her spine and leaned over the podium, making eye contact with key members of the crowd. Her pause was almost past the point of dramatic emphasis when she boomed, "I invite anyone who agrees with my way of thinking to join me in forming a consortium to make sure we get what we need around here. And what we need is that casino."

A roar, whether in agreement or disapproval, filled the room.

"Like I need a cow with two heads!" a voice called from the rear.

"We have to keep this meeting orderly." Bespectacled Joseph Trent spoke with surprising vigor. I'd only seen him in his day job behind the prescription counter at Trent Pharmacy, where he sported a perpetually worried look and a mild manner. "You want a civilized town, you have to behave civilly to each other."

A woman two rows from the stage looked ready to leap over the seats and commandeer the mike. She shouted, "We need to keep our town safe. No gambling, no whores, no —"

A gabble of voices drowned her out and

bodies blocked her way. People were on their feet, surging forward, placards bobbing dangerously close to heads and limbs. How had a town meeting about Oneida Gaming's plan to build a casino turned into this cacophony of greed and guilt? From my spot near the far left aisle I felt my own anger grow. This wasn't why I moved from Brooklyn to a small town one hundred miles to the north.

"I need some fresh air, you know, to clear my head," I said. "If I don't come back inside, I'll wait for you at the car."

Nora shook her head. "You go ahead. Melissa can drive me home. I'll talk to you tomorrow."

I shouldered my way past three overall-clad women and pushed toward the side exit. But knots of people, jabbering and poking each other in the chest as though that would make their point, made forward progress impossible. I felt like Sisyphus, only instead of rolling a rock up the hill I was trying to roll myself.

"Hey, Lili, take a lesson from the martial arts. Resistance doesn't work." Seth Selinsky pressed his hand against the small of my back, turning me the way a tug turns a loaded ship. The swell of people pushed us toward the stage. Elbows and fingers and, once, a sharp-cornered pocketbook worthy of the Queen, jabbed various soft places on my body. When the crowd thinned, Seth took my hand and drew me past four laughing teens up the steps to the stage. Before I knew it, we were pushing through a heavy metal door and into the quiet of the parking lot.

"Go with the flow — isn't that a karate principle? Anyway, it worked this time. Thanks, Seth." Even in the dark, his eyes seemed to gleam, but I couldn't tell whether it was pleasure, mischief, or a simple biological reaction to the absence of light.

"You going with the flow on the casino?" He sounded curious. We'd been to dinner the Saturday before but we hadn't talked about the casino. As we walked through the ranks of parked cars, his shoulder brushed against mine. I moved away, still on edge after being in the middle of an unpredictable crowd. He was a single man who made a better than good living as a mortgage broker, and his livelihood depended on city people wanting to move to the southern half of Columbia County. It seemed a fair guess that he'd oppose the casino. We'd gone out at least a dozen times, but hormones and politics didn't seem like a good mix.

"I'm a NIMBY on this one. I don't want

to wake up one morning and find that I gave up the energy and diversity of Brooklyn for a garish, late-night, traffic-generating magnet for sleazebags and desperados."

His laugh was one of the things I liked best about Seth. "Not In Marino's Back Yard, eh? Listen, I've got to go to Philadelphia next weekend to a mortgage products seminar. Deadly dull but there's a Picasso exhibit at the museum that I plan to see even if I have to play hooky to do it. If you'd like to join me, I'd love the company."

"Thanks, but I've got a gallery opening in New Hampshire." Saying yes would have been a nice but problematic complication, ushering in a new era of weekends away, which might lead to shared vacations and who knew what else. I wasn't ready for *maybe never* either, so I was relieved to have a valid reason to decline.

Seth's smile might have been a dodged-the-bullet expression that mirrored my own relief, or simple cordiality. He took two steps toward me with The Look on his face, but before he could take me into his arms, shouts churned the warm spring night. I looked over my shoulder to see several dozen people in the rectangle of light spilling from the open doorway. Had the meeting ended already? They were only up to the eighth speaker, with ten more on the list and scores more who would try to get their sixty seconds of airtime before the mandatory ten o'clock end of the session.

"Something's wrong," Seth said, as the wail of a siren got louder and the twin high beams of a county emergency vehicle split the darkness. He started toward the building at a lope and picked up speed. I ran behind him.

The ambulance screeched to a halt at the open doorway. A tall man carrying a large plastic box and a shorter guy wielding a walkie-talkie hopped down and waded into the noisy crowd. When the cluster of onlookers stepped aside to let the two men pass, I saw Susan Clemants, sitting on the curb and holding a bloodstained handkerchief to her forehead.

Glad for my subway rush hour training, I pushed past several people to get closer to Susan. Except for the dark streak of blood that trickled toward her eye and the vacant, glazed look on her pale face, she appeared to be unhurt. Kneeling, I restrained my impulse to touch her shoulder or stroke her hair or otherwise comfort her and let the taller EMT poke and prod and check her out, while the shorter one, a sandy-haired blond boy I'd seen around town, held the crowd back.

"Susan, it's me, Lili. The paramedics are going to take care of you. Is there anything you need? Jack's still away on his fishing trip, right?"

Her pale lips parted, but before she could say anything, her eyelids fluttered and her body went slack.

CHAPTER 2

Country hospitals are quiet. Oddly, people smile less than they did in Brooklyn. A ponytailed doctor with pretty blue eyes bent over a now-awake Susan, probed at the raw wound, then frowned as she waited for an answer.

Susan's color had returned along with her consciousness. "No, I don't know what hit my head. All I know is I was getting off the stage after I spoke. This thing came flying from somewhere to my left. And when it hit me, it hurt like hell."

"Looks like it was probably a rock," the doctor said softly. "There's grit in there and I have to get it out. I'm going to numb it and then muck around until it's clean. It'll take ten, twelve stitches, but I know how to sew a fine seam. If you manage the wound care properly, it won't get infected. So, you okay with me going ahead?"

Susan nodded, grabbed my hand, and

held tight for the twenty minute procedure. I averted my eyes and let my mind drift. I'd followed behind the ambulance in my car and navigated the bustle of the ER in that state I call essential reality. Only Susan and her needs existed. Now that the doctor was taking care of her, I had the mental space to wonder about what had happened in that packed auditorium in the few minutes after Seth and I left.

A rock had been thrown. The tactic brought to mind thirteen-year-old boys whose frustrations had reached desperation levels in a dates-and-oil exporting country. It wasn't the kind of behavior I expected from members of this small, congenial community.

Susan had expressed what turned out to be the minority opinion — that the casino was a morally righteous project that should be endorsed by the town in the name of justice. Nora said she'd called it a reparation. Didn't that come from the word repair? What would it take to repair the friendships that were close to shredding over this issue? Nora, Elizabeth, Melissa, and Susan had helped each other flourish in the rich Walden Corners soil. I'd read lately about how marigolds and tomatoes, planted near each other, made for a healthier garden. But my friends were behaving more like dill and carrots, natural enemies that interfered with the other's ability to reach its true potential.

"What's funny?" Susan said in a constricted voice.

The doctor murmured an apology and swabbed her forehead with more clear liquid.

I must have laughed out loud without realizing it. I had slipped so easily into country metaphors, replacing all the real-estate figures of speech that had been my native tongue when I lived in Brooklyn.

"I was just thinking about marigolds and tomatoes and dill and carrots. You feeling better? You sure look better." Except for the Herman Munster zipper that would grace her forehead for a while, she did seem almost like herself again.

"Thanks for staying with me, Lili. I guess what hurts even more than my head is that they all disappeared. Melissa, Elizabeth, even Nora. At least, that's the way it seemed."

"They were probably stuck in the crowd somewhere," I said, only half believing myself. "I'm sure they wouldn't let a difference of opinion cancel out more than twenty-five years of friendship."

Susan's silence spoke volumes.

By the time I'd driven Susan home, helped her undress, and waited while she left a message at school saying that she wouldn't be in in the morning, I felt lightheaded, my energy gone. But I still had to drive twelve miles on two-lane country roads and not hit any stray cows that had wandered onto the road in search of bovine companionship. I'd ridden the subway to my parents' house in Brooklyn in this state countless nights after long talk sessions following a City College philosophy seminar or after tedious, noisy parties that were meant to prove that we were smart, accomplished, and desirable. That took a different kind of concentration, one that assessed the eyes and the body language of other riders.

This took being able to see in the dark.

After a little more than a year of living in the country, eight miles from the town of Walden Corners and far enough from my old life to feel excited, still, by the possibilities of a new start, the beacon of my front porch light had the power to give me a floaty, happy feeling. I parked and stood in the darkness, enjoying the sound of the peepers. How friendly, how peaceful. An hour with a book and I'd call it a night.

Sheltered by the sky, covered by the stars, nourished by the scent of green, new life . . . this was what I'd sought. I wrapped myself in my *bono fortuna* and walked up the back stairs, feeling lighter, happier. The comfort of my own small space — big enough for me, with its fifteen-by-fifteen foot living room with a wall of built-in bookshelves and a fireplace, three snug bedrooms, and a kitchen with enough elbow room for four friends to kibbitz shoulder-to-shoulder while I cooked — colored everything with hope, and I felt some of my worry wash away. Perhaps the fight over the casino could be transformed into a teachable moment about how to resolve differences without destroying relationships.

As a volunteer community mediator, I understood that process. It worked well in a small room with an impartial facilitator. People walked in with a set of demands and, hopefully, walked out with an understanding that settling their dispute would let them put all that energy to other, better uses. No way would I get in the middle, though, with these four women. They'd get around to talking eventually, but they weren't ready, not yet.

I kicked off my shoes and stared at the blinking message machine in the kitchen.

No more trouble, I pleaded silently, not tonight.

I wasn't enough of a math whiz to calculate the odds that all four messages were cheery greetings or even obnoxious sales pitches from adenoidal telemarketers trying to pay the rent by selling Flex-o-rama Workout Shorts. I hit the play button and started unloading the dish drain. Melissa, calling five minutes after I'd left to remind me about the meeting. A hang-up. A Ms. Janeway, heavy on the Mizz, inquiring about my schedule and the possibility of my writing a manual for new employees for her hotel in Boston. And then my brother's voice, exultant, excited.

"Call me. Doesn't matter how late. Just call me," he said.

As I dialed, I wished I had a bottle of champagne waiting in the refrigerator so that I could pop the cork as Neil answered the phone. I would give him the chance to say it, but I knew exactly what his message meant. He picked up after the first ring.

"Port St. Lucie, here I come! Yahooo!!!" Dance music and loud voices in the background forced him to shout, and I pictured a crowd of happy, sweaty celebrants bumping hips, cheering my brother's good fortune.

"You better get me some good seats. I'm not driving all the way to Shea Stadium just to sit in the nosebleed bleachers." My laughter was unexpected, and I just let it roll out until I could breathe again. "Shortstop or second base? Oh, Neil, that's so great. I'm so excited. I can't stand it, this is so —"

"Second base. Just for now. They promised me shortstop within two years. Dreams come true, Lili. Hold on. I feel another one coming on." The only sound I heard was the raucous noise in the background. After a second his "Yahoo!" split the air.

I yahooed with him, holding back the questions. There would be time for details — when he had to leave, the length of the contract, what his agent's cut would be. For now, after three years in the minor leagues and a lifetime of preparation, my brother was finally going to live a dream that had sustained him since he was five years old. He would play baseball for the Mets.

"Mom's already all worried about can I take care of myself on the road, and all the women who'll be swarming me just to get near the glamour and the money. She's gonna drive me nuts, I swear."

"Not tonight — don't let anyone spoil tonight. I'm sending huge hugs, Neil. And

31

raising a glass to your success. I am so happy I can hardly stand it. Go back to your celebration."

"I love you, Lili. Talk to you tomorrow."

I guess that's how the universe maintains equilibrium. One Neil triumph cancels out one Susan disaster.

After a night of tossing and checking the clock every half hour, the sound of rain on my tin roof made me want to reach for a book and spend the morning with it propped on my knees as a cup of tea cooled on my bedside table. I managed the fantasy for about half an hour, but by seven I roused myself and stood under tepid water, washing away the lethargy and preparing for another busy day. Breakfast, a brisk walk with my umbrella keeping everything but my shoes and socks dry, and then two hours at the computer working on a brochure for a luxury spa finished off the morning.

I called Susan, got no answer, and hoped that meant that she was feeling well enough to use her time off to run some errands.

I'd been good, had earned time in my gourd studio, transformed from the third bedroom into a space filled with tools, brushes, embellishments, and shelves and shelves of gourds. Entering that space always made my heart beat a little faster. When I first told my Brooklyn friend Karen Gerber about decorated gourds, the pink-tipped spikes of her brown hair seemed to stand up even straighter.

"You've gone cuckoo over a *vegetable?*" she'd said. "I thought I could trust you out of my sight for a couple of weeks. Why didn't you go to St. Barth's or Martha's Vineyard or even, God forbid, a Hampton on your vacation? But no, you disappeared into the wilds of West Virginia and Kentucky and North Carolina. And came back a changed woman."

"I still love good cheese and I read the book review section of the Sunday *Times* first. I like to sit around with my friends and dish. And I will always love walking down Fifth Avenue when there's a foot of snow on the ground. What do you know about gourds, anyway? Ever meet one? They're really magical."

A *whatever* sigh wafted across the booth of our favorite Brooklyn diner. Even after I showed her a gourd I'd bought, a hard-shelled kettle gourd with a Native American design pyrographed on its round belly, she merely cocked one of her thick brows.

"Look at these colors," I said, running my finger over the translucent richness of the rust, green, and chestnut hues of the designs. "You know, no two gourds are exactly alike. A natural canvas, that's what they are. And unique."

"Very unique," she said, laughing at our longstanding language joke.

"Extremely unique," I answered.

But other people, at fine craft fairs all over the country, did get it, and after three years my gourds were being accepted into juried shows and were selling to collectors. The twelve gourds I was driving up to a New Hampshire gallery on the weekend, a new series featuring designs based on African textiles and colored to approximate the muted tones of natural dyes, sat on a shelf awaiting their bubble wrap protection. The long-necked dipper that I'd been yearning to start rested on my work table, gleaming in the overhead light.

Dipper gourds, used for decades in the South. Huge kettle gourds that held grain in Central America. Gourds with skins fixed tight to make drums in Africa and Polynesia. When I picked up one of these humble vegetables, I felt a kinship that transcended time and geography, a connection to people I'd never met but who had the same appreciation of friends and family, of the land and its bounty.

If Karen could hear my thoughts she'd roll her eyes and proclaim me sappy. I smiled as I cupped the rounded bottom of the dipper gourd in my hand and turned it to see all its bumps and markings. Vines, that's what it needed, twining up the graceful neck and joining at the top. I marked two long curves, selected a stylus for my pyrography tool, flipped on its transformer, and pulled on my respirator mask. Beyond sappy, she'd say, but Karen wasn't here to watch as I closed my eyes and said my version of a prayer of thanks for the gourd and for my part in transforming it.

Still in that peaceful state, I reached for the gourd. And was nearly startled out of my chair by the shrill of the telephone. My first impulse was to ignore it, but I thought about Susan, alone, maybe even afraid. I reached for the receiver.

"Lili? Hi, it's Connie Lovett. I've been knocking on your door but I guess you didn't hear me."

Her graciousness and that trace of Southern drawl kept the accusation out of her voice, but a flush of guilt crept up my cheeks. Tuesday. Today was Tuesday, my regular appointment teaching her how to work with gourds.

"I'm so sorry, Connie," I said as I walked

through the hall toward the kitchen. "I must have been lost in gourd space again."

By the time I'd finished my sentence, I was pulling open the door. The rain had stopped and the sun shone brightly behind Connie. She looked good today, for someone undergoing chemotherapy for cancer. The treatments had turned this beautiful, energetic woman with snapping dark eyes and the clearest porcelain skin into a pale but brave version of herself. She stepped inside, gave me a quick hug, and adjusted the bright blue scarf that covered her head.

"Well, you're here, and I'm glad. I'm so excited I could hardly eat my breakfast. Can we start? I don't want to take up our time chatting when I could be learning."

She seldom spoke about her illness these days. We'd met the summer before, when we both reached for the same watermelon at a farm stand outside of Hudson. One laugh led to another, and Connie and I started meeting at The Creamery for coffee and conversation most Thursday afternoons. A social worker with cases all over lower Columbia County, Connie had to learn how to treat herself with the same care she offered to her clients after she got her diagnosis in February. "Just be my friend," she'd said after I asked her how I could help.

"Don't treat me like a sick person."

I'd honored those boundaries she'd established, shutting off the questions and the sympathy she clearly didn't want.

"Then I guess you're ready to cut your first gourd," I said as she followed me down the narrow hall to the studio.

"Can't wait! I've been dreaming designs, and I've started a scrapbook to collect ideas. I'm so excited about this." She stopped in the doorway and shook her head. "I hear you were with Susan at the hospital."

"Doc says she'll be fine. I still can't believe that anyone would think that you can get what you want by hurting someone who disagrees with you."

"All that person wanted," Connie said quietly, "was to lash out at someone. The casino — that's not what it was about. The person who hurt her was angry in his heart. I want the casino to be defeated, but I wouldn't get physical about it."

"You're right. Listen, let's forget all that for a while. Pick your gourd, Connie. Any one. Look. Touch. Smell. Whatever moves you to choose one of these babies."

"Oh, Lili, this is like my birthday and Christmas, but better because I don't have to write thank you notes afterward." Her eyes shone with pleasure as she moved from shelf to shelf, a tentative hand exploring the surface of one, then another gourd. When she picked a medium-sized pear-shaped gourd, her face glowed with pleasure.

"I know," she said happily. "The first lesson is cutting a straight rim. I can't wait to make waves and —"

"Straight cuts this time. First you have to decide where you want the cut to be."

I watched as she looked intently at the bumps and the coloring, turned the gourd, set it on the work table and knelt until it was at her eye level. Then she touched it about two-thirds of the way from the base.

"Great, now set the gourd on the table and then make a stack of books at the height of the cut. That's where you'll rest the pencil, and then you turn the gourd against the pencil, and voila! A perfect, even, straight rim."

Laughing, Connie followed my instructions. I showed her how to adjust the respirator mask so that it was snug yet comfortable, then demonstrated how to make a starting cut with the Exacto knife and how to control the small jigsaw.

"But you'd better tuck your scarf in," I said, pointing to the dangling ends of bright blue cotton that hung over her shoulder.

In response, she pulled the covering from

her head. "Nobody else but Mel has seen me like this."

I smiled and pushed back the lump in my throat so that I could say, "Well, you look gorgeous. I mean it. Your eyes stand out and your head's such a lovely shape, and those earrings are the perfect touch. You'd captivate presidents and rock stars just the way you are. But now let's captivate this gourd, okay?"

For an hour we lost ourselves in the concentration of work. She cut the rim, scraped out dried fibers, sanded the inside with a focus that I'm sure she used to bring to her clients.

"Oh, dear, I have to run, Lili. Doctor Axelrod gets so busy. I hate to screw up his schedule." She grabbed her scarf from the chair and deftly wrapped it around her head.

If I didn't know her, I might have missed the fleeting expression of apprehension that flickered across Connie's face, replaced by a crooked smile.

"Did I tell you?" she said. "No more endless chemo drip, at least for a while. We've started something new. A pill, can you believe it? This one sounds good."

"Fingers crossed, Connie. See you next week." I squeezed her shoulder and walked to the door with her, watched as she got into her car and waved before she drove off.

These Tuesday sessions were going to be harder on me than I'd anticipated. I wanted to give her the respite she craved. I wanted to hug her tight and keep her safe.

CHAPTER 3

The daffodils were a surprise. First three, then nine, and finally hundreds of them appeared in clusters around the three acres on which my cottage sat. I wondered whether Tom Ford, the mutual fund manager who had paid me for a huge corporate writing job by transferring ownership of the house and its three acres to me, was the person responsible for such a glory of sunshine. As I walked the edges of my yard with my afternoon cup of Earl Grey, I pictured him wearing a pair of worn jeans and a soft flannel shirt, sandy hair held back by a baseball cap as he bent over, trowel in hand, preparing the earth and then setting each bulb in its damp, earthen nest.

But of course that wasn't an accurate picture. Or, if it was, I had no way of knowing that. Never having met the man despite endless telephone and computer communications, having seen no pictures of him, knowing not one single person who had ever been in his presence, I could only conjure fantasies. Lately, I realized that each new imagined version had much less to do with Tom than it did with what was bothering me, or intriguing me, or exciting me on any given day.

This afternoon it was the profusion of daffodils. The sky still glittered with the hard blue of winter and the clouds had sharp edges. Even the light felt cold until it landed on the daffodils and their cheery yellow. They were a declaration of possibilities, and they pushed away thoughts of the casino, of Connie, of Susan for a while.

But my mind didn't stay quiet for long. Sometimes it felt as though I'd traded too much to do in Brooklyn for too much to do in Walden Corners. The parts of my new life were beginning to add up to more than one whole. I surely couldn't add one more thing, but what could I give up?

Certainly not my gourd work — the joy of learning new techniques, of figuring out what images and colors and shapes and textures I wanted to explore. Not the friendships, first with Nora, and then with Susan, Melissa, and even, after a rough start, Elizabeth. I couldn't pay my bills without the freelance writing jobs. Seth? Give up the man who cooked for me a couple of times in the past six months and loved the same music I did, and surprised me with the intensity of his feelings about the travesty of CEOs who made thousands of times the salary than the workers? Not yet. Surely not my once a week sessions as a volunteer mediator, which satisfied a deep need to help others and do something that took me totally outside of my own musings. Not teaching Connie.

And not my thirty minute daily walks. They'd led to the unexpected bonus of discovering the yearly cycle of nature. I was stopping not only to smell the roses, but to watch the daffodils go from tight green buds to this profusion of happiness.

This afternoon, I didn't have much time to contemplate nature. I had a mediation case scheduled at three, and I had to leave in ten minutes. I combed my hair, checked that my sweater didn't have any rips or stains, and was about to leave for Hudson when the phone rang.

"Lili?"

My mother sounded anxious. I immediately thought about my father and his Parkinson's disease. He had learned to live with the shaking, but was still terrified of the occasional episodes when he froze, unable to move or even speak. "Yes, Mom. What's wrong?"

"Neil."

A relieved laugh escaped before I said, "Mom, I know he's going to be on the road a lot, but this is his dream. Let him enjoy it in peace. He's wanted to play for the Mets since —"

"He's in the hospital."

The room did a wavery spin, and I leaned against the wall for support. "He's going to be all right?"

Her silence gave me too much time to imagine awful things. Finally, she said, "Yes. If you mean will he live, and will he have all his faculties. But he's got a compound fracture of his tibia."

"Damn." I should be grateful that my brother was alive. Instead, I was furious. I resisted the impulse to slam the receiver down and go back out and wander among the daffodils. "What happened?"

"He was so happy, Lili. He came over to say good-bye. Brought his two big bags to the apartment, and then he ate a tuna fish and lettuce and tomato sandwich, brushed his teeth, hugged me and promised to hit a home run his first game for me. He didn't want me to come downstairs, so I watched from the window. Next thing I knew, some doctor was on the phone. I can't stand it. I'm going to lose my mind here."

Exasperated, I snapped, "This isn't about you, Mom. How did Neil get hurt?"

"He was at the airport. Getting his bags out of the trunk. Some geezer from New Jersey lost control of his car and pinned your brother against a concrete column. You don't have to be mean to me. That won't fix Neil."

"You're right. Sorry." I stopped short of a full apology. "Where is he?"

"He's at New York Hospital, you know, over on the East Side. The team doctor's with him. I'm going there now. I wanted to call you girls first. Charlie and Ellie won't be home for three days. I can't reach them until then."

My brother Charlie and his new wife Ellie were on their honeymoon somewhere in Costa Rica. My sister Anne, who put the most distance between herself and the rest of the family, lived in Fairfax, about forty minutes from San Francisco, and had a terrifically busy and supremely well-ordered life that had little room for the rest of us, except on Christmas, my father's favorite holiday, Passover, which my mother observed to celebrate her contribution to the family's diversity, and birthdays of numerical significance.

"I'm coming down, Mom." I hadn't stayed in my parents' house since I was twenty. "I'll stay at Karen's, so you and Dad can have your quiet. Dad know yet?"

"No. I'm going to tell him now. He'll be glad you're coming. We can't protect him from everything but we can help comfort him. I love you, Lili. I'm glad you'll be here."

"I love you, too, Mom." And I did, despite our often prickly exchanges. If only she would figure out why she had to drink to deal with the world. If only I could accept that part of her without letting it put a gaping chasm between us.

First, I phoned the mediation center and told the director that I'd have to reschedule because of a family emergency. She wasn't thrilled, but in true mediator style she acknowledged my dilemma, asked for a couple of alternative dates and times, and then wished me good luck. I threw some clean underwear and a couple of long-sleeved cotton tees into my backpack, watered my plants, turned on the timer so the lights would go on and off at normal people hours, and headed for my car. I was halfway down the drive when I screeched to a stop.

Neil would love daffodils. I gathered enough to fill a large vase, wrapped the stems in wet newspaper and a plastic bag, and headed for the Taconic Parkway.

He looked so peaceful I almost backed out of the blue and beige room, but his voice drew me forward.

"Sunshine in a jar." His voice was weak, his smile goofy and good-natured. "They smell nice."

"Well, sure, better than bleach and bedpans." I set the daffodils on the windowsill and reached for his hand. As soon as I saw the apparatus hooked up to my brother's right arm, I understood. Neil Marino was high, self-administering a painkiller, probably morphine, and turning the world into his own private funhouse. With the oxygen flowing into his nostrils and the drug into his veins, he was protected from the worst of it. Or so I thought.

"I'm out for the season. They have to pay me, but they had to fill my spot on the roster. They did not let a single blade of grass grow under their spikes. You were right, Lili. You knew."

I looked at his sweet face and realized that the glazed expression was the result of a great effort to keep from crying. He probably felt little physical discomfort, but he was enough aware of his situation to know that more than his leg had been shattered in that stupid accident.

"What did I know, sweetie?"

"Homework's not done until it's in the teacher's hands. That's what you told me. Third grade." This time, the smile that wrinkled his face made its way to the corners of his dark brown eyes. "I never forgot that."

"*I* said that?"

I vaguely remembered reacting to the confused little boy who had brought home a D in math on his report card and couldn't understand why. He was diligent about doing his assignments, but also pretty consistent about leaving the worksheets in his bedroom. He was insulted that Mr. Wallace didn't believe that he'd done the homework. Five times in three weeks had earned him the D. Ten years older, I'd been eager to teach him the ways of the world.

A large-bosomed woman with dyed black hair bustled into the room, ignoring me and cooing at Neil. Like most women who find themselves in my brother's presence, she was already under the spell of his boyish good looks, a definitely manly physique, and the kind of self-effacing charm that can't be faked.

"Temp's up a little, honey. We need to keep you quiet so that the drugs and some good rest can fix you right up." Her blue eyes avoided mine, but it was clear the last part of that message was meant for me. She leaned closer to Neil. "Anything you need?"

"Thanks, I'm fine. Mary, this is my sister, Lili. Lili, Mary's been taking care of me since I got here. She's got the healing touch. I'll be right again in no time." Neil's voice, stronger at the start of his little introduction, trailed off and he sank back against the pillows.

"Glad to meet you. Thanks for taking care of my brother."

Mary smiled a hello before backing away from his bedside. Neil seemed to have drifted off again into a drug-induced sleep. As Mary made notes on his chart and straightened the bedside table, I studied Neil's face. At twenty-four he'd been on his way to his dream. That furrow between his eyes spoke volumes about the pain he felt, no matter how sedated. The breath I'd been holding for hours escaped in a huge sigh, and I grabbed my jacket and headed for the doorway, leaving Mary to watch over a sleeping Neil.

CHAPTER 4

"See here, where the x-ray shows several breaks? He needs a metal plate here." The doctor pointed to a jagged gray line that looked like an Etch-A-Sketch rendering of a flock of geese in flight. "He may need additional surgeries. Or not. We'll make that decision later. We'll keep him here for a week, teach him to walk on crutches and how to get up and down stairs. When we release him, he's going to need rest, physical therapy, and hope."

His head shaking more than usual, my father said what none of us could bring ourselves to ask. "Will he be able to play again?"

The doctor's face remained expressionless. "I left my crystal ball at home. I'm afraid I can't give you a guarantee. The surgery is the first step. If he's diligent about his physical therapy, it's possible. If he's not, he could spend the rest of his life with limited range of motion in that leg."

My mother hugged me. "Then the answer is yes, he'll play again. My boy is dedicated. He'll do whatever it takes. Thank you, Doctor Reichman."

But the man in the white coat didn't join the celebratory round of smiles and hugs. He fingered the stethoscope around his neck, pursed his mouth, and then said, "Don't expect him to be the same old Neil except with a broken leg. His dreams have been shattered, too, and that may prove harder to heal. I'll see you again when we're done in the OR."

Not the same old Neil? A rush of fear and sadness overwhelmed me. I couldn't fix his leg, as I might mend a broken gourd. Nor could I demand that Neil face this challenge with a smile, or that the doctors give him a pill that would allow him to forget his old dreams and shape new ones that could be navigated with a limp. I could only offer my brother encouragement and practical help in the form of providing rides to physical therapy and doing laundry and other domestic chores for a while.

For once, my mother didn't have anything to say. She sank back into the leather chair in the family waiting room, her eyes damp with tears as she ran a finger along the seam of her jacket. Dad gripped my hand and held on. His palm felt warm and dry, like paper that had been left in the sun. After a few seconds, he pulled away and I noticed that he'd jammed his shaking fist into his trouser pocket.

"Okay," I said. "Neil's alive. That's the biggest deal. And nothing has affected his brain or any other important system. So we have to remember that it's going to be hard, but he needs us to be loving and not so worried that we turn him into a perpetual patient."

My mother's eyes narrowed and she pushed to the edge of her chair. "You mean, *I* shouldn't turn him into a patient. I have no such intention. He's a grown man, and I'll always be his mother but I don't need him to be dependent on me. Speak for yourself, Lili."

"I was." Funny how easy it was to choose my words carefully in a mediation session, and how that skill went out the window when I was with my mother and my sister. I liked women, valued my friendships, but I still hadn't figured out how to connect to those two. "Maybe we should get something to eat. The doctor won't be out of there for three or four hours."

We rode the elevator to the ground floor.

Outside, the world was going about its normal business while my brother was having his leg put back together. I told my parents I'd catch up to them in a few minutes and I lingered behind as they walked down the street, their shoulders bowed with the weight of Neil's condition. When they were half a block ahead, I punched in Susan's number, half expecting an answering machine. Instead, her chirpy voice greeted me.

"You're home. I thought maybe I'd get a message machine. No headaches? No seeing double? Nothing?"

Her laugh was clear and strong. "Nothing. Only the pain of knowing that my perfect face won't ever be in a Revlon commercial. Jack's home, so that's a big relief. Thanks for staying with me, Lili. That mattered. A lot."

"Just lucky I was out there in the parking lot." I wanted to say that anyone would have done the same. "Listen, my brother's been in an accident and I'm down here in the city. I just wanted to let you know why I haven't stopped in to see you."

"No, don't worry about that. He's going to be all right?"

"That's what the doc says. He's out for the season and it's not clear yet whether he'll ever play ball again. Professionally, anyway. He'll need rest, a positive attitude, and a good physical therapist."

"And are you going to be all right?" Susan's voice was quiet, concerned.

"Oh, I'm just tired. Haven't slept well in the past couple of nights. Between you and my brother —"

"Hey, don't you worry about me. And your brother? He can get everything he needs plus fresh air and some time to get back on his feet — so to speak — in Walden Corners. Trisha Stern, you remember, she was at the casino meeting? She worked for the New York Liberty, you know, the women's pro basketball team, for five or six years, then married my principal, Jonathan Kirschbaum. She's a terrific physical therapist."

And, just like that, I knew what I would do. It was one of those moments in which everything felt so completely right that I was grateful to be on the receiving end of such good luck.

"Susan, that's so perfect. I'm so happy to know about Trisha. That's great, thanks so much. I have to run. Talk to you soon. Thanks a gazillion times!"

She'd provided me with some good ammunition to use when Neil was well enough

— and clearheaded enough — to make decisions about his post-op care. I'd give him a real choice. He could go to his apartment and have someone come in to help him — and do too much himself and probably reinjure his leg and end up on the receiving end of a disability check. He could go to Mom's — and have her hover and get chatty and then weepy every evening as the number of Glenlivets rose. Or he could come to my house — and let me bring him his meals, hook him up with a great physical therapist, and be only as much company as he wanted.

I thought I knew which one he'd choose.

"Go home, Lili."

He said it with one of his deep-dimpled smiles, so I joined the game. I kept my tone light when I said, "Tired of my face? Or is it my conversation? Anyway, I was about to leave. My mediation case was rescheduled for six this evening and I want to do some laundry before then."

"Good. Plus, you've got that gallery opening. You have a whole life to live. And most of it takes place one hundred miles from here. Your offer is great, but I can't think that far ahead." The speech left Neil tired, and he sank into the pillows, his smile still bright.

I nodded and leaned over and kissed his stubbly cheek, then rubbed a finger over the one-day growth. "Isn't it your leg that's a problem? Your hand and arm are still okay, right?"

Neil smiled. "This is not laziness. I'm growing a beard. I'm not going to shave until the docs and the team tell me I can play again."

I suppressed the obvious question and settled for a little mood-boosting. "Then you probably won't get past your first whisker trim. You've convinced me. I'm going home. But I'll call you. I want you to think about it. No pressure, but I might not talk to you again if you don't come back with me when they let you out."

"No pressure, but if you aren't careful, you're gonna put Mom out of a job," my brother said, squeezing my hand.

I thought about Neil's comment all the way up the Taconic Parkway. A pounding rain had forced me to slow to under fifty miles an hour as my worn wipers smeared the fat drops across the window. April showers — except this was a deluge that would have made whales happy. I stuck Janis Joplin's

Pearl into the tape player. My mother used to sing along with everything, but this one always felt like a special talisman when she needed extra strength. Maybe I *had* absorbed parts of her — and maybe that wasn't so bad.

By the time I pulled into my driveway the rain had stopped. I navigated past three pond-size puddles and made my way to the back door.

I tossed my keys on the kitchen counter, dumped my backpack on the floor, and walked directly to the bathroom. I'd used the restroom at the Stewart's where I'd stopped for gas on the way home, but I'd also fueled up with a large container of coffee. My sense of relief was cut short by the plink of water hitting the toe of my left sneaker.

The stain on my new white bath mat matched the one darkening the ceiling tile. My bathroom had sprung a leak.

It must have started slowly, unnoticed. Water — a silent traveler that moves along the smallest slope and finds an opening, any unsealed place, the tiniest space. Patient, persistent it makes its way along the path of least resistance, even if that means cutting through sandstone and shale. If the great river valleys of this beautiful green earth can be formed by water wearing away the rock, then a ceiling covered in acoustic tiles had little chance against its power. Tom Ford had apologized for those cottage cheese tiles, had said he'd meant to replace them, and so had I. But neither of us had gotten around to it.

I stood in the 1950s green-and-black, functional but far from beautiful space. No way to tell from here where the leak was coming from, but if I pushed up the ceiling tile, maybe I'd see something obvious. I grabbed the flashlight I kept on my bedside table, pulled a folding stepstool into the middle of floor, and climbed up, bracing against the wall with my right hand. With my left, I pushed up on the tile with the large, damp ring in the center and moved it aside.

A rifle crashed to the floor, just missing my head.

Funny how many things can go through a person's mind at once. I waited for a flash and the searing pain that I'd heard accompanies a gunshot wound. I wondered whether Tom Ford had stashed the gun in the attic and I'd missed it when I moved in. Or maybe someone was trying to get me arrested for possession of an illegal weapon because I'd been helpful to Susan Clemants, who supported the casino.

The next thought was that whoever put that rifle in my attic might still be in my house. And might be dangerous.

I was careful stepping down from the ladder. Then I grabbed my pack from the kitchen counter and ran to the car. I backed down the driveway, turned left onto Iron Mill Road and headed toward Walden Corners. By the time I'd gone about a quarter mile, sanity returned. I didn't need to drive eight miles into town to report what I'd found. I had my cell phone.

The brilliant sun made the rain-soaked grass sparkle. I pulled over into the shade of a graceful willow and dialed the number for Michele Castro, at the Columbia County Sheriff's Department. Maddeningly, the phone rang and rang but nobody picked up. Great. Law enforcement was taking a coffee break? My annoyance became jittery frustration as the phone continued to ring. Eight times, ten. I was about to hang up when a tentative male voice said, "Hello? I mean, Sheriff's Department."

"Can I speak to Michele Castro?" The man who answered might well have been a janitor or a computer geek — he hardly sounded as though he knew his way around a crime scene.

"She's out in the field," the voice said. For a second, I was confused at the notion of Michele Castro tromping through beds of alfalfa, but then I realized that was cop talk.

"What about Sheriff Murphy?"

"Not here," the voice intoned.

Exasperated, I nearly tossed the cell phone into the newly green bushes, but instead I took a deep breath and said, "Listen, I live on Iron Mill Road. I found a rifle in my attic and I want to report it. I'm afraid to go back into the house myself because the person who put it there might be —"

"Hold on. Stay where you are. What did you say your name is?"

"Lili Marino," I said. Generic disco music filled my ear. As I waited in confusion, a white and blue police car screamed past me, screeched to a halt about one hundred yards down the road, and then backed up, fishtailing on the blacktop until it came to a stop in front of me.

Either that dispatcher was more efficient than I thought, or the officer in the cruiser was more interested in me than she should have been.

CHAPTER 5

Michele Castro stepped out of the cruiser and approached me, her right hand resting lightly on the revolver that hung at her hip. I still couldn't get past the cheerleader image — blond hair pulled back into a low ponytail, steady green eyes rimmed by lashes that didn't need mascara, a figure made to wear tailored jeans and snug, colorful T-shirts. "Stand up and hold your hands out at your sides," she said.

Confused, my heart pounding, I obeyed.

She continued to take careful steps forward, her eyes locked onto mine. Static crackled from some piece of equipment hanging from her belt. Her face seemed to be cast in stone — no twitching, no movement, no expression at all to give away her feelings. We might not be friends, but I hardly expected her to treat me like a criminal because I'd discovered a gun in my attic in a truly freakish way.

"What are you doing parked by the side of the road?" Her right hand gripped the handle of the gun.

"I — didn't you get my message? About the rifle?" My idea of a perfect Thursday afternoon did not include standing in the dappled shade of a large willow facing off against a law enforcement officer growling questions at me.

"Answer my question. How come you were parked at the side of the road?"

My frustration ballooned into exasperation. "I just called your office from my cell phone. Someone left a . . . I don't know . . . I found a rifle. It fell out of my bathroom ceiling. I thought whoever put it there might still be in my house so I left. And I called the sheriff's department and then you came and here we are."

Her face softened, but only for a second before hardening back into a stern, official mask. "What kind of rifle?"

"The kind that shoots." The words were out before I could deflect my smart remark into something that might not raise her hackles. My father's handguns were familiar to me, but rifles? Not in Brooklyn. "I don't know. It was big, so I knew it was a rifle, but that's all I can tell you."

"Where is it now?" She didn't brush away

the gnat that flew in front of her face, but she did blink. Somehow, I found that reassuring.

"On the floor in my bathroom. Right where it fell. I didn't touch it, and I didn't move it. It would be fine with me if you came back to the house and just took it away. I don't want it or anything. I mean, I want to get rid of it, you know." Babbling through my nervousness, I maintained eye contact with Michele Castro, Columbia County undersheriff, who watched me with a cool, analytical stare.

An hour earlier, I would have said that my biggest problem was figuring out how to juggle too many demanding parts of my life. Ten minutes ago, I'd have said that the only way my name and the word suspect would be linked would be if my mother had phoned me and said, "Lili Marino, is this fellow you're dating a usual suspect or is he someone ready to settle down?"

I began to feel like a bantamweight mouse being batted around by a Sumo cat. My impatience with this little charade bubbled over. "Are you going to get the rifle or not?"

"Where were you this morning?" she replied.

Great — that wasn't a question a cop asked without a reason, and that reason was surely bad news for me. "Driving home from New York City. Where I was visiting my brother in the hospital. And, yes, I was alone. Maybe a gas station attendant at the Stewart's at Oyster Point would remember me. You make it sound like you're going to haul me in for murder," I said to lighten the tone.

"That depends on what forensics finds out about the rifle." She motioned me into the rear seat of the cruiser and called in her position on the walkie-talkie she pulled from her belt.

Murder? She was probably just sticking to her script, ticking off procedural requirements one by one.

At least I wasn't spread-eagled against the hood of my car, enduring a pat down in full view of any neighbor who happened to drive by. As my breathing slowed, my mind started into gear again. Michele Castro was going to a lot of trouble, asking me questions and making me wait in the patrol car. Something big, perhaps even unthinkable, had happened. Nothing as simple as an accident along this quiet country road. Clearly, it had something to do with a rifle. Hunting out of season? That wouldn't be serious enough to treat me as though I were a . . . murderer. That was the word I'd been trying to avoid.

In the rearview mirror, I watched Castro's normally pretty face screw into a look of puzzlement as she paced from one side of the road to the other. Finally, she flicked off the walkie-talkie and opened the door on the driver's side.

"I need to see the rifle you found."

"Good, I'd love to have you take it away." But I felt no relief. Her still-tense expression told me that this wasn't going to be a quick and easy jaunt.

"And we need to search your house. We can do it two hours from now, after we get a warrant, or we can do it now with your permission."

My head dropped against the seat back. I didn't need this, not when I had so many other things demanding my attention. No clear answers came out of the soup that was my brain, but I heard my Dad's voice echoing in my head.

If you're ever in a jam, don't be stupid. Lawyer up. It's the only smart thing.

He'd told me that when he was on the job, the only judgment he made when someone called a lawyer was that they had brains. Not every cop felt the way he did, he'd said, but that didn't matter. The smart ones protected themselves.

"I'll give you my answer in a minute. After I call my lawyer. Can I get out and have a little privacy?"

Castro's steady gaze was accompanied by a curt nod. I climbed from the cruiser, walked a few steps down the road, and punched in Elizabeth Conklin's number. I explained the situation in two seconds, and then she put me on hold. Now it was my turn to pace. Disintegrating tissue wads dotted the ditch, along with crushed beer cans and cigarette packs. On the other side of the road, a torn gym bag and a formerly white sock lay abandoned. The detritus of bored teens, I thought, on their way to becoming joyless adults. What was Elizabeth doing? The minutes dripped by like molasses in January. Finally, I heard a click and a voice.

"Listen very carefully. Marjorie Mellon was found in the woods about a quarter mile from your house. Somebody shot her with a rifle. Are you sure you didn't touch the one in your bathroom?"

I stopped pacing. Marjorie Mellon, dead? Near my house? Her bouncing steel gray curls bobbed into my mind, her brown eyes flashing beneath them. Every bit of her moved when she spoke about starting a consortium to support the casino. Now she was dead.

"Lili? You didn't touch the rifle. That's right, isn't it?" Elizabeth sounded exasperated.

"I didn't. I don't think I did. I was too scared. When it fell out of the ceiling, it scared the crap out of me. What do I do now?"

"You let them take the rifle, and you let them search your house. They'd get their warrant, so there's no use appearing uncooperative. Meanwhile, I'll call B.H., just in case."

"B.H.?" Was I supposed to understand, or was this some kind of lawyer code I hadn't learned?

"Sorry. B. H. Hovanian, the smartest criminal defense lawyer north of the city. You probably won't need him, but I want to alert him. Like I said, just in case. And call me when the cops leave."

She clicked off before I could say thank you. And before she could say *Don't worry, this will blow over in a couple of hours.* But then, Elizabeth wasn't much of a hand holder. I'd known that for months. Maybe the lawyer, whom I hoped was a combination of Gerry Spence folksy and Alan Dershowitz passionate, was a good idea. It was a stretch to think I'd need his services, but he'd probably be better to work with than Elizabeth, whose clients came to her for wills and pre-nups and business contracts.

Michele Castro walked towards me, her head tilted in a question.

"Okay, I'm ready. Let's go. You can take the rifle and you can search my house." So, she'd get what she wanted and I'd go on with my life. After I made a couple of important points. "But I didn't murder Marjorie Mellon. First of all, I hardly know the woman, so why would I kill her? Second of all . . . Oh, hell, *you* know I didn't do it."

Michele Castro didn't show a flicker of emotion. "I don't know anything yet. I need you to come down to the department and get fingerprinted and give a formal statement about the rifle. And I need you to stick around for a couple of days."

My throat closed up. "A couple of days? I can't. I have to go to New Hampshire tomorrow. You know, it's not so far. I'm in a new show at a prestigious gallery there. My work has to be set up for a show on Saturday afternoon. I'm not going to run away or anything. But I have to be at that opening."

She shrugged. "I can't force you to stay. But I can make sure you have a police escort the whole weekend. And I still need you to come to Hudson and give me a statement and get fingerprinted — after I follow you to your house so we can get that rifle and check things out."

I doubted that the sheriff's department had the manpower to spare someone to babysit me for a trip to New Hampshire, but even if Michele Castro wasn't making idle threats, no way would she stop me from going to New Hampshire.

"Fine. I'll come by this afternoon. And that escort? You want to try for Officer Garrison? He looks like he'd know how to behave around a bunch of patrons of the arts."

Her boyfriend would, in fact, not be bad company for a weekend. She glared at me and then strutted off to her car and gunned the engine while I managed to turn the car without landing in the ditch.

I'd been mugged once on a deserted street on the Lower East Side, and hustled by a couple of would-be thieves on the subway, but I'd never felt as helpless as I did when three members of the Columbia County Sheriff's Department tossed my small home. They went through every drawer and closet, every box and bag, impersonally peering beneath T-shirts and under towels. They opened every container in my gourd studio, and pawed through each folder in my file cabinet, until I was ready to scream.

But they were relatively neat and they were efficient and they made an attempt to be courteous and even apologetic. Nobody answered my questions about how the rifle might have gotten into my attic — they just poked through everything and then left. Michele Castro directed traffic, and directed herself to go through my underwear drawer. At least she was the one to learn that I had thirty pairs of the same off-brand panties, in red, blue, purple, and white. What she didn't know was that they served as a private, color-coded reminder to help me get through the day — red when I needed energy, blue when I wanted to be calm, purple when I had to be assertive, and white when I felt in need of a spiritual boost.

Today, I should have been wearing one of each color.

Not that it would have helped. My feeling of violation gave way to a weariness that felt bone deep. I still had to get fingerprinted and then go to the mediation session. But not before I spent ten minutes lying on the sofa and staring out the window at the sparrows fighting over the seed in the feeder. Which helped me remember that Elizabeth had asked me to call her when Castro and company were gone.

"He wants you to meet him at the Creamery tomorrow morning at ten," she said when I'd identified myself.

"Who? What are you talking about?" Puzzles and word games, usually among my favorite forms of entertainment, were more annoying than intriguing right now.

"The lawyer, the one I said I'd call. B.H., remember? He thinks this may get some attention because of the casino connection and he wants to meet you before the news hits the fan."

"Tell him I'll meet him tonight at nine," I said. Even my attorney wasn't going to stop me from making that gallery opening.

I'd been through the messy ink-and-roll procedure once before, when I applied for a job at a bank. That time, I hadn't cleaned one of my fingers thoroughly and had ruined a perfectly fine yellow cotton sweater. This time I'd be more careful. As double insurance I threw an old denim work shirt that was stained with leather dye and gilder's paste over my mediation slacks and sweater, and then drove into Hudson.

Warren Street buzzed with activity as the county prepared for the return of seasonal visitors. I was still too protective of the slow, uncrowded quiet of my new life to welcome the intrusion of Them — city people. If that casino was built, the stream would turn into a flood. Maybe, too, I just didn't get the appeal of gambling because I was missing the gene that got excited when the dice stopped or a little ball rolled into my number. Instead, the gene that hated losing kept me from getting involved in matters of pure chance. Either way, I'd heard about how gambling joints changed not only the look of a town but also its feel. The culture of neighborliness became corrupted into theme-park friendliness that disappeared when the money ran out. All the arguments about jobs and expanding the tax base and seeing that justice was served for Native Americans wouldn't convince me that a casino was the only way to achieve those good ends.

Inside the sheriff's department, the smell of disinfectant nearly knocked me over. I was reminded that policing was a job in which you might be exposed to bad odors and bodily wastes, and in a county jail that would happen regularly, especially in the drunk tank. I shivered with distaste and headed for the desk.

"Hi, is Officer Castro around? She asked me to come by." I smiled in the direction of the heavily mascaraed woman on the other side of the counter, but she continued to stare at her computer screen as though I hadn't said a word.

Seconds marched by, my patience seeping away with each tick of the clock. Public servants, my foot. Public torturers was more like it. "Hello!" I shouted as I slammed my hand on the counter and sent two papers fluttering to the floor. "Anybody home?"

Glaring, the woman glanced away from the fallen papers and pushed her chair back. She pointed to a sign on the counter.

PRESS THE BUZZER FOR ATTENTION.

In the uninflected voice of someone who has never heard the melody of human speech she said, "No need to be sarcastic. What can I do for you?"

The notice was as clear as my regret. "Sorry. I didn't see the sign. Michele Castro wanted me to come in."

The woman followed my speech with her eyes, not her ears. I waited while she dialed an extension, spoke into the receiver, and then motioned me to a seat on a bench. How would it be to live in a silent world, to not hear music, to have only your eyes, your nose, your skin to alert you to changes or dangers in the world? Maybe it was peaceful. No traffic, no jackhammers, no shouting.

I was so lost in thought that I didn't hear Castro's footsteps. Startled by her sudden appearance in front of me, I jumped up to a standing position.

Funny, I'd made myself deaf for a few seconds.

"You all right?" she asked, and when I nodded she led me down the corridor to her small office. As I had last fall after I'd found Nora's husband's body in a pond, I sat across from her, wrote out my statement on the yellow legal pad she pushed toward me, and tried to include every detail. Without looking up, I knew Castro's eyes were on me. When I was finished, I handed her the paper.

"Am I still a suspect?" I asked, keeping my voice light. "Do I still need a babysitter this weekend?"

Michele Castro pushed her ponytail behind her shoulder. Fine lines crisscrossed her tan cheek, and a frown furrow had begun to form between her plucked brows. She was too young to be sporting worry lines, but there they were. The stress of work, the sun, irregular hours, eating food that came from a chemistry lab instead of a farm, had all left their mark on her. For a second, I wanted to send her home with a hot meal and some expensive skin cream. The impulse didn't last long.

"You and everybody else in town. But, yes, you. The rifle was in your house and you have no corroborated alibi for the time of Marjorie Mellon's death. Not yet, anyway, until I check out your statement. So, yes. That's why I told you to stick around town, that's why I needed to search your house, and that's why you're here now." Her chair squeaked as she leaned back. "We're looking at some other people too. I'm not going to say who."

Great. Other people. The only thing that kept me from utter despair was the knowledge that my prints were not on that rifle. Thank goodness I hadn't touched it.

"When will you check my prints against the ones on the rifle? Because if they don't match, then I move down on your list, don't I?"

"As soon as we can." She got up and poured herself coffee, gestured to ask if I wanted any but I declined in the interests of my stomach.

"Okay. Whatever that means. Is it all right if I have someone come out and fix my roof? I mean, I found the rifle because my roof has a leak somewhere. I don't want to be charged with tampering with evidence or anything, but I don't want the whole house to get ruined." No rain was forecast in the near future. Still, I didn't want to watch my bathtub go floating down Iron Mill Road because my damaged shingles were evidence in a murder case. She could take all the pictures she wanted, but I intended to have that leak fixed before the week was over.

Before she could answer, her phone rang. "Castro," she said in her official voice. She tapped the eraser end of a pencil as she listened. Once, her eyes cut to me before she scribbled something on the note paper in a neat cube on her desk. "Don't let anyone near it," she said, standing and motioning me to the door. "I'll be there in ten minutes."

It had sparked Castro's interest enough for her to almost forget that I was supposed to be fingerprinted.

"I don't know where the fingerprint room is," I said matter-of-factly.

With an exasperated sigh, Castro led me to another small room, told the lab tech what she wanted, and then kept going down the hall. The technician, an overweight boy whose hair was cut so close I could see whitish patches of scalp, mimed his way through the printing procedure. With my encounter at the front desk still fresh in my mind, I went along with his gestures. He pointed to the table, then grasped my thumb with a hand so soft it startled me. Gently, he rolled each finger first in ink and then onto the paper. The silence doubled my apprehension. To distract myself I tried to remember the lyrics of an old Bob Marley song about some kind of vibrations. The words didn't stick. Instead, I found myself traveling through a labyrinth of disturbing questions about casinos and friendships in jeopardy, about Marjorie Mellon lying dead in the woods, and Connie Lovett living fiercely, and Neil trying to recover from having his dreams crushed.

What could I, should I do to change any of this? That question wasn't real, I knew — I'd given up thinking I could fix everything a long time ago. Maybe my mediation session would restore my belief that I had at least some power to make certain things right again.

CHAPTER 6

The room was calm and dignified, in a low budget kind of way. Posters of mountains and a shining sea brightened the beige walls and three healthy pothos plants lined the windowsill. They helped set a tone that made dealing with angry people easier. I was too late to sit quietly and close my eyes and concentrate on my breathing, a practice that allowed my personal concerns to recede. Neil and Connie and Susan and that rifle hovered at the edges of my consciousness. Marjorie drifted among them. No use trying to make them disappear completely, not today.

The case file listed Mr. Smith as complainant and Mr. Caterra as respondent. To encourage fairness, the mediation center's policy was to tell the mediator very little about a conflict. I only knew that this was a business dispute involving a contractor and a homeowner — a relief, because this wouldn't be the best time for me to deal with the high emotions of a truant teen or a child custody case and maintain my equanimity.

The two men sitting on benches across from each other in the waiting area couldn't have been more different, although they looked familiar to me. I'd seen them before, around town, in the Agway, at a casino meeting, perhaps. One was tall, with a balding head tonsured in white, a navy button-down shirt, and knife-creased khakis. Smith, the homeowner/complainant, I decided. The muscular man sitting across from him wore paint-spattered jeans and T-shirt. His hair hung to his shoulders. Caterra, the contractor.

I called them into the room and we took seats around the battered library table.

"Hi, my name is Lili Marino. Thanks for coming in. I know we're getting a bit of a late start, but we always try to accommodate everyone's schedules. If time runs short, we can schedule another meeting." Both men nodded at me, avoiding eye contact with each other. "Please tell me your names so that I can pronounce them correctly."

The shorter man flipped his hair off his shoulder and grinned. "I never heard a single person pronounce my name wrong.

What can you do to Smith?"

I felt my cheeks redden. I'd violated a basic principle of mediation by making assumptions about these two men based on their appearance.

I explained that mediation was voluntary and confidential, which meant that I couldn't be called on to testify in court about anything that happened during the sessions. They'd be the ones to determine the outcome. "I'm not a judge. I'm here to help you talk to each other. We've found that the process works best if we observe a couple of guidelines. First, one person at a time speaks. I've given you paper and pencil so that you can write down what you want to say when someone else is talking. Can you both agree to let one person at a time speak?"

Mr. Caterra sat taller in his chair and rubbed his bald spot. He said, "No problem."

Good. But it was Mr. Muscular Smith I was more concerned about. He'd been sitting with his arms folded across his chest, scowling and shaking his head. After a few seconds, I said, "Mr. Smith? Do you agree?"

He unfolded his arms and slapped the table. "He's all agreeable now because we're in public, but I don't care if it's one person or three people speaking, if he talks trash to me I'm out of here and in court. He cheated me, he promised to do work on my bathroom and he did a crappy job and used crappy materials. He charged me for the good stuff and pocketed the difference. Plus, he's taking *my* money, the money he stole from me, and giving it to that group that thinks building the damn casino is gonna solve everybody's damn problems."

No matter where I went, I couldn't get away from the casino.

"You'll have a chance to talk about everything that's on your mind, Mr. Smith. But I want to know if you can agree to let one person at a time speak."

"He's got a temper and he —"

"Shut up, Caterra. I can talk for myself." Mr. Smith gripped his pencil so tightly it nearly snapped. "I'll try."

He didn't say that going to court was an expensive, time-consuming alternative that he wanted to avoid, but I could see it on his face. So far, so good — nobody had leaped across the table or made threatening gestures or stormed out of the room.

For the next fifteen minutes, first Smith and then Caterra told their stories. Smith claimed that he had hired Caterra to redo his bathroom, that the work had taken a little over a week as specified, and that he had paid $4,359 for labor and materials. He slapped a sheaf of receipts on the table, each marked paid. And then he told how a week later, a leak had caused his bathroom to collapse into the dining room downstairs. He slapped another thicket of papers on the table — estimates of damage to his table, a family heirloom, and the repair of the plumbing, the sheetrock, and all painting. He claimed that Caterra had used inferior materials and had neglected to seal and caulk crucial joints. He wanted full compensation for all the repairs and restoration, plus enough money to cover the two days he'd had to miss work.

"He thinks he's gonna get a piece of the construction work for that casino? I'll make sure that doesn't happen. I'll take this jerk to court and then the whole county will know what scum he is and how he screws over honest, hardworking families. Just because I don't have a college degree don't mean you can run your little scam right over me like a Sherman tank," Smith declared between clenched teeth.

There it was. In business disputes, respect was almost always one of the unspoken concerns. "So, Mr. Smith, there's been some damage done to your furniture and your dining room ceiling. You believe that Mr. Caterra used materials and processes that were inappropriate to repair your leak. You also feel that Mr. Smith hasn't treated you respectfully, and you're upset that some of the money you paid him might go to help bring a casino you don't support to Walden Corners. Did I get that right?"

Smith scowled, but he nodded. Then it was Caterra's turn.

Caterra denied everything. He had used materials that were within Smith's budget and his workman had properly sealed joints and edges. The problem, he said, was that Smith had dumped sludge from his motorcycle down the new drain, causing a backup and the subsequent flooding.

"And how I spend the money I earn is my business. If I want to buy a million purple lollipops or give it to a girl who wants to open a massage parlor then that's what I'll do. But let's get this clear. You're blowing foul air all over town — I want you to stop telling people I'm a crook. If you continue to badmouth me, I'll sue your butt for defamation," Caterra said with a smile, "and enjoy every minute of it."

And there was the other unspoken concern. Reputation — a businessman's make or break commodity. Again, I summarized what Caterra had said, ending with a recognition that he was concerned about maintaining his reputation in the community. Caterra smiled at me, as though it was our little secret that he was going to win this case, but I ignored his manipulation.

"Gentlemen," I said, "it seems that there's a lot more to talk about, but we can't do it tonight. It's eight o'clock, and the center is closing. Can we come back next week, same time, same place, and pick up where we left off?"

I expected grumbling from Smith, and he didn't disappoint me. In the end, though, they both agreed to return to try to work things out.

My day had been longer and filled with more surprise challenges than I'd anticipated. And it wasn't over yet.

B. H. Hovanian didn't look anything like I'd imagined. His brown hair was cut short enough to qualify as military, his strong nose and wide mouth were just right to balance his cleft chin, and his long-lashed dark eyes softened the hard edges of his face. His six-foot-four frame was sturdy; he either had great genes or he worked out regularly. A couple of years the far side of forty, he gave the appearance of being someone who strode instead of walking, who guffawed instead of laughing, who wept instead of crying.

He listened while I told him in detail about coming home to find the rifle, leaving the house, calling the sheriff's office. He offered one piece of news — Marjorie Mellon's car had been found in the town parking lot. He asked all the same questions as Michele Castro, about where I'd been and who had seen me, and then he probed in a different direction.

"What was your relationship to Marjorie Mellon?" The challenge in his gaze didn't diminish as he leaned back and watched my face.

"Relationship? We didn't have one." This part was easy. Telling the truth, letting my frustration give my voice a slight edge. He was supposed to be on my side, not trying to catch me in a lie. "I might have met her, let's see, two times. Once at the Santa parade last year, and once when I was looking for a book that I'd misplaced and went to Seth Selinsky's office after hours when she was cleaning. I didn't say hello to her at the casino meeting. I'm not sure she even knew who I was."

"You made public statements that you oppose the casino. Is that right?" He sat with his back straight and his hands folded on the marble top of the café table, an untouched cup of double espresso to his right.

"Me and at least three hundred other people. I don't think it's a good idea. But, actually, I didn't get up and speak against it, not yet." I watched as he lifted his cup, sipped noisily, and then set it down again. This was a man who understood timing, and I was growing impatient with the interview. "Listen, I don't know what you're after here. I haven't been charged with anything, I didn't do anything, and I would like to go on with my very busy life now, if you don't mind."

His laugh made Frank Vargas look up from the ham and brie sandwich he was preparing behind the counter. "I don't mind what you do. You should know, though, that this isn't over for you. You'll be in the spotlight for a while."

"Well, that won't last long because I didn't do anything." A little of my defensiveness melted. This man, with his dark, darting eyes, and in language that demonstrated an ability to hold apparently contradictory thoughts about a topic, was a new experience for me, and I didn't quite know how to respond to him.

B. H. Hovanian's chuckle managed to

convey both amusement and skepticism. "Everyone swears they're innocent."

"And sometimes it's even true. If I'm a suspect because I didn't like the idea of the casino coming in and ruining the character of the town, then about two-thirds of the citizens of Walden Corners are suspects, too."

"Two-thirds of the citizens in Walden Corners didn't have what will probably prove to be the murder weapon concealed in the ceiling of their bathroom," he reminded me.

Even if I were pure in heart, mind, and deed that might not mean anything to a sheriff's department that needed to find someone to hang. My father's voice whispered again in my ear. *Don't be stubborn, Lili. Lawyer up.*

"Will you work with me?" I asked.

"If you can pay my fee." He scribbled something and then passed a business card across the table. "Here's my beeper number. If Castro or anyone comes at you with something else, some supposedly vital new evidence or new charge, call me. Meanwhile, I have to get on with my case. Cases," he corrected himself.

"You're not doing this as a favor to me. I'll pay your regular hourly rate. So don't rush me out with a dismissive wave of your hand. I have another question."

To his credit, he didn't roll his eyes or sigh, nor did he offer pretend apologies. He just sat there, large-knuckled hands folded atop the table, and waited.

"What's your name? I feel weird calling you B.H. It sounds too much like a camera store in Manhattan or something." He might take for granted that his physical size and his reputation would be imposing, that not telling his real name to an adversary or even a client would create a power imbalance, but I was not about to buy that brand of intimidation.

His head dropped forward, and when he picked it up again a huge smile brightened his face. "Berge Hartounian. Call me whatever you like. My ex-wife had a lot of names for me, but you probably won't be using those."

I laughed. Now that the full Armenian glory of his name was revealed, I felt silly to have been so prickly.

"Here's my real question," I said. "If the sheriff's department is already convinced that I'm the one they want, how will they find the killer? I'm not willing to sit around and be railroaded just because the local bureaucracy suffers from a lack of imagination."

I expected to be treated to a speech about letting the law enforcement agencies do their job. But B. H. Hovanian's sigh was not followed by a lecture. Instead, he said, "Can you afford a private investigator? I'd guess that once you pay all your bills, including mine, the answer is no. So we'll have to convince the sheriff's department that you were nowhere near those woods today. You'll do that by providing me with as much corroboration for every statement you make as you can, and you'll share any thoughts or observations you might have with me. About other possibilities, I mean."

"So you agree? That they may not work too hard to find someone else."

He leaned back and clasped his hands across his belt, eyes droopy and mouth quirked into a smile. "You sound like a lawyer. I didn't say that. I happen to know that Anita, Marjorie's self-indulgent daughter, stands to inherit a comfortable house, ten acres of land, a lucrative business, and who knows what else. She lives in Tennessee in a small town and has a husband who hires on with a logging company when he feels like working. Our Anita didn't show up on time for work this morning. Rolled in about two hours late."

"Do the police know this?"

He shook his head. "Not yet. I only just heard that last part myself. And I didn't say our local law enforcement agency is incompetent. I just think it's prudent to be precise and thorough."

CHAPTER 7

"He said yes, and I didn't even have to badger him much."

My friend Karen, who knew how to smile with her voice over the phone, said, "That's great, Lili. I know how much you wanted that. I'm just disappointed because it means you won't be hanging out here in Brooklyn with me."

Our visits were always wonderful, satisfying . . . and difficult to end. Even after a year, Karen and I missed the almost daily contact we'd grown so accustomed to when we lived within walking distance of each other.

"So, you'll have to come up and help me keep my brother entertained," I said as lightly as I could.

"Ach, you forget so soon. A working woman can't just pick up and go off on a whim. It's a big responsibility, this new job. I love my old folks. My new lady thinks I'm her friend Tatiana from Moscow and she wants to play Russian rhyming games with me. I'm so lucky. The bills get paid, I get to paint, and then I work four days a week with Alzheimer's patients who just want someone to come into their world and share it with them."

This time, I could picture her cheeks lifting in a real smile, her big brown eyes glinting with pleasure. "You know, I could see it in your face when you talked about those people last week."

"Can't help it," she said. "But how did you get Neil to go along with your plan?"

"All he needed to hear was that I was uneasy because that rifle had fallen out of my ceiling and a murdered woman had been found a quarter mile away, and I was suddenly high on the list of suspects, in the pretty green eyes of the law. Told me that he'd get copies of his prescriptions and detailed instructions for the physical therapist from his doc, and then he'd be there to support me. Keep the suspect company."

"What about the Mets?" A note of worry crept into her voice. "Such gnarly timing."

"The Mets are being good to him, at least for now. His agent's got them convinced that he'll be back for the last quarter of the season. They're even giving him a car and driver to bring him up here. ETA is noon on Monday."

"Which means that you can go to New Hampshire. That's so perfect! You'll have at least one less worry on your mind. And that will make the gallery opening even more fun. Besides, who can have a bad time drinking champagne, eating lovely cheese and grapes, and being surrounded by admirers who want to know everything about your gourds? May you sell all your wares to total strangers who then tell all their friends and increase your sales until you need to hire apprentices to do . . . whatever a gourd apprentice might do."

Even if she rolled her eyes whenever the G word came up, Karen knew how to celebrate, and for that I would always love her.

My brother's cheekbones were as prominent as a Russian Cossack's and his dimple a little harder to see because he had less flesh than usual. But his spirits were good, and he managed on his crutches as though they'd become a part of his body.

The driver who carried his bags into the living room looked around, his expression shifting from dismay to pity. I read volumes into that look. What was the newest second baseman of the Mets doing in a place like this when he could be getting home massages, takeout from Whole Foods, and visits from his mates? The driver set Neil's bags in the corner, refused my offer of coffee, and hurried away from this luxury-free zone and headed back to his leather-seated, climate-controlled limo as quickly as he could.

Neil wobbled as he made his way to the corner of the sofa. I'd arranged a few things on the end table to make him comfortable — a tray with a carafe of water and a glass, some grapes, a couple of Civil War histories I knew he hadn't read, and a bell, which he jingled and then set back with an amused shake of his head.

"I have to go over the rules with you. You're not gonna hover. You're not gonna ask me twelve times an hour how I'm feeling. And you absolutely will not listen in when I'm on the phone." His grin lit up the whole living room as he propped his leg on the pillow I'd set on a chair in front of the sofa.

"Wouldn't have entered my mind. To listen in, I mean. But now I may have to. Does this mean someone special is going to call? Tell."

But he smiled his canary-eating smile and

said, "How was the gallery opening?"

"Better than I expected. I'll show you the article when it comes out." Not only had I sold nine pieces, I'd been interviewed by a reporter from the *Manchester Herald*. I didn't mention to my brother that I also spent a quarter of my earnings on a spectacular piece of glass, cranberry with undulating silver waves, that would live on my windowsill until I needed to come up with a special-occasion gift for a very good friend.

"And just to be clear," I said, "it's not hovering to ask if you need anything. Besides, I *do* have other things to do than sit around and watch you veg out in front of the television or play Spider on your laptop. Oh, before I forget — you think you'll be up to a houseful of beautiful, intriguing, smart poker players on Friday night?"

"If I'm not," he said, "that probably means you should rush me to the emergency room. Sure, it'll be great to meet your friends." Neil waved a fistful of prescriptions at me. "I have enough to last me a day or two. Doctor Reichman said that I need to start the physical therapy tomorrow. Today I'm allowed to slide by with a couple of leg lifts."

I took the papers from him. By the look on his drawn face, Neil was likely to spend at least part of the afternoon napping. That would be a good time for me to drive into town, get his drugs, pick up the new respirator mask that Bob James at Primitive Originals had mailed, and still be back before my brother noticed my absence.

"I'm going to make a quick run into town. I've got my cell phone. Call if you need anything. Here's the remote and today's *Hudson Register*."

"My leg's broken but I can still see," he said, grinning. "This seems like the perfect place to get some rest. It smells good here, like the air is green. And it's quiet — no car alarms, no Mom. But you — you look so tired, Lili. You can't let this murder thing interfere with your sleep."

I didn't want to talk about my insomnia or my suspect status. Instead, I kissed his forehead and headed for town, happy that he was comfortable, glad that I could give him this space for a while.

"I can have these for you in ninety minutes." Mr. Trent peered at me over the top of his granny glasses. With his short-cut gray hair, pink skin, and white jacket he looked like a pharmacist in a television commercial. But Joseph Trent's jacket had fraying sleeves and a couple of faded stains that spoke of years of wear, as did the runner that led from the front of the store to the prescription counter at the back. He tugged at the surgical glove on his right hand and went on sliding pills into a bottle.

"I don't mean to rush you, but if you could get to it sooner, I'd really appreciate it. I left my brother home alone, and he's not so great on his crutches yet."

Mr. Trent counted out the last three pills, stripped off the latex glove, and then looked up at me, frowning. "He should have someone with him."

"I can't be in two places at once." Who was he to tell me how to take care of Neil? I turned away to give myself time to regroup so that I wouldn't yell at this well-meaning but officious man.

"You haven't been sleeping well, have you? Those circles under your eyes, they're new." Suddenly, the same Mr. Trent who was so ready to berate me sounded concerned, solicitous — and he had nailed one of the reasons for my curtness.

"No. It's been a rough week. I —" Why hadn't I thought of this before? Maybe I didn't need to spend the early hours of every morning playing computer solitaire or watching bad movies on TV. The man behind the counter was a pharmacist, after all. "Is there something you can recommend that would help me sleep?"

Mr. Trent folded his arms across his chest and shook his head slowly. As his brows knitted together in concentration, I realized that I was in for a lecture. When he stepped from behind the counter, I looked down at his shoes. They were scuffed and worn. Backing up two steps, I forced my gaze to meet his.

"If you're asking me to suggest drugs, forget it. Go to that new Walgreens down the road. Cut rate prices — half my customers left. What they're finding out is that nobody there cares about anything except making money. Thank goodness the rest of my customers still want to do business with a member of the community. Someone who knows them."

I nodded, not knowing for sure whether I really wanted his advice or just a quick in-and-out to buy what I needed.

"I can give you something, though, a natural herbal remedy." Joseph Trent's face relaxed a little. "It's called valerian. Try it first. And make sure you get at least forty-five minutes of exercise every day. Learn some kind of meditation or a relaxation technique where you do deep breathing. No caffeine after noon. And be sure you drink a glass of warm milk at bedtime. I'll have your brother's meds ready in fifteen minutes. And I'll get you those capsules. Here," he said as he went behind the counter again, reached down and handed me a brochure about good nutrition, "read this while I'm working on your order."

Of course, he was right, even though I bristled at his condescension. Until the night of the casino hearing, my usual pattern was to read for half an hour, fall asleep instantly, and stay asleep for seven hours. I didn't need drugs. I'd look up valerian on the Internet when I got home. A glass of warm milk — that sounded so Laura Ingalls Wilder. But even though my little house wasn't on the prairie, treating my insomnia with such a homey remedy felt like just the right thing to do.

I was digging in my purse for my credit card when someone called my name. I turned to see Connie Lovett standing beside the lotions and skin creams, her face paler than usual. Even though a fuchsia and violet scarf covered her head and her nylon jacket matched the energetic hues of the scarf, something about her felt colorless, listless, as though all the vibrancy had seeped out of her. But she managed a smile as I approached.

"Hey, Lili. I've been sketching designs, and I think I know what I want to do on that gourd we cut." She waved a prescription and looked over at Mr. Trent, who nodded at her and went on typing Neil's label. "Can't tell if the new chemo is working. It'll take about a month to see any results, the doctor tells me. Meanwhile, I figure it's my job to enjoy myself. How's your brother doing?"

The way news seemed to travel — almost like that water in my ceiling — was one aspect of country life I might never get used to. If it were anyone but Connie I might even try to trace the path of the news about my brother's accident and his recuperation at my house, just to satisfy my curiosity. Nobody else seemed to be bothered by relative strangers knowing the intimate details of their lives, but maybe that's what made small town life work — fewer secrets meant better behavior.

"He's getting used to the idea that it might be a while before he can play ball again. Listen, I'd better get back with his medication before he hobbles down the road to see what's keeping me. See you Tuesday." I hugged her, taking care not to squeeze too tight.

"Ten o'clock. See you then." In the few

minutes we'd been talking, some color had crept into her cheeks. Looking at her at that moment it was easy to forget that she was facing a life-threatening illness.

Easy for me to forget. I'd wager that little fact was present every second in some corner of Connie Lovett's mind.

I drove home lost in a blur of thought, and tiptoed my way up the back stairs and then through the kitchen to the hall so that I could peek into the living room. As I'd hoped, Neil lay on the sofa, eyes shut and mouth open. His gentle snores made me smile. I was about to put the sleeping remedy in the medicine cabinet when the phone rang. I grabbed it before it could ring a second time.

"Oh dear, poor Marjorie. And so close to your house. What's going on, Lili? She takes a strong stand in favor of the casino and gets killed? They said that Marjorie's body was found by a couple of teenagers walking in the woods about a quarter mile away from your house. You go away for three days and come back to find a rifle in your kitchen?" Nora's concern, as much for Marjorie's murder as it was for me, pitched her voice several notes higher than usual.

I shifted the telephone to my other ear and pulled a couple of yellow leaves off the basil plant on the kitchen windowsill. "Sheesh, news travels fast around here. Except, the rifle was in my bathroom ceiling."

"You don't have to keep a rifle in your ceiling. If you're feeling like you need protection, it would be much easier to buy a dog or just pick one up from the pound. Okay, bad joke. You sound shaky. You all right?"

My throat swelled. The tight place in my chest expanded, and I took a huge deep breath. I hadn't realized the depth of my distress, hadn't checked in with myself in days.

"It's everything. My brother. Marjorie, of course. Connie Lovett and what that illness is doing to her. Finding the rifle." Delivering a catalog of woes was supposed to help lighten the burden, but the more I spoke the worse everything seemed.

"Overload," she said. I could practically see her ticking off each item on her fingers. "Everything doesn't have to be a major big deal to count as a source of stress, you know. Scrambling to juggle your freelance work and never knowing when you'll get paid. Sitting in a mediation room every week with people who want to kill each other. And now you have to fix that leak in

102

your roof, too. Let's see — is that it, or do I have to start on my toes?"

I might as well complete the list, even though one item affected Nora directly. "I keep getting up at four in the morning with my mind racing and I can't get back to sleep. And this casino thing — I hate how it's turned the poker group into warring camps. Have you spoken to Susan? She needs her friends now, and instead —"

"Whoa. Yes, I've seen her. And so has Melissa. She's doing better. Just that scar and a little shakiness. Her classes have sent her funny cards and flowers and she's going back to work on Monday."

Heat rose to my face. I should have known that these women wouldn't let one of their own suffer through a trauma without offering support. But the omission of one name nearly deafened me in the silence.

"And Elizabeth?" I listened for a response, and when it didn't come my anger spilled over. "I don't get it. How can she do that? That's like not talking to your sister because of some stupid argument and ten years later you can't remember the argument but you still won't make a move to fix things. She's conveniently forgotten how everyone — including Susan — tried to understand when she represented that cement plant that would have polluted four counties on either side of the river."

"Eight years. Elizabeth hasn't spoken to her sister in eight years." Nora sighed again. "She phoned Susan yesterday, so that's something, even if it wasn't face to face. You know the tolerance you're demanding of Elizabeth? Maybe you should think about extending it to her as well."

Sometimes, I do need to have another person point out the obvious. But I didn't much like being forced to think that way when what I really wanted was to be bothered by Elizabeth's apparent lack of compassion. I reached for an almond and crunched noisily.

"Melissa's so confused about the Susan situation. She's been upset and only half-present, even at work." Nora sounded like the one who was upset. "I'm the new partner at the Taconic Inn, so it's been delicate, figuring out how to tell Melissa that the business is going to suffer unless she finds a way to come back to her real self. The casino and Susan are only part of what's bothering her. She hasn't been right since her Aunt Bernice died. Bernie was almost like a mother to her."

It had been devastating for Melissa to watch her aunt die. She'd talked frequently about Bernie, who had Parkinson's for years, about how she gave herself shots whenever things got bad. And they'd helped. Until a month ago. I knew too well how it was with that illness. My father's good days gave us hope, and the bad ones left us watching and waiting to make sure his medicine was working. Melissa must have been as grateful as I was that modern medicine had come up with a drug that shortened the bad episodes.

"You know what the trouble is? I can see both sides. Both sides of the casino issue, and both sides of the Susan thing. Sometimes I wish I could keep things much, much simpler. But then I'd be someone else."

"Someone I wouldn't like half as much. Enough of this stuff. Scooter wants to know how your brother is. I mean, I do too, we all do, but you know sixteen-year-olds — everything's either the worst or the best. Neil's going to be all right, isn't he?"

I filled Nora in on my brother's condition and on my call to Trisha Stern, who assured me that she could help him. She let me ramble for a while, and then her voice lit up with that I-know-a-secret sound.

"You know how you hate it when people say everything happens for a reason? You know, your house burns to the ground for a reason. Your husband is murdered for a reason." Her voice caught as she said the words that some well-meaning person had probably delivered to her last fall, thinking they would be a comfort. "You got grounded by Michele Castro so that your brother would have an excuse to say he'd come up and stay with you."

"Grounded — that didn't happen. I went to that gallery opening. I told her that if she wanted to send somebody to tag along behind me, that was skin off her behind, not mine." My inner adolescent, never far from the surface, was enjoying this brief excursion into the daylight.

Nora laughed. "I never thought I'd hear a thirty-four-year-old white woman sound like my sixteen-year-old African-American son. Anyway, you just keep that in mind — that Neil feels good that he can provide you with some company while you're going through your own ordeal. That lets him feel he's doing something for you, instead of being a burden."

"Lemonade," I said as I heard Neil stirring in the living room. "You really do know how to make lemonade."

CHAPTER 8

The sounds of laughter that accompanied the footsteps on my back porch were a welcome break from thinking about Marjorie Mellon, Michele Castro, and the murder that had gotten a little too close to home. And from the four-hour stint I'd just put in working on a brochure for Boite Blanc, a small, white cave of a restaurant about to open on a side street of Great Barrington, Massachusetts. My friends tumbled into the kitchen clutching their sides and looking at Elizabeth, who took her time as she played out the moment for its dramatic value.

Susan wasn't with them.

Elizabeth set her purse on the counter, unbuttoned her lavender suede jacket, and waited until all eyes were on her before she said, "And the pirate answered, 'Aargh, it's driving me nuts!' "

Everyone dissolved again into laughter that left them holding onto the butcher block or each other for support. Convulsed with belly laughs that reduced them to helplessness, they were irresistible. Despite my worry about Susan, I laughed with them. Neil laughed too. The sound was so infectious I was afraid they would keep going until they collapsed in a puddle on the floor.

Finally, everyone resumed normal breathing. I looked around the circle of women gathered at the kitchen island and said, "Don't even tell me the start of that joke. Bad enough that I have a Bob Marley song stuck in my head for days. You know my brother Neil is staying with me for a while."

I made introductions all around, and Neil asked each of my friends a question that told them he was really interested in their lives. This was one of the skills he'd learned from Mom, who used it to her advantage in her job as event planner for the office of the mayor of New York City. Neil simply used it to make everyone love him — or at least, to feel comfortable in his presence.

He'd saved Melissa for last. "Lili tells me you're expanding your business. That sounds so exciting. When will you open the second place?"

"With Nora's help I'll be ready to cut the ribbon on the bed-and-breakfast in about a month," Melissa said, smoothing her already perfect brown bob. Whenever she talked about the inn or the new B&B, she glowed, but a little extra shimmer surrounded her now. "We've picked out wallpaper and linens for upstairs. Now all we have to do is make sure the contractors, three brothers from Chatham, show up on time. Our ads should start running in the *Wall Street Journal* and *New York Magazine* next week."

I didn't bother to suppress my sigh of relief that Melissa wasn't using Tony Caterra to do her renovation. If she told me that she'd hired him, I'd really be stuck. As a mediator, I couldn't warn her away. All the facts weren't in yet, but I still couldn't say whether or not he'd turn out to be a crook who pocketed money that should have gone into paying workmen who knew what they were doing and to materials that actually could do what they were meant to do. As her friend, I wouldn't be able to remain quiet. A little creative information delivery — I'd have figured out a way.

"You're covering lots of bases at once. Sounds like you're ready to hit a great double," Neil said. He shook his head. "Sorry about the baseball thing."

Melissa smiled, holding out her hand as if to stop his apology. "Well, if I didn't cover all those bases, my business would strike out before the first inning. I'd hate to be thrown out of the game before I even got on deck."

The rest of us groaned, but Neil said, "Now I understand why Lili's so happy here. Beautiful scenery, clean air, a chance to do the work she loves. Plus, she's surrounded by smart people. Well, great to meet you all. Good luck, everyone."

"In poker, unlike in life, somebody's got to lose," I said. "Are we going to stand around chatting up my brother or are we going to play cards? And where's Susan?"

I added that last question as casually as I could. Neil offered a salute and then swung forward on his crutches and disappeared down the hall. I carried the tray of cut vegetables to the living room, placed it on the low bookcase that doubled as a buffet, and waited for my friends to settle in to their seats. Nobody jumped to answer me.

"Well? Is she coming? Did anyone talk to her?"

Melissa pushed her hair behind her pretty ears and then reached for her wineglass. Elizabeth's mouth opened and then fell shut.

"I spoke to her earlier. She wasn't sure if she could —" A smile of relief melted

Nora's frown. "That must be Susan now," she said, nodding toward the headlights that had appeared in my driveway.

Elizabeth sat straighter in her chair. An uncomfortable evening lay ahead of us, unless someone could figure out a way to change the mood.

I went to the kitchen and pulled the door open. Susan shrugged off her down vest and pushed her red curls off her shoulders, a half-smile lifting the corners of her mouth.

I hugged her, hard and quick, and then stood back. "Great! We couldn't start without you. Everyone's inside."

A tiny twitch appeared at the outer corner of her eye, just below the bright scar, her badge of honor. "I almost didn't come," she said softly.

"I'm glad you did." I waited for her to lead, and then followed into the living room, where everyone smiled and said hello and pushed chairs around to make room.

I sat down, fanned a deck of cards, and said, "Okay, everybody, pick a card to see who's dealer."

Melissa reached for a card in the middle of the deck and slapped it on the table. "Ace of spades. Contest's over."

Instead of the groans and good-natured banter I expected, Melissa's shoulders straightened, Nora's lips pressed together, and Elizabeth slouched in her chair, legs stretched out in front of her. Susan and I looked at each other and waited to find out what the joke was.

"What?" I said finally.

Glances were exchanged around the table, and finally Melissa said, "We need to talk before we play. About what's going on with you."

"You're in trouble." Elizabeth wasn't asking a question, she was making a very direct statement, and her tone and her expression made my stomach do a flip. "B. H. Hovanian filled me in on what's been happening."

"You're cutting yourself off, Lili, and that's not good. When you cut yourself off from your friends, we don't have the chance to share our collective wisdom. And you don't get the benefit of knowing that you have the support of people who care about what happens to you." Melissa sounded as though she'd rehearsed this speech.

Without my permission, a lone tear trickled down my face. The stone that had been pressing on my chest levitated a few inches and I started to breathe more easily.

But my brain did not engage, and I found myself speechless. My first impulse, to defend myself and say that I was over-whelmed by a sea of details that I had to juggle until the list became more manage-able, would only make me look even more foolish. I did the only thing I could think of — the simplest thing.

"Thank you," I said. "I just came to that conclusion myself, sort of. Okay, so one of the things that's bothering me is how the casino debate is affecting this group. There's a huge undercurrent of . . . I don't know, tension for sure. But something else."

"Hostility? Is that what you're having such a hard time saying?" Elizabeth's lips tight-ened. "You seem to think that people can just turn off their feelings so that they can sit down to a nice, friendly game of cards. Well, it doesn't work that way."

Susan pushed her chair away from the table, stood and leaned over in Elizabeth's direction. "Why not? Why can't we leave our political differences out of this? It's not like I'm advocating ritual human sacrifice. I really don't get it, this cold shoulder. As though all these years hadn't even hap-pened. And that goes for you, too." She turned to face Nora. "And you," she said, swiveling to confront Melissa.

Each woman broke eye contact before Susan did. Her green eyes flashed with anger, and I resisted the impulse to jump in and try to fix things. That wouldn't have worked — even if I had any idea how to do that. Finally, Nora rose and stood in front of Susan.

"You're right. I'm sorry for shutting you out." She pulled Susan into a hug and then stood back. "I don't want this to go one second longer."

"Me too." Melissa reached for Susan's hand. "I'm sorry."

Susan nodded, squeezed Melissa's hand, and then looked over at Elizabeth.

Each tick of the kitchen clock echoed through the house. My heart did a double-time accompaniment as I studied the table. It was the only way I could avoid staring at Elizabeth.

Finally, she took a swig from her water glass and said, "I'm angry, Susan. You refuse to admit what a tragic impact that casino will have on our town. I still love you but I hate what you say and what you do about this. I don't know if I can —"

"Your choice. You can accept that we think differently about this and not let the differences erase thirty years of friendship. Or you can decide that the only people who can be your friends are people who agree with you." Susan sat down again, her eyes still fixed on Elizabeth.

A twitch played along Elizabeth's upper lip. She looked away, took several slow, deep breaths, folded a paper napkin in half and then in half again. "Okay, you want me to be honest? I don't know if I can just, as you call it, accept our differences, I truly don't. Best I can say is that I'll try to set them aside tonight. More than that?" She shrugged. "I really don't know."

Now it was up to Susan. Her freckles seemed to dance across her face as she scrunched her forehead. When she nodded, she still wasn't smiling. "Okay, I can deal with that. Like they say in those twelve-step programs, one day at a time. Well, I guess this is one poker game at a time. Melissa, it was your deal, right?"

Before Melissa could answer, I said, "I'm really glad the air got cleared a little but there's one more thing I want to talk about before we play. I need some help figuring out this whole Marjorie thing."

Nora stood up, bustling about with glasses and the wine bottle. "See? Great minds do think alike. We thought we'd do a little brainstorming before the game. Everybody up for this?"

An emphatic chorus of yeses followed.

"Great. So — no censoring, anything

goes," I said as Nora set a nearly full glass of Cabernet in front of me.

"No alligatoring," Melissa said. "You know, snapping your jaws to say something negative when anyone puts an idea out there."

"Quantity counts. Keep the ideas coming," Susan said, scooping up three baby carrots. With delicate precision, she started eating them one by one, as though they were tiny logs being fed into a chipper. She started giggling, and Nora and Melissa laughed with her. Elizabeth looked away.

"Otherwise, we'll be spinning our wheels." Nora peered over her raised wineglass at me. "And we can't do that when Lili needs our help."

Everyone stared at me for a long, silent moment.

Being the center of attention was fine with me, as long as I was the one who sought the spotlight. Having it thrust on me was harder. I'd been loathe to admit that I needed help ever since childhood, because it meant . . . what? I wasn't sure. I don't have a problem acknowledging that I'm not perfect, that I don't have answers to every question, that other people really do have expertise, training, and life experience that I don't have. So, why should it be so hard to accept help from a group of women I considered my friends?

I'd thought about this so many times, and the answer had always been the same.

If I needed help, that meant I couldn't manage my life on my own. If I couldn't manage my life on my own, my safety depended on the whims and moods of other people. The first part was certainly true. My life was full, rich, and complex, and some situations required knowledge I didn't have. That's why plumbers and pharmacists and mortgage brokers were sometimes necessary. But those were the people I paid to help me. If they let me down, I'd just call another one.

The yellow pages didn't have a category called "Friends."

If I had to leave my beating heart in someone else's care for a while, I'd trust my friend Karen with it, no questions asked. I almost felt the same about Nora. I probably should have about the others, but I wasn't quite there yet. I could sit here and wonder until I turned mauve, or —

A rush of energy and a desire to plunge ahead rose up so suddenly I didn't have a chance to question it, or to quell it.

"Marjorie Mellon was murdered," I said. "She was shot in the back of the head. Her body was found half a mile from my house. The rifle that fired the shot that killed her was stashed in my attic. Those are the facts."

"Not all of them." Susan had scribbled down everything I'd said, and now she looked up from her paper. "She made a public statement that she was in favor of the casino. And she called for other people who wanted it to join her in a consortium to find ways to support it."

"So, who was against the casino? Most of us." Nora avoided Susan's gaze and took a sip of her wine. "And Connie Lovett."

"And Seth Selinsky," I said quietly. "And Trisha Stern. And at least a hundred others."

"The real question," said practical Nora, "is what do we do now? I mean, how can we get useful information?"

We exchanged shrugs and sheepish glances as we waited for a spark to ignite a bonfire of great ideas.

"In New York after September 11th, the slogan was 'See something, say something.' I always thought it was kind of lame," I admitted, "but it makes sense in this situation. We keep our eyes and ears open, maybe ask a couple of discreet questions — *discreetly* — and then follow up if something strikes us as odd."

"So," Melissa said, "what's odd?"

Odd, in Brooklyn, consisted of asking a total stranger to watch your bag while you went to the restroom. Here in Walden Corners, nobody would look twice if you left your car unlocked, but they'd roll their eyes if a neighbor suddenly decided to paint the gazebo purple. The discussion continued with example after example, each one stretching the envelope a little more, until Nora said, "Odd in this group is stopping the jokes and getting down to business. We're trying to help Lili here. No more fun allowed."

Everyone laughed, of course. I realized that the most likely outcome of all this activity was that we'd feel a little more like we were in control. As though we might contribute to discovering the truth, thereby saving me from wrongful prosecution, even if all we found was crumbs. Another corner of my mind was sure that with so many smart, resourceful friends working toward the same end, I'd be suspicion-free in short order.

"So, would you say that Nathaniel Bartle going to Poughkeepsie and coming back with a generator and two wooden crates is odd?" Susan shook her head. "He's always been the totally PC do-the-right-thing activist, the last one I'd figure for a survivalist.

Maybe he's thinking that the casino is going to bring the cowboys into town, to fight off the very Indians . . . I mean, Native Americans, he's trying to help."

Nora nodded. "And what about Trisha Stern? I've seen her walking her land and hanging mirrors in trees and carrying bowls of burning stuff that make thick, black smoke. She's had this glazed look in her eye ever since the meetings started. Maybe she's getting in touch with a higher power, or maybe she's gone off the deep end."

"I'm sorry to say this, but wasn't Seth pretty adamant that the casino would cost him business?" Elizabeth glanced at me and then looked away. "He's been so distracted lately, he hardly even remembers to say hello if you bump into him. Melissa, you have any ideas?"

Melissa shuddered, as though she'd been awakened from a bad dream. "Sorry, I was just thinking about my Aunt Bernie. She loved puzzles — she was so sharp she would have made sense of all this. It's not fair, it's just not fair. We were so optimistic about the new treatment, we thought we had all the time in the world. Now I can't stand that I put off stopping by at her house that last week."

Connie and her doctor had been so sure

she'd be feeling better by now. I could barely imagine how it must feel to watch someone you considered a second mother not respond to treatment. I reached out to close my hand over Melissa's. "It sucks, you're right. I'm so sorry."

Melissa squeezed my hand and smiled. "Enough of that. Look, Lili was right. Maybe just being conscious of odd behavior is a good place to start. For now, I think, we'll have to settle for being observers."

"And poker players," Nora said. "Who has the next highest card? Oops, looks like my jack of clubs is it."

The others looked at her meaningfully. I nodded, ready for her to scoop up the cards on the table and start the deal.

"So I get to say this part. It's not just the suspect thing, Lili. We're all a little worried about you. You're under a lot of stress right now, and it shows. We're here to help however we can — run errands, come over and take care of house stuff. Even stay with your brother for a couple of hours to give you a break."

Susan, her eyes twinkling, looked at Melissa and nodded. "From the look on your face, I'd say that you'll be the first volunteer, right?"

"Okay, enough of that, you guys." Melissa's voice had dropped to a whisper as she pointed to the hall, in the direction in which Neil had disappeared. "Neil Marino is cute and charming and he's eleven years younger than I am, so back off."

She passed me the bowl of vegetables. "And, yes, I'd be happy to come over to let you run errands or whatever. But you have to do something, too. You have to promise to take us up on these offers. You've been looking so tired lately. I know I'm not a doctor, but maybe you should think about getting something that would help you sleep."

I laughed. "Warm milk and a clear conscience. And valerian. Mr. Trent gave me some. It's supposed to be Nature's sleeping pill or something. I'll be all right, once Michele Castro decides to leave me alone. Listen, I don't know how else to say this, but thanks."

"No thanks yet. We haven't done anything. Good intentions won't take the place of good ideas." Elizabeth snatched a celery stalk from the vegetable tray and looked at it as though it had stepped out of a Martian spaceship. "Whatever happened to chips and dip? I think one way to find out who murdered Marjorie is for all of us to go to her funeral on Wednesday. And we need to get more active in the whole casino thing."

"Well, of course. I was planning to go to the service anyway. And to all the casino meetings." Nora's face brightened. "But now we'll have a focus. We'll talk to people, get them to open up and maybe reveal something. There's a meeting next week at the Lovetts' barn. The posters have been plastered all over town. 'If you want to keep our town small and friendly yada yada. . . .' Some of us should go. Nobody would think twice about that."

My heart thudded. The only one whose presence at that meeting would raise suspicion was Susan. Before I could figure out how to say anything, Susan laughed and then pointed her finger at each of us around the table.

"I'm the only one who can go to the *other* meeting," she said, grinning. "You'll have to trust me to be your eyes and ears and bring you back a full report. If any of the rest of you went to the Lovetts, nobody would say a word because you've already stood up and been counted. Against. All of you. What you might not know is that there's talk of a supporters' meeting at Nathaniel's bowling alley. It's closed on Tuesdays and that's when it's scheduled. You want me to go?"

Nora was the first to break the silence. "Of course. That's perfect. It'll be harder for you to cover a lot of ground because you're only one person, but you're right, Susan. You're the only one who can go to Nathaniel's."

"I'll take good notes. Everyone takes notes at these things, except mine will be a little different." She slipped the cards back into the deck, shuffled, and then fanned the cards out in the middle of the table. "Okay, now this is for real. High card deals."

I placed my hand atop the cards and waited until everyone looked at me. I was the only one smiling. "Aha, see? You only like it when you know what the script is. You engineered this whole conversation. But you forgot that I don't take orders very well. So before we play, I get to say something too."

They all sat closer to the edge of their chairs. If I could have, I would have scooped them into a group hug, the way my friends used to in fifth grade in Brooklyn.

What, I wondered, was stopping me?

"Okay, everyone stand up," I ordered. Nora, Susan, and Melissa pushed their chairs back and came to where I was standing in the middle of the room. My eyes met Elizabeth's, and I saw a challenge that six months earlier might have ruined the moment for me. But I knew enough now to reach for her hand and tug her to her feet. I raised my arms to start the circle, and Susan grabbed me on one side and Nora on the other. Melissa and then Elizabeth joined the huddle.

"Now, get closer. Closer." I waited until our noses were practically touching. "Okay, now everyone repeat after me. One for all and all for —"

"Lili!" Nora shouted. "We shall prevail. Just think of us as your enforcers."

"My Gourdfellas, only this time we're on the right side of the law."

I felt like a winner without ever seeing what cards I'd been dealt.

CHAPTER 9

Trisha Stern might have been the most cheerful person I'd ever met. Luckily, it was a bearable cheerfulness, because it seemed to come from a genuinely optimistic view of the world. With her short, wispy hair and blue eyes that crinkled when she smiled, she looked like an elf sent to lead my brother to a hidden treasure.

"You are so lucky it wasn't your femur," she said as she coaxed Neil to raise his leg a little higher. "Would have taken longer, might have been harder on the weight bearing. And you're in such good shape, too. You just have to work a little harder for the next eight weeks, keep your upper body strength — no, don't point your toes, flex — and get some cardio in, you'll be okay."

Sweating with the strain, Neil finally dropped his leg and swabbed his face with a towel. "Were you this hard on the girls?" he asked, grinning.

"Harder. And the New York Liberty complained less." She handed him the water bottle. "All right, sixty seconds of rest. Then we'll work those lats."

In just a week, Neil had made remarkable progress. He was especially pleased that his right leg, which he insisted was a little skinnier than his left when he arrived, was already starting to regain its muscle. He started his upper body workout, lifting the hand weights he'd brought from home. Sweat popped out first on his face and then on his torso as he went through his reps. I waved as I headed for the gourd studio, relieved that Trisha had turned out to be more than competent. Forty minutes gave me just enough time to finish staining one of the pieces I wanted to show at the Welburn Gourd Festival in June.

Neil and I had settled into a pleasant routine, and life would have been good and comfortable except for the sword of suspicion hanging over my head. We ate breakfast and lunch whenever and wherever the spirit moved us, but dinner was served at seven o'clock at the table, television off. We'd fallen happily into the routine of our mother's house. Its virtues, against which we complained when we were children, were apparent to us now.

I was so absorbed in applying the leather dye and watching it run and spread along the gourd surface that I was startled when the telephone rang. I reached for the receiver, nearly spilling a large container of Buckskin all over myself. My voice might have had the slightest edge to it when I said hello.

"Lili?" the familiar male voice asked.

"Tom. You weren't exactly who I expected when I picked up the phone. Sorry if I sounded weird. I nearly turned myself brown when . . . never mind, you didn't call to hear my problems. What can I do for you?"

After I'd left messages in Vermont and at his offices in New York City last winter when I was looking for information about money Nora's husband had invested, Tom Ford had made it clear that he didn't want me to call him. I'd been more than happy to honor his request. Now he was the one who had crossed that line. What could be important enough for him to violate his own ban and telephone?

"That proposed casino sounds like a little bit of hell about to be dropped into paradise," he said. "Who can I contact about it?"

I refrained from asking him why anyone

would care what he thought about the matter. He'd owned this cottage for five years, had never socialized with a single soul in the community, and then had moved three thousand miles away.

"I guess the mayor or the head of the town council. Mayor's name is Fred Patronski, and Joseph Trent is the council leader. I'm sure if you write to them at the Walden Corners Administrative Center it will get to them." If he thought I was going to spend time looking up the address when he could find it just as easily on the Internet, he was missing some marbles. In fact, he could have found Patronski's and Trent's names that way, too. And yet he'd phoned me.

"Right, sure, I should have thought of that. Everything all right at the house?"

The answer to that question depended entirely on the person doing the asking. "Fine," I said. "I'm having some roofing work done, and I put in a garden. Everything's fine."

"I miss the place." I'd never heard him sound wistful before, but the note of longing in his voice was clear. "It's beautiful here and they have great coffee and it's a terrific spot to feel the spirit of Manifest Destiny and all that. But it doesn't have the settled, lush feel of Columbia County. Listen, I read about Marjorie Mellon and the rifle."

Was he about to solve at least part of the mystery? I held my breath and waited for him to go on.

"I had an idea about how it got there," he said. "You know that louvered window? The one at the east end of the attic where the fan is? Someone can climb up the maple tree and just push on the fan and drop the rifle in. Pull the fan back into place and that's that."

And maybe leave behind fingerprints or clothing fibers. Before I could say more, Tom cleared his throat. "Anyway, I'm sure things will work out for you. But this casino idea — it would be criminal to destroy that part of the Hudson Valley with a casino. Jobs, taxes, reparations — nothing is worth the price of ruining the peace and beauty of the area."

I sighed. Understanding what it was like to have to scramble for a job was not Tom Ford's greatest asset. What did he, the manager of a failed mutual fund who had then picked himself up and rebuilt the business so that he could pay off the investors he'd burned, know about real struggle? I doubted whether he'd ever had dinner with someone who had to decide whether to buy groceries or pay for health insurance. His dinner companions were more likely to fret about whether to go to Valencia or Cozumel for a winter break.

When it came right down to it, the real question was whether he'd ever had dinner with someone.

"The people who support the casino think Walden Corners needs to expand its tax base and its employment opportunities," I explained.

"They're right. But there are other ways. They don't have to support a blight. Well, thanks for the information, Lili."

"Wait!" Before he hung up, I wanted to tap the well of ideas that was his brain. "How else? What would be a good alternative to the casino?"

"I'd need to think about that more before I say. But I'm sure there's something. Look, I have to go. I'm late for a meeting. I *am* glad that things are working out for you at the cottage."

Except for the little matter of Marjorie's murder.

Without waiting for a good-bye from me he hung up, ensuring that my frustration would remain at a simmer for the rest of the hour. I pictured him, dark hair slicked back and tinted glasses shielding his feral green eyes from the sun glare bouncing off

Puget Sound. Tom the Arrogant, who took what he needed and then moved on, was terribly efficient at getting a reaction from me. I should have known, should have been prepared. Should have told him to take his request and —

No need to allow those buttons to be pushed, I reminded myself. That gives him the power, and that's not right. I closed my eyes, let out a whoosh of air, and then started to work on my gourd again. I glanced at the clock. Only five minutes left of Trisha's session with my brother, and I really wanted to catch her before she left so I could tell her how much I appreciated what she was doing for Neil.

Besides, I liked her. I wiped my hands on my work jeans and got to the living room just in time to see her pack up her equipment. The sound of running water in the bathroom meant that Neil was washing up after his workout.

"I'm so glad you're helping my brother. When he was trying to figure out what to do for rehab, he perked right up when I told him about you. You're just the right combination of tough and tender to make him work his hardest. I'm really grateful."

She bent to secure the buckles on her bag and then stood, face flushed and eyes twinkling. "He's got the grit. That'll serve him well."

I couldn't read whether she meant serve him well in recovering and playing the second half of the season or serve him well in building a new life without baseball.

"How do you like the change from the big city?" she asked.

Glad for the opening, I said, "Made it through four seasons, and I still love it here. How about you? You seem so at home. You don't miss New York?"

Her smile made her look even younger, and the twinkle in her eye brightened. "Sometimes I think I married Jonathan just to be able to live in that great house. I love the stillness of winter and the way everything wakes up in the spring. I love the abundance of summer — did you ever can thirty-six quarts of tomatoes? Amazing! Fall — wow, I never seem to get my eyes open wide enough to take in all that spectacular beauty. You'll have to come for lunch when Neil's a little more mobile. Our own stream. A meadow surrounded by trees. The crocuses are almost gone, but we've got a fantastic tulip bed that should be at its peak next week. And you can't even hear the traffic from Route 9G or Walden Road."

Which was right where the casino would

be built. No wonder she was so against the whole idea. She was protecting her backyard. Literally.

"The casino would change everything, wouldn't it? It's such a complicated issue, so many points on both sides." Playing the innocent wasn't my strongest suit, but I hoped Trisha Stern didn't know me well enough to recognize a change in my tone.

She was still smiling when she said, "Two sides to every question. It does look like enough people are against it that it won't go through. The people who want that casino are really only halfhearted about it. No match for how passionate the rest of us are about seeing it doesn't happen. They aren't well organized, they just spout theories about taxes and justice."

Not well organized now that Marjorie was dead.

"See you next time," I said. A glimmer of suspicion flitted into my mind and then floated away. No, Trisha Stern wouldn't go to *any* length to protect her new life. No way.

She hefted her blue nylon bag onto her shoulder and waited until Neil made his way back to the sofa. When he was settled in, she patted his arm. "You're really doing great. Don't forget to do those healing visualizations."

I watched her walk to her car. Where was Trisha Stern the day that Marjorie was killed? What about her husband and the other families who bordered the ten acre plot just outside of town?

But I didn't have time to add to my mental list of questions. The spot Trisha's car had occupied was hardly cool when Seth Selinsky's silver pickup truck took its place. He carried a stack of magazines and a bakery box, and wore neat grey slacks, a black and white checked shirt, and a soft, satisfied smile.

"I know, you were in the neighborhood." I stepped aside to let him come in, not even trying to hide my pleasure in seeing him.

As he passed, he lingered in front of me. "Mmm, you smell good. Better, even, than these butter cookies. No, I made this trip to bring you and your brother some cookies and see if there's anything I can do to help."

"You're not only cute and a good cook but also a gentleman. Even a scholar, when it comes to mortgages. I'll make some coffee and introduce you. Not in that order."

Seth put the white box on the kitchen counter and followed me to the living room. Shiny and relaxed, Neil had taken up his usual spot on the sofa and was tapping away on his computer. Seth walked over to my brother, stuck out his hand, and said, "Hi, Seth Selinsky. Sorry about the leg. Tough break. Your first at bat, man. A two and three count."

Neil shut the cover of his laptop and pointed to the chair on the other side of the coffee table. "You ever play?"

What happened to perfectly nice and articulate men that made them talk in half sentences? I stood back, watching my brother and the man I was dating circle each other conversationally. For all that my presence mattered, I could have been a doorknob. Amused, I went to the kitchen and got the coffee started, loaded a tray with cups, saucers, plates, cookies, napkins. If this happened all the time, I'd probably be annoyed. For now, their little game tickled me.

When I carried the tray into the living room, the conversation hadn't gotten very far.

"Sure, I was on the disabled list for two weeks. But that was in college. It's different for you." Seth's lean legs stuck out into the middle of my living room floor, a sight that made me smile despite myself.

I deposited the tray on the coffee table and kissed the top of Neil's head. "See? Your fans find you wherever you are."

Neil grinned at Seth and then raised his eyebrow at me. "*Your* fan, you mean. You think Seth really came to see me? We've been talking baseball. Among other things."

I made the family gesture, index fingers making a backward circular motion to signify eye-rolling. "I'm much too mature to be goaded into asking what other things," I said as I lowered myself to the chair across from Seth.

"Good," he said. "Then we don't have to give up our secrets. Listen, I stopped by with a business proposition."

Neil did a Groucho Marx with his eyebrows and an imaginary cigar.

"Rick Luney says you're quick, smart and always hit the mark for him. Well, for me, too, but he's talking about the business writing you've done for him. I need a new brochure for MidHudson Mortgage. We're trying to carve out a bigger piece of the second home market. If I can let people know we're here, and just what we can do for them that their city mortgage broker can't, then I think I can double my client list."

I needed to find another gallery to carry my gourds, and I needed someone to help me get my garden started, and I needed to figure out a way to make sure my friends continued to talk to each other despite their political differences, but I definitely did not need another freelance writing job. I was working four days a week already, with jobs lined up through June. Besides, what would working for Seth do to our not-quite relationship? And what would saying no mean?

I was about to find out.

"I'm flattered. And I'm also loaded right now. So many writing clients I can hardly keep up. I wouldn't be doing either of us any good if I took on your brochure before July. I'm sure you want to take advantage of the spring and summer influx of city folks. I can recommend a couple of other writers, though, people whose work I know and who I think would do a great job for you."

Seth's brown eyes clouded. His genial expression didn't change, but it seemed like he was holding his breath. Whether he was having a temper tantrum or waiting for me to change my mind, I couldn't tell. This was the first time I'd seen him show a petulant side. Finally he said, "That works, I guess. Are any of them as pretty and as smart as you are?"

"One fellow I know is probably prettier and more tuned to city things but I'm smarter. And then there's my mentor, who describes herself as "Rubenesque." She's one of the brightest people I know." Maybe I'd gotten too defensive too quickly. Seth's smile still beamed in my direction. When I glanced over at Neil, he seemed to be enjoying the sparring match. "Besides, you probably don't want a murder suspect to have a hand in your brochure."

Neil's eyes widened and Seth's laugh filled the room.

"I'm sorry." Seth's grin was replaced by a thoughtful frown. "You think you're a serious suspect in Marjorie's murder? That's crazy. She was the focal point for the pro-casino group. What Marjorie did that nobody else bothered to do was to organize. She knew the power she'd wield if she had the backing of prominent businesspeople and town opinion-makers. 'Consortium.' That's her word. Mine is 'gang.' And if Castro and Murphy are smart, that's where they'll put their energies. Looking at people who would feel threatened if Marjorie succeeded."

Neil was suddenly alert, his attention apparently ignited by the fire in Seth's voice. "So you really think that whoever killed that woman was against the casino? People would get that hot about a place to have a little entertainment?"

"Some of these people." I rubbed a finger along the soapstone elephant my brother Charlie had brought me from Tanzania. "At least that's how it sounded at that meeting when somebody got hot enough to throw a rock that hit Susan just above her eye."

"It's about protecting their safe, quiet little corner of the world." Seth reached for his coffee cup, took a tentative sip, and set it back on the coaster. "You learn a lot when you're in the business of helping people buy a house. Sometimes feeling in control is more important than money, sex, career, whatever. Walden Corners — they don't want anything about it to change unless they say it should."

"And that's worth killing to protect? If Marjorie's out of the picture does that mean the support for the casino will fall apart?" Neil winced in pain as he dropped his leg to the floor and reached for his crutches. "Hold that answer. I'll be right back. You guys go ahead, solve the world's problems, clean the windows, and build stronger levees in Louisiana. I should be back by the time you're finished."

Without a word, Seth stood beside Neil and offered his arm. This time, Neil was either tired enough or weak enough to accept. I gathered the empty cups and plates and took them into the kitchen. The rhythmic thunk-plunk of Neil's forward progress faded as he made his way to the bathroom.

I was about to sweep the crumbs into the garbage when I felt Seth's strong arms draw me to him. He kissed the side of my neck before he said, "I miss you."

I turned so I could look into his eyes. "Me, too. But it can't be helped, at least not for now. He's getting stronger, but I don't feel comfortable leaving him alone for more than an hour. So we'll have to satisfy other appetites for a while. You want to whip up dinner next Wednesday? I'll make dessert."

"A threesome?" He smiled as he said it, and kissed the top of my head.

"I was thinking more along the lines of four. Why don't you bring Ron? I know your son is a sports nut. He'd probably get a kick out of meeting a professional baseball player. And Neil would love to have an adoring audience."

"Not exactly what comes to mind when I think about spending time with you, but actually it's a great idea. You can do dessert. Your brother eat falafel and baba ganoush?"

A new culinary adventure — I'd encouraged Seth to indulge his love for cooking, but until now the menu had been creative versions of standard fare.

"You know anyone from Brooklyn who doesn't? That sounds like fun. But I don't know how to make baklava. Isn't that the thing to go with Middle Eastern food?"

"Where's your vision, your pioneering spirit? Dare to eat pie! I'll see you at seven."

I was very glad that he was still standing in the doorway when the phone rang, for two reasons. His kiss was delicious and the warmth that rushed through my body left no room for anxiety. And, second, he was the voice of reason when Michele Castro told me her news.

CHAPTER 10

"Good, you're there. The report just came in. That rifle is the murder weapon. And the lab says the prints on the rifle aren't yours," she said.

I sank back against the kitchen counter in relief. My smile must have been big enough to light the dark side of the moon, and I allowed myself a tiny whoop of pleasure. "I told you I never touched it."

"There's something else. Don't go anywhere. I'll be there in ten minutes."

Right away, I knew that the something wasn't going to make me open another bottle of champagne. "What?" I asked, trying to submerge the feeling of dread that kept bobbing to the surface.

"Just don't go anywhere." And then the line went dead.

Seth's eyes were full of questions I wasn't ready to answer. With trembling fingers I dialed B. H. Hovanian's number.

"He's in court," a male voice informed me. "Can't reach him for at least twenty minutes. He'll phone you as soon as he gets out. Cross my heart."

I hung up and met Seth's worried gaze. "Castro is on her way here. She says my prints weren't on the rifle but that there's — her words — something else."

Neil appeared in the kitchen doorway. "What's this? You getting carted away?"

"Maybe." My mind wouldn't get still and my body twitched at the thought of jail. "But not likely. This is America, not some dark, wooded Eastern European country that Kafka created. Not me — I'm not letting my imagination run away with me. Whatever Michele Castro thinks she has, it has nothing to do with me. Even so, I wish that lawyer would call."

"I know a couple of real estate attorneys," Seth suggested with his teasing smile. "But you rest easy, Lili. If it's under a million, I can post bail."

"You may be sorry you said that. Listen, you guys go back in the living room. I need to catch my breath here." Seth might have been joking, but a second visit and that warning tone in Michele Castro's voice made me wonder whether I'd have to take him up on his offer. To calm myself, I washed the dishes, letting the warm water and the mindlessness of the task soothe me.

It's nothing, I told myself. It couldn't be anything because I had nothing to do with Marjorie Mellon or her murder. My prints weren't on the rifle. They might say that I'd worn gloves, but I hoped the sheriff's department would be sensible and say case closed, at least the one that had me at the center of it.

It didn't sound as though Michele Castro was about to do that.

By the time I finished wiping down the counters, the sound of a car in my driveway announced Castro's arrival.

I walked into the living room, where Neil reached for my hand, squeezing it hard enough to break the spell of my worry. "It's gonna be fine. You didn't do anything, so what could happen?"

Seth stood behind me and placed both hands on my shoulders. "It's just some routine thing, I'm sure. You'll see, some detail she wants to check out with you."

The knock was firm and brisk. I inhaled, nodded to myself, and then opened the wood door but left the screen door closed, latched so that nobody could simply pull it open. On the other side of the screen stood Michele Castro. A burly uniformed officer with a suety complexion and a shirt that was straining to hold back his girth stood behind her.

The sight of him did stop the breath in my chest for a second.

But I didn't wobble and faint, and I did not invite them in. This wasn't a social call requiring that I offer them pleasantries and cookies. I glanced at my watch. Ten more minutes until that lawyer would be out of court — and I could get some rational, informed advice.

"You want to talk to me," I said.

Castro's green eyes narrowed, peering first at me and then over my shoulder into the living room. "I need to come in. *We* need to come inside."

"Why?" I felt Seth's presence behind me, heard Neil thumping to the door. My backup — that didn't exactly put us on equal footing, but it gave my spine a little extra steel.

The steel melted the next second when Michele Castro whipped out a paper and pressed it against the screen. I glanced at the document, my heart sinking. A search warrant, signed by a Judge Michaels. Why hadn't Hovanian called so that I could ask him what was going on? As the daughter of a former NYPD detective, I knew enough to realize that unless some *i* wasn't dotted or a *t* crossed definitively, these officers of the law had the right to come into my home — again — and search through my belongings. What I didn't understand was what they hoped to find in a second search.

"Hey, I'm Neil Marino." My brother waved and flashed a smile at Castro. "Nice to meet you."

She smiled back, her eyes lingering on him before she squared her shoulders as she remembered what she was doing on my front porch. "Look, I'm sorry to disturb you all, but I've got a job to do here. I need to come inside."

"Would you mind telling us what this is about? From what my sister told me, you already searched her home. Pretty thoroughly, too."

I had to hand it to my brother — he made his question sound like he was bestowing high praise for a job well done instead of challenging the necessity for yet another search.

This time, Castro's response was pure cop. "Sorry, this is an ongoing investigation. I need to see all of your computers, Ms. Marino. And your printers, too."

It was a good thing so many people were crowded in the doorway, because her words made me dizzy. My computers and printers? What in the world would she want with them? I looked at the warrant still pressed against the screen. Letters danced on the page. No, it couldn't really say that they could confiscate my computer and my printer. I tapped Neil's shoulder, pointed to the line in question, gathered my thoughts.

"I need them." Even I could hear that my voice was strained and high, and I struggled to lower it. Calm. I had to stay calm. "I only have one computer and it contains confidential client files. My livelihood depends on it. And all the personal things — my banking and a journal and lots of other things that are private. My printer doesn't have anything on it. What do you want that for? You can't just come in here and take them away."

She pointed to the lines that told me she could.

"Look, I can read. But I'm not letting you in here until I speak to my attorney. This is ridiculous, you know it is. You already checked the rifle, you didn't find anything, and you know I had nothing to do with Marjorie's murder. So this constitutes harassment, and it interferes with my right to earn a livelihood, and it's an invasion of my privacy." Each word made Castro's eyes darker and her mouth tighter, but I was not about to let her steamroll her way over my life. "So I'm going to ask you to wait out there, and I'll call my attorney, and then I'll follow his advice. Whatever it is."

Whenever it was that I actually reached him. I stepped back into the living room, aware that Seth had taken my place at the screen door. "Hey, Michele," he said, his voice warm and friendly. "You can understand, right, how upsetting this is. Maybe if you could tell her why you —"

"Seth, you know I can't. It's part of an ongoing investigation."

Just then the phone rang, and I ran the rest of the way to the kitchen and grabbed the receiver.

"I have three minutes," the voice on the other end said. "Speak."

I was glad my folksy country lawyer stereotype had already been shattered. "Michele Castro is standing on my porch with a paper that looks like a search warrant. It says she can take my computer and my printer. Judge Michaels signed it. Do I have to give it to her?"

"Yes. But why does she want it? I know, she didn't tell you. I'll be out of here in ten minutes and I'll see what I can find out. I'll be in touch. Give her what the warrant says. Don't give her a hard time over this."

"Too late," I said quietly.

"Well, then chalk it up to you being the entertainment for the afternoon. I'll call you later."

Somehow, I trusted the man. He made me feel a lot of things, and right now the most important one was — safe. He was direct and he knew how Walden Corners worked, and I was glad to have him on my side.

When I got back to the living room, the big cop was still standing with his hands clasped in front of him but Seth, Neil, and Michele were laughing. Great — my stalwarts were doing a fine job of keeping the enemy off guard.

"Are you sure I can't just show you some file, or make you a copy of the things you're interested in? I've got two jobs that I worked on for three weeks. It would kill me to have to call my clients and return the money they already paid me." Despite Hovanian's advice, I didn't want to give up my link to work, all my client files, my ability to communicate with Albuquerque or Amman or Alicante whenever I needed to.

"I need the computer and the printer." Michele Castro frowned, looked directly into my eyes, then glanced at Seth and Neil before she said, "Before I leave, you can make a back-up of those two work files."

"And her address book?" Seth said. "She can't do business without that."

"You're pushing it, Seth. Quit while you're ahead. That's good advice for gamblers. Of all kinds," she said, her gaze staying on my face. "Okay, the address book, the two files, and that's it. Now, please open the door and let us in."

Neil hobbled back to the sofa, Seth stood watch at the window, and I led the under-sheriff and the deputy to my office, where the laptop I'd bought three months earlier sat in sleep mode. It took her less than twenty minutes to read the two files I needed to finish for my clients, look over my address book, back them up to a disk that she handed over to me, and unplug the cables and connectors.

"You can use my laptop for work," Neil said as Michele Castro brushed past him with my computer in a plastic bag. "As long as you give me a chance to check my email and Google myself every day to see if I'm fired."

I hugged him, and then punched his shoulder. "Not going to happen. Getting fired, I mean. Thanks."

Seth leaned against the windowsill and together we watched the deputy load the equipment into the cruiser. "Makes you feel a little like a television star, doesn't it?" he said. "You know, like the guy who's made millions with his Mafia connection and now has a starring role on *America's Most Wanted.*"

That kind of celebrity I didn't need.

Hovanian summoned me to his office an hour later. The building, formerly a bank with a columned facade and two-story-high windows, sat at the northeast corner of the main intersection of town. The downstairs space now housed an antiques conglomerate called The Goods, while the upstairs was divided into space for three offices: B. H. Hovanian, Seth's MidHudson Mortgage, and something that called itself Luney's Toons, Rick Luney's advertising agency that specialized in producing radio, television, and print ads for local businesses.

Hovanian's secretary, a young man with a blond pompadour and a manner that suggested he would have been wearing an ascot if the weather were the least bit chilly, hung my jacket in a closet, offered me coffee, and engaged me in small talk until the man himself made his appearance seven minutes later.

"Hold my calls, David. We'll be in the

conference room." He stood aside to let me in and pointed in the direction of a long table surrounded by eight burgundy leather chairs.

"Just so you know — I suggested that Castro check that attic window, as you asked me to. She found clothing fibers on the window frame. Maybe they're old, but maybe someone did get into your house that way."

I nodded and I drew my chair closer to the table. When I looked into his dark eyes, I caught a flicker, a frisson of . . . *something* that made me forget the matter at hand for a second. I pulled myself back to business and said, "So, why did she take my computer and my printer, and when will I get them back?"

"You wrote a note to Marjorie Mellon telling her that you had no intention of letting a casino come into Walden Corners to spoil your new home." He sat with his back straight and his hands folded on the gleaming mahogany table. The air smelled vaguely of balsam and furniture polish.

"I *what?*" I would have been less surprised if he'd told me that I'd won the lottery. And certainly more pleased.

"That's why they took your computer and printer. Someone found a note folded into a small square in Wonderland Toy Town. In the bathroom, to be precise. Right near the supplies that Marjorie used every Tuesday to clean the place. Castro says it probably fell out of her pocket the last time she was there." He never took his eyes off mine, even when I failed to say anything in response to the news he'd just dropped as casually as a beekeeper drops a swarming hive.

Finally, I said, "I didn't write any note. Wonderland toys — maybe she should check with the people who work there or shop there. It's a great store, all those wooden train sets and great old board games. Lots of people are in and out of Wonderland. Don't they cater to the city crowd?"

He picked up his gold pen, and turned it between lean, strong fingers. "They'll examine the print on the note and run some tests and then they'll determine whether or not it came from your computer or your printer. That's the easy part. They won't get a match. And they won't find your prints."

What was the hard part, then? Why wouldn't that clear me? "So, if there's no match and no prints on the note, then why —"

I didn't need to finish my own question. The answer was obvious. I might have written it somewhere else. After all, I'd said that I was in the city for several days before Marjorie was killed. And if I did write the note on another computer, I might have been careful enough to make sure my fingerprints didn't turn up on the paper. Which meant that I was still a suspect.

"Okay, I get it. Listen, someone is setting me up. I know everyone must say the same thing, but this time it's true." I sank wearily into my chair. "What did the note say?"

Hovanian smiled with angelic amusement. "Now, that's such a good question. But since you haven't been arrested yet, I don't get to demand that the sheriff's office tell me the contents of the note, and they're not volunteering. If we can find out what the note says, then maybe we'll be able to shift the spotlight away from you to someone else. Another person who clashed with Marjorie."

"I didn't clash with Marjorie." I bristled at the thought that he believed even that part of the sheriff's wrongheaded theory. "Not any more than any other opponent of the casino, probably less. Look, this is really starting to worry me. Why would someone pick me to blame?"

"You know," he said, "I've been asking myself the very same question. From what I gather, you've been accepted by most of the residents of Walden Corners, because of your connection to Nora Johnson and that gang she hangs out with."

Was this tall, rugged-looking man suggesting that I was an uninteresting, unappealing, asocial misfit who would have been shunned if Nora hadn't been my friend? That I wouldn't have been tolerated unless someone had vetted me to the satisfaction of the long-time movers and shakers — such as they were — of this inconsequential little crossroads that called itself a town?

Then I caught myself and laughed at how quickly my defensiveness had colored my thinking. His take was probably right on, given the nature of small towns. Even in Brooklyn, where each neighborhood functioned a bit like a separate village, it had helped when I'd first arrived in Carroll Gardens to have Karen as a guide to ease my entry into new situations.

"Okay, so if Nora and Elizabeth and Susan and Melissa granted me the Walden Corners seal of approval, why would someone think that I'd be an easy target? I mean, wouldn't it make sense to think I'd have backers and resources?" My mind raced, trying to see myself from the perspective of a murderer looking for a patsy. It was harder than I would have imagined.

I was a mediator because I disliked conflict — I wanted to help make life a little easier or more fun for the people around me. I worked hard and kept my lawn trimmed. I was a pretty good daughter, sister, and friend, usually. None of these qualities was especially remarkable. The thing that set me apart from some of my neighbors was a factor of timing: thirteen months in Columbia County, instead of eight generations. But this was a community that relied on weekenders from New York City to drive its economic engine at least partway down the road to prosperity, so even that part of my background was unremarkable.

"Maybe it wasn't a conscious decision." My lawyer took off his dark-framed glasses and rubbed his eyes, then squinted across the table at me before putting the glasses back on. This time, his gaze was steady. "Maybe your house just happened to be near where Marjorie was killed, and it turned out to be a convenient spot to hide the murder weapon. Once the rifle was discovered, the opportunity to shore up the case against you was too good to pass up. Theoretically."

I sank back into my chair. "Fine. So we're back where we started. Someone put a gun in my house. Then they said, 'Aha! Let's make it look like Lili Marino killed Marjorie Mellon.' Which, in a fit of creativity, led them to cleverly forge a note that appeared to be from me and drop it in the bathroom of the local toy store. To make sure the fickle finger of fate — and Michele Castro — continue to camp out on my stoop."

His laugh, more like a bark than a giggle, startled me. "That's a very original job of mixing metaphors," he said. "I just hope that finger doesn't drop anything else on your doorstep."

CHAPTER 11

Maybe my time would have been better spent staying home and working on Neil's computer on the forty-page summary of health care options for one of my longstanding New York City corporate clients, but I put the task aside and prepared to go off into the night in my what-you-see-is-what-you-get persona.

Instead of wearing a trench coat, dark glasses, and a shoe phone, I deliberately chose plain, dark clothing so that I would draw as little attention to myself as possible — I would be just another interested citizen attending the anti-casino meeting, and maybe I'd stumble across a nugget of information that would help me clear my name.

At least I had companions in deception. Nora, Elizabeth, and Melissa would be there too, extra eyes and ears to cover the large crowd and poke into dark corners that hid secrets and lies, while Susan put in an appearance at the pro-casino gathering. It seemed like an unbalanced use of person-power, but Susan was the only one of us who could go to Nathaniel's bowling alley without standing out like a pineapple in a tomato patch.

"Scooter and Armel get there on time?" Nora asked. "Those boys were so excited. A professional baseball player. My son and his best friend, going to spend the evening with a pro. They must have said it at least a zillion times."

"Ten minutes early." I smiled at the memory of how Scooter's usual cool had evaporated under Neil's high wattage smile. Armel, his best buddy, had been speechless until Neil told a joke I only half heard, about third basemen and chewing tobacco. "By the time I left they were talking NASCAR and making bets on whether Mike Piazza would be a Hall of Famer."

Nora stared down at her shoes. "He really misses his father. It's good for him, hanging out with Neil."

"Good for all of them. I'm glad my brother's getting a taste of the adulation that he would have had if he were playing."

"He'll get to have that, only a little later than he thought." Nora looked around, her eyes fixing on a corner of the barn where two gourds sat on a wood plank. "It's great that Connie and Mel have this big barn. Good place for a meeting. Are those the gourds she worked on with you? Who would have thought of putting Art Deco designs on a gourd?"

I nodded, trying not to let my pride show too much. They *were* good — Connie was a quick study, and I loved teaching her.

"They're wonderful." Melissa clutched her jacket closer. "It could be ten degrees warmer in here, but at least it's not February. They're talking about sunshine and sixty degrees again tomorrow. Well, at least Marjorie had a nice day last week for her farewell."

We were all quiet. The service in the plain white church had been jammed, mourners and the merely curious vying for seats. I had put on my invisible shield and slipped into a pew next to Nora, even though the thought of sitting around with Marjorie's family made me feel like an imposter. The stares and whispers of suspicion subsided when the preacher began his talk, except for an occasional glance that only reminded me to sit up straight.

Elizabeth nodded. "I heard that Connie had breakfast with Marjorie's daughter that day. Anita Mellon — she's always been the last person I'd expect to be Connie's friend."

"Other way around, I'd say." Melissa brushed her silky hair off her shoulder. "Connie's the one who was always trying to get Anita to go to school or to dress more . . . conservatively."

Before I could ask what she meant, Melissa turned to me and said, "Listen, I forgot to tell you something."

Those were not words I wanted to hear. Nora, Elizabeth, and I leaned in closer. I smelled lilac shampoo, cinnamon breath mints, and a citrusy scent that reminded me of my favorite bubble bath. Melissa put an arm around me and said, "Watch out for Seth. Someone said he's written a big check to the pro-casino group. He may be a double agent. You know, showing up here just to see what we're up to, so he can report back."

"Who's someone?" I demanded. If the already small dating pool were to be cut by one, I wanted to be the one to do the slashing for my own reasons, not because I'd believed a rumor about one of the few eligible and interesting men around. Seth had declared himself as against the casino . . . or, at least that's how I'd interpreted what he'd said. The idea that he'd give money to the other side was disturbing — if it were true.

"Two different sources. That's all I can say." Melissa looked directly at me. "You can find out, right? Don't you think he'd tell you things the rest of us couldn't ask?"

I groaned. Now they were suggesting that I spy on the man I was dating. If I didn't do it, the seed of doubt might continue to grow, but I'd have to take my chances.

"Not my style to lead a man on." I hoped my smile communicated a what-me-worry attitude. "If it comes up, fine, I'll have an opening. But I won't manipulate Seth into —"

"Speak of the devil," Elizabeth said, her eyes tracking a path from the door to a point about two feet from the four of us.

"Ladies." Seth's brown eyes crinkled as he smiled. He leaned toward me and brushed my cheek with a kiss. "Ready with some good strategies?"

"Ready to listen and see what sounds good and what doesn't." Which was truly what I was doing at this meeting. He smelled good, a fresh herbal scent that didn't overpower, and he looked good, in his white sweater and jeans. "What about you?"

One of Elizabeth's eyebrows rose. Nora

blinked and turned away.

"We need to counter all the negatives with positive proposals. Think of responses that would satisfy the long list of concerns the other guys have developed. Problem is, anything we come up with is bound to be more complicated and take a lot more effort, and it can't be reduced to a slogan that we can plaster all over town." His voice had risen in volume as he spoke, and his eyes shone with excitement. "We need to find a way to bring more compatible businesses to town, and convince the casino supporters that the projected revenues are offset by some tangible, predictable costs and, more important, by some intangible and unanticipated costs."

"Such as?" Melissa cocked her head and smiled, but her crossed arms sent the message that she wasn't completely convinced by what he was saying.

Seth smiled back at her, then looked past us to a group gathered near a rusting plow. "That's one of the things I'm going to talk about in a bit. Listen, I have to check something out. See you later."

When he was ten steps away, Nora whispered, "If he's on the other side, he's a pretty damn good actor."

"Well, *I* haven't ever thought of him as

performing." I blushed, realizing how many different ways my friends could take that statement. Seth Selinsky might hold back some of his feelings on occasion — he certainly imposed limits and boundaries, which was not only fine with me but definitely in sync with the way I operated in this relationship. But despite a baloney radar system in fine working order, I'd never worried that he was pretending about anything.

That didn't mean I was right.

"We'd better mingle," Nora said, looking over the crowd, "or the only goods we'll get will be on each other."

It would have been nice if we all clasped hands and touched foreheads in a huddle again, but instead everyone nodded and walked off in different directions. The smell of old hay wafted up to me as I made my way to the closest knot of people. Joseph Trent, Trisha Stern, and Sue Evans, the owner of Wonderland Toy Town, nodded their hellos as I joined the small circle.

"Lili, hi, we were just talking about a new idea." Trisha brushed her pixie bangs away from her forehead. "It's an original, all right."

Sue Evans didn't respond to my inquiring look, and I bit back questions about who had found the note and what it said. With her brightly colored patchwork jacket, broomstick skirt, and long silver earrings, she was declaring herself Creative. I wondered what else she might have invented in the past couple of days. A note, perhaps, that had somehow made its way to the store bathroom?

"I want to build an arts complex. Small theater, large concert space. Places for art workshops, writing classes, that kind of thing. Use local labor to build and maintain it, and wherever possible to be the artists. It would be a way to enhance the identity of the community, build on what Rhinebeck's already started." She fingered the large orange stone that hung from a leather thong at her throat. Her smile turned a notch brighter. "You might even think about offering gourd classes there."

I tried to return a smile but I'd have to stop gritting my teeth and get rid of my suspicious mindset before anyone believed me. Was she, as Karen would say, sucking up? Trying to buy my support? I preferred to think of her offer as enthusiastic and generous.

"You really think a theater and some classes will generate the same tax revenues as a casino? And how does that answer the social justice problem and help out the tribes who were treated so badly — and continue to be? Don't get me wrong, I don't want that casino. But Marjorie Mellon identified a concern and was preparing to do something about it. And she'd managed to address issues that Nathaniel Bartle and Susan Clemants raised." The challenge in my voice seemed to startle Trisha, who frowned when I glanced in her direction.

Joseph Trent, who looked better in his faded green sweater than his usual pharmacist whites, *tsk*ed twice. "You don't have to be so negative. Some problems can't be solved by thinking about things in the same old way. Who says it's possible to make up for what the Europeans did when they colonized America? It doesn't make sense to spend energy on problems that can't be solved."

"So, we just forget the past and move on? Isn't that a little like condoning what was done?"

"Not at all." Trent's color and his voice rose. "It's a lot like saying that we're not the ones responsible and we have to figure out how to move forward."

The toy store owner nodded her vigorous agreement. "That's right. And anyway, we don't want to create new woes with our solutions to old problems. Which is what the casino would do."

I wanted to steer the conversation back to Marjorie, but before I could, Trisha Stern said, "The casino won't just create problems. It's bound to ruin a way of life that's been embraced by a lot of people for a long time. I just can't see what's to be gained if we take what little we have left of natural beauty and turn it into something ugly. There's got to be a better way to solve all the problems, I just know it."

I'd never seen her so worked up. And I wasn't the only one — Joseph Trent and Sue Evans looked surprised as well. Her intensity raised the pesky specter of suspicion again. Was Trisha Stern really capable of murdering Marjorie Mellon to protect her corner of the universe? Could she come up with a devious little plan to pin it all on me? Even if she could pull off both those things, it was hard to see how she could come into my house every day to work with my brother and chat pleasantly about crocuses and canning tomatoes.

I set my questions aside and searched for one more provocative comment that might encourage someone to reveal a dark secret.

"Look, some people who are for the casino aren't simply greedy." I was winging it here, but I pushed on. "Like Nathaniel and Susan. And personally, I'm not so sure that Marjorie was only after money. She sounded like she really did believe that a lot of good would come out of it. Besides, I'm not even sure she was killed because of her stand in favor of the casino."

Trisha laughed uncomfortably, Joseph Trent frowned and looked down at his scuffed shoes, and Sue Evans took a step back, as though that would protect her from being contaminated by the idea I'd just dropped into the middle of the circle.

"I don't mean to be rude or anything, but you'd be better off if that were true, right?" Trisha glanced over at the makeshift stage. "Looks like the meeting's going to start."

The hard surfaces of the Lovett barn had turned the conversations into a roar, and I was glad when the microphone squealed and Mel Lovett tapped on it for attention. The roar subsided enough for his voice to be heard when he said, "Thanks for coming out tonight. We have a lot of work to do if we're going to be ready for next week's meeting. The final vote is the week after that, so we can't waste time."

"The town council doesn't have enough votes to pass the thing," Trisha whispered. "People are defecting like crazy. I don't think there's anyone around, now that poor Marjorie's gone, who can get enough support to present a unified front and make a difference for their side."

Only Trisha had acknowledged out loud that Marjorie's death might make a difference in the outcome of the vote. But I didn't have time to try to get her or anyone else to say more, because Mel tapped on the microphone again and said, "And so I'd like to introduce our first speaker, Randall Smith. Randy, come on up."

My mediation homeowner — I felt my fists clench against my sides. I had at least one more session with the Smith-Caterra case, and I'd hate to have to excuse myself because Randall Smith had said things at this meeting that might prejudice me. I didn't trust Tony Caterra, probably wouldn't hire him to change a washer in my sink until I saw how the case went, but he was still entitled to my impartiality. Would Randall Smith say something helpful about how to defeat the casino — or was this going to turn into a public forum on his mistreatment at the hands of his former contractor?

You're not here to win a political battle or get details for a mediation case, I reminded myself. You're here to see if you can find out anything about who might have killed

Marjorie Mellon.

Smith, his long hair pulled back into a ponytail, had cleaned up his act for the occasion. He placed two hands on the stack of boards that served as a makeshift podium and scanned the crowd, a huge smile on his face. "I'm just an ordinary guy. I go to work, come home and eat whatever I'm served while I watch television. I hang out with my buddies, I drive my kids to soccer practice, and I grumble when my wife hands me the 'honey-do' list."

A smattering of laughter rippled through the crowd. Mel Lovett smiled at Connie as she nestled her head against his shoulder. Joseph Trent, too, glanced at his wife, an almost pretty woman who looked as though she could use a day off and a wardrobe makeover. It didn't seem to bother them that Smith's comments perpetuated the tired sexist cliché of marriage as an arrangement to get needs met by putting up with boring but necessary obligations. If the person I wanted to spend the rest of my life with talked about me that way in public, the next time he'd see me would be in divorce court.

Lighten up, I told myself, and listen.

"And I like it that way. I like everything about my life. Well, except for a couple of

171

plumbing problems and these twelve gray hairs." He stopped again, waiting for the laughter that never came. "So I just want to make sure that we keep Walden Corners the way it is. Well, not exactly the way it is. Those guys have a point about we need to figure out how to bring in more tax money. But this is definitely not the way to do it. We need to bring a small manufacturer out here. Get the roads in shape so a trucking company can take care of all their needs. Make sure we have a labor force and affordable housing and good schools to keep them happy. Then other businesses would come in, see? And, man, it would mean jobs, everybody from people on the line to secretaries. Then, with all those extra jobs, we'd need more barbers and grocery stores and restaurants, and, well . . . it keeps on keepin' on, if you know what I mean."

Elizabeth appeared beside me. "Great idea," she whispered, "except that manufacturing is going overseas. Cheap labor, cheap taxes. He thinks it's still 1950, maybe, because that's as far as he ever studied in school."

"Now, I know some of you think it's crazy because we've outsourced so much manufacturing," Randy Smith said, as though he'd heard Elizabeth, and probably half the people in the auditorium. "But we can help turn the tide. We can start a 'made in America' thing. And Walden Corners can open its very own flag company. So that's all I have to say. I hope you give it some thought."

For a man who had shown me nothing but anger and petulance, Randy Smith had come up with a creative idea. I didn't love the idea of a manufacturing facility — I'd want to see the environmental impact studies that proved it was safe — but it certainly would help the unemployment situation and bolster the tax base.

"You know his brother-in-law and father and two cousins are just about to run out of unemployment benefits. That doesn't exactly make Randall Smith an altruistic man, but at least he's thinking." Elizabeth scribbled notes on her pad, then looked up at the podium again. "Okay, pay attention, girls and boys. Here comes Seth."

It took a while for Seth to plug in his computer. The microphone buzzed, and he stood back, looking as relaxed as he had the last time we'd spent an hour in my kitchen cooking a complicated recipe for pork posole.

"I won't take too much of our time here tonight. I just have a couple of things to say." His voice sounded as though a very intimate personal conversation had been accidentally amplified. He *was* a good actor . . . but wasn't that required of all good salespeople? That was his job, after all. The details of what he said might be different from the words of a guy who sold refrigerators, but the ideas were the same. You had to convince a customer that you were the one who could get her what she didn't even know she wanted, in the most convenient and most satisfying way.

"The ideas I've heard — and will hear — tonight are good ones," he said. "Some seem like they'd be easier to accomplish, others seem like they'd suit the population of Walden Corners and Columbia County better, still others seem like they'd have the best chance to generate the most money to get the town what it needs."

So far, he hadn't said anything new, but as I glanced around I realized that the crowd was paying attention in a way that they hadn't earlier.

Seth clicked a remote that started a PowerPoint presentation. The first screen showed a photograph of three police cars pulled up at odd angles in front of a big windowless building. "This is only one of seventeen incidents last year at a casino in

Wisconsin in which the local police force had to be called out."

He clicked to the next screen. A bar graph with several pairs of elements appeared. "The line in blue represents the year before the casino came to town, and the line in red represents the year after. This first measurement is town revenue. You can see how much it jumped in one year. That's pretty good. But when you look at these other things, it's a different story. The number of automobile accidents involving drunk drivers — higher. The cost of maintaining the town police force and the jail, higher. And most interesting to me, in this particular town, the percentage of kids who graduated from high school in four years dropped by five percent and the number of divorces increased by eleven percent."

I was reminded of the old saying about "Lies, damn lies, and statistics." Other things might have happened in that town to account for those numbers. A factory might have closed, leaving families desperate and dysfunctional. The mayor might have hired a bunch of incompetents to run the show. Where was he going with this? He clicked the remote and the next screen came up.

The picture, of a pond surrounded by graceful willows, benches, and in the background, a complex of two-story garden apartments, was captioned with the words GRACIOUS LIVING FOR ADULTS.

"This is emphatically not what we used to call an old age home," he said. "It's more like a high-end condo with a wide range of services. Store, beauty salon, a medical center."

He spoke about the number of jobs the facility would generate, about the tax revenues it would raise, and about how the nature of the community would be preserved. "Best of all," he said as though he was sharing a delicious secret, "my friend Sue Evans has said that the arts complex she proposed might well live side by side with this new development, so it's a total win-win situation."

I couldn't think of a single objection, except that I hated the idea of any group of people being isolated from the natural mix of ages, genders, backgrounds. Still, if someone else wanted to live that way, I wouldn't stop them. It might not be a bad thing to have a retirement community in Walden Corners. If city people could be convinced to spend their golden years here, they'd bring money and a desire for high-end consumables that would make my own life practically perfect. After all, Parma proscuitto and brine-cured olives were indulgences that made daily life feel like a party.

The crowd responded with enthusiastic applause, and Seth closed his computer, unplugged it, and stepped down from the makeshift stage, leaving me with the big questions still running like a news crawl at the bottom of my screen.

Had he really given money to the other side? And if he had, what did that mean?

CHAPTER 12

The kitchen of Melissa's Taconic Inn still smelled of herbs and melted butter. The staff, under Nora's supervision, had been encouraged to try new things, some of which had been more successful than others. The chicken with herbed dumplings had gone over better than the *bacalau,* a Portuguese salt cod dish that even some city people shunned, not knowing what they were missing. Nora had talked about how she was struggling to find the balance between being innovative and trying too hard. Whatever had come out of the kitchen a couple of hours earlier smelled as though it fit squarely on the Big Hit side of the ledger.

Melissa and Elizabeth waved and Nora pointed me to a chair and sat down beside me.

"I just called Scooter and told him we'd be a little late. He didn't seem to mind one bit. Told me to tell you your brother is totally awesome."

"He sure is." Melissa blushed and shook her head. "You know what I mean. He plays pro ball *and* he's a nice, unspoiled guy. That's an unusual combination."

"So you're buying season tickets to the Mets home games?" Nora asked with a twinkle. "That means more work for me, partner. So maybe we need to renegotiate our arrangement."

I definitely needed to avoid making comments about Melissa and Neil, but that didn't mean everyone else would.

Before Melissa could respond, Susan breezed in, all twinkle and high energy. Elizabeth was the only one who didn't smile a hello at her.

"Do you think anyone followed me here?" Susan peered under the long, scarred butcher block work table and then grinned. "Nope, we're safe. I can't wait to tell you what I found out."

Nora took down one of the chalkboards the staff used to list daily specials, and looked expectantly in Susan's direction. "Spill it, girl. We're ready."

"Nathaniel Bartle has gotten together with Oneida Gaming and they're planning a sweat lodge ceremony to purify their hearts before they go to the next meeting. Where they plan to convince the town council to change the procedure. They want to cut out the public referendum and let the town council vote decide."

My jaw dropped. According to established procedure, the nine-member town council could make recommendations, but a referendum had to follow. Of course, the county and the state hadn't yet passed the bills that would grant their seals of approval to expanding gaming into Columbia County, never mind Walden Corners. If too many people in our town and too many people in the entire county disapproved, it was likely that nothing would go forward. But if town councils thought they could skip right to what *they* wanted instead of having voters decide . . . I didn't even want to think about the chaos that was sure to follow.

"If you don't like the rules, change them? Isn't that, like, illegal or something?" I still found it hard to believe that a man of principle would suggest such a thing. Nathaniel Bartle, gentle and compassionate, had embraced the end of providing justice for Native Americans by accepting the means of behaving unethically. "And the rest of them went along with it?"

Susan pushed a springy red curl away

from her forehead. "Some of them. Tony Caterra said that he knew that five of the council members would vote yes. He practically guaranteed it. But someone else said that it would take a referendum after the council vote to clear a rules change like that, so they were back where they started."

I noticed that Susan was referring to what *they* were planning. What had happened to her sense of *we?* Now didn't seem the right time to ask, so I said, "Did anyone say anything about Marjorie?"

"Everyone." Susan shook her head. "Every single soul there said what a lovely service it was and how the pastor had said such nice things. They all talked about what a shame that she was gone, but nobody seemed to care about her life — just her death and the loss it would be to their cause. I could hardly stand to listen to them talk about her as though she were a tool that had gone missing and now they were terribly inconvenienced."

"Wow, that's harsh. Didn't her friends speak up?"

"She was a loner." Nora handed slices of white cake with chocolate frosting all around. "Did her work, mostly at night. She was pretty active in the local Rotary, you know, again the business thing. But I never heard of anyone having dinner at her house. Never saw her out shopping with anyone. I'd say she wanted it that way."

Elizabeth's eyebrow rose, punctuating the skepticism in her voice. "Nobody really wants it that way. I always think there's either a little bit of misanthropist or a lot of fear of being hurt in people who stick to themselves as much as she did. You know, as though the rest of us weren't good enough, or were bound to do something nasty. Anyway, Marjorie really was a loner. Even her daughter didn't have much to do with her."

"What's her daughter like?" I didn't know much about Anita or any other aspect of Marjorie's personal life. I had built a picture of Marjorie Mellon based on what I'd heard, and on three brief encounters. It all added up to an energetic, self-aware person whose sarcasm provided a facade to keep any tender parts hidden from view.

"Anita. She moved to Tennessee right after high school. Of course, she came back for the funeral, but she didn't stay long. At least, not in Marjorie's house, the house where she grew up. She went to school with us, but she ran with a different crowd." Melissa shook her head. "Connie was the school social worker then. She tried to help Anita sort things out, but nothing seemed to get through to her. I always thought she wanted bright lights and big city, but she ended up in an even smaller town in Tennessee. Maybe she just needed to get away from Marjorie's constant carping and criticism."

"Anyone else hear anything?" Elizabeth glanced at her watch, her eyes suddenly tired.

"Listen, it's late." I was aware that everyone, especially Susan, had to be up early the next morning. "We can do this another time. You all have to get to work tomorrow, so maybe we should just —"

"Keep going. We should keep going." Nora pointed to the wall clock. "At least another twenty minutes. You know what they say about how important it is to collect information while it's fresh? So let's do that."

I grinned. "I thought you didn't have time to watch television. Okay, so did you hear anything else, Susan?"

Susan shook her head. "Nothing worth mentioning. Everyone seemed a little down, everyone still wants the casino to go through, nobody acted any more strange or upset than usual. What about you guys? You hear anything?"

"Trisha Stern certainly had something to

say to me as I was leaving." Melissa poked at her slice of cake. "She went on and on about how Marjorie's ideas threatened her comfort and her privacy, you know, with the casino right next door. She made it pretty clear that she's been terribly upset. And that it's gotten so bad that Jonathan's thinking about applying for a job in some school district up in the Adirondacks."

"He can't do that!" Susan's dismay turned to anger. "He's the best principal I've ever met, certainly the best one I ever worked for. If Trisha is so upset about the casino, she should talk him into selling the house and buying something else. Maybe a little farther out of town."

That wouldn't be a true solution, at least not for the woman who had stood in my kitchen and rhapsodized over the wonders of living in her home, on that particular piece of land, surrounded by the those very trees and fields.

"You know, our meeting was quiet, too," Melissa said, "except that most people were pleased, happy that it looked like the casino would be defeated. There were lots of good ideas for things that might bring money into town. The only person who didn't sound so optimistic was Connie. She looks so tired, so pale. I can't help thinking she doesn't want to spend whatever time she has left fighting against a casino."

We were all quiet. The Connie I knew would want this controversy to be resolved so that she could give her attention to other, happier things.

"You're right, Connie hasn't been looking so good lately," Nora said. "I wish I could help her, but right now I feel like we need to concentrate on things we *can* change. Okay, we went to a meeting. And there was all that high energy. All those proposals to bring new businesses into town. What do you think about Seth's retirement-slash-arts center?"

Melissa's eyes narrowed and she smiled. "Maybe I could run a concession stand. Sell chocolate cupcakes and fancy madeleines and coffee drinks and Italian sodas. And maybe even get to hear some good concerts. Sounds like a decent idea to me."

It sounded like putting up with a lot of extra traffic in return for some potentially diverting theater to me, but saying so probably wouldn't go over too well with my Walden Corners friends. "Well, it's better than the casino, that's for sure. Don't you feel like we're this big family trying to figure out how to live with insufficient resources to meet our needs? And it just keeps getting worse."

Susan poked at the crumbs on her plate. "If we were a big family, we'd probably be eating beans five nights a week and squabbling about whether we should switch to peanut butter. Listen, you guys haven't said anything new about your meeting. Didn't anyone hear anything that we should . . . I hate to use the word, but that we should *investigate?*"

We looked at each other. The clock above the stove ticked loudly. Nobody said anything.

"Joseph Trent made this weird remark. About Marjorie's murder muddying the waters around the casino issue. And you know what? I think he's right." Melissa drummed her fingers on the table. "It puts all the discussions on a whole 'nother level. Emotionally, I mean. Everyone's afraid and upset. So nobody is thinking clearly."

"Maybe that's what the killer had in mind." As soon as I said it, it sounded wrong to me. "Nah, way too complicated. Whoever killed Marjorie wanted her dead for personal reasons. Wanted to keep her from leading the charge to bring in the casino maybe. Or maybe it was something else. But it doesn't seem likely that it was just to create a diversion."

Nora sighed. "We've been sitting here for over an hour and haven't said a single helpful or interesting thing. Maybe we're just being too passive about this. Maybe we need to go out there and actively talk to people. About how they felt about Marjorie. About where they were when she was killed."

"And you think you'll get the truth?" Elizabeth's tone was sharp, almost mocking. "You'll get evasions and polite lies. That's how people protect themselves around here. And you'll also get a heap of ridicule for playing at being detectives. And then they'll start calling the town Cabot Cove and we'll all look like fools. I think we've gone about as far as we can with this. Gene Murphy and Michele Castro aren't sitting on their behinds. They're out asking the questions. It's okay for them to do it. It's not okay for us."

"We're not just in it for the fun," Susan snapped. "Lili's a prime suspect."

I could have hugged her, but Elizabeth turned to me, a challenge in her eyes. "What about Seth? You find out about those donations?"

Despite my annoyance, I forced a smile. "All I found out is that he thinks Gracious Living for Adults is a good investment.

Sheesh, I can't wait until I'm old enough to cut myself off completely from kids and new ideas and . . . I guess other folks can choose that if they want to, but the big old messy world is just exactly where I want to be. So, no, I didn't find out any more about those checks tonight."

"I did," Susan said softly.

You could have dropped an elephant into the middle of the kitchen and nobody would have moved.

She blushed from her freckled neck to the roots of her carrot hair. "I gave two hundred dollars to the same person Seth did."

Melissa paled and clenched the table, but Nora leaned forward and smiled, inviting Susan to continue.

"Nathaniel is taking donations for a scholarship fund for the Phillips family. You know, Rod Phillips, that farmhand who died last week? He's got two kids in high school and of course he didn't have life insurance or any other assets. They'll get some kind of death benefit from Social Security, but not nearly enough to live on. They'll get welfare and food stamps and a lifetime of struggling to find work that pays enough to let them live with dignity." Susan's eyes filled with tears. "I know those kids. Robbie and Rhonda. They come in wearing hand-medowns, they're tired all the time because they worked right alongside Rod in the barn before and after school. But they were still making A's and B's. His wife left him about two years ago. Just after he was diagnosed with brain cancer. Can you imagine, walking out on a sick husband?"

All the fun and even most of the urgency had gone out of our little spy game. We talked for a while about how unpredictable life was. If things really did happen in threes then Rod, Aunt Bernie, and Marjorie made up one very sad and unfortunate set.

We each wrote out checks for the Phillips scholarship fund, gave them to Susan to deliver to Nathaniel, and then went our separate ways into the dark night. Alone. As we had come into the world, and as Rod, Bernice, and Marjorie went out.

CHAPTER 13

They looked cute, three strapping guys asleep with the television blaring. They hadn't heard me drive up, nor had they heard my footsteps up the front stairs, through the door, into the living room. Scooter's eyes moved under his closed lids, and I wondered what he was seeing in his dreams. His café au lait cheeks were kissed by a blush of color, hinting at some interesting possibilities. Scooter's best friend and constant companion, Armel, curled into the armchair, looked like a fair, gangly angel who'd forgotten his wings and needed to have his blond hair trimmed. Neil groaned softly, his hand moving across the growth of beard that almost looked good after nearly two weeks. His forehead wrinkled the way it did when he was in pain.

The computer sat silently beckoning, inviting me to write another three pages on that health care booklet before I went to bed. After I got everyone safely tucked away, I thought. I'll do it then.

"Scooter," I said softly, and Neil's eyes flew open.

"Movie must have been way too exciting for us," he said, smiling and scratching at his beard. He uncapped the prescription bottle and shook out a large white pill, gulped it down with a slug of water. "I better go to bed before I get too wobbly. Your meeting go okay?"

Before I could answer, Scooter stretched and sighed and his eyes fluttered open. "Wow, I fell asleep. Some help I am. Sorry, Neil."

Armel sat straight up and smiled beatifically. "I guess I missed the end of the movie," he said softly.

"Buddy, we all conked out," Neil said with a grin. "Must have used it all up playing blackjack. You gonna be all right driving home?"

I'd forgotten how much Scooter had grown until he pushed himself out of his chair and stood next to Armel, who was wrestling his way into a pale gray sweatshirt. They weren't my children — I'd known them about a year, but even so I felt the tug of bittersweet and contradictory wishes, that they'd stay the cute, sweet boys who stumbled over their own feet and had clear moral centers, and that they'd hurry up and finish growing into adults so I could know how their stories turned out.

Swigging the last of what appeared to be a warm Coke, Scooter picked up his backpack and stuck his hand into one of the side pockets, then rummaged in the main compartment. "Sure, I'm fine to drive home, not like some *old* person who has to go to sleep at ten o'clock. Hey, you see where I put my car keys?"

"I thought they were in your pack," Armel said, frowning.

I glanced at the obvious places in the living room. "Put them in your jacket?"

Scooter shook his head. "No jacket. I know I didn't leave them in the car. Maybe they're in the kitchen."

Neil smiled as Scooter bounded out of the room. "He's right. Only us old folks could be tired so early. Or us old folks on medication, anyway. I'm gonna try to do without that little pink pill tomorrow night. I hate the idea of getting addicted to sleeping pills."

I didn't say that maybe I'd try to do *with* a couple of the pills that Joseph Trent had given me. When I took one two nights earlier, I'd fallen asleep within fifteen minutes, but I still awoke with a million thoughts racing through my head four hours later. It was wearing me down, and nothing anyone else suggested seemed to do the trick.

"Hey, what's this?" Scooter's voice, loud and clear all the way from the kitchen, sounded half amused and just a little frightened.

Armel frowned and then bounded out of the room.

I glanced at Neil, whose raised eyebrows told me that he was fixed on the frightened part, and followed Armel. A dime store address book lay on the center island, its cover worn and the pages crinkled, as though they had been left out in the rain.

I'd never seen it before.

Pressed against the counter, a puzzled expression scrunching up his face, Scooter eyed me warily. "It was under the stove," he said in a small voice.

Pale and wide-eyed, Armel hung back in the doorway as I reached for the book and then dropped it back on the butcher block as though it was on fire. Across the top of the cover, the name Marjorie Mellon was written in a cramped hand. When I started breathing again, my brain went into over-drive, scrambling around the questions of how that book had gotten into my kitchen and what I needed to do about it, now that Scooter's, and more important, *my* fingerprints were all over the thing.

"I don't know how this got here, Scooter. I have to make some phone calls. You find your keys?"

"They were in my pants pocket. I guess I didn't feel them until I bent down to look on the floor and under stuff." The wary look on his face softened to concern. "Whatever it is, I hope it's not more bad news for you, Lili. You're in trouble, right?"

I shook my head. "No, it's just that I don't understand what's going on yet. It's like people who say they're lost. They just haven't figured out how to get where they need to go. It may take a while for things to get straightened out. You go home, Scooter, Armel. And thanks for staying with Neil."

Awkwardly, Scooter reached over and gave me a one-armed hug, then both boys disappeared in the direction of the living room. I barely heard the low male voices as I stared at the book on the counter. Someone could have come in while Neil, Armel, and Scooter slept, or even during a night when I hadn't paid attention to bedtime routines.

So much for not locking doors in the country.

After I heard the front door slam —
Scooter and Armel were still teens after all,
boys whose movements were as large as
their hearts — I went back into the living
room.

"So what now?" Neil's eyes were already a
little droopy, and he blinked as he waited
for my answer.

"Now I call my lawyer. And then I do
whatever he tells me. Which is, I'm sure, to
call the cops and tell them the truth. You
didn't hear anything tonight, no cars, no
doors creaking open, no footsteps?"

My mind raced to catalog the people who
were at the anti-casino meeting, and to
remember what Susan had said about who'd
been at the pro group. The swirl of names
immediately got mixed up with the meeting
two weeks earlier. I saw Jonathan Kirschbaum sitting in one of the back rows and
yet I didn't remember talking to him tonight. I couldn't picture him in the barn,
but given his wife's strong feelings I couldn't
imagine that he'd miss a chance to oppose
the casino. Nathaniel Bartle, Ira Jackson, Joseph Trent, Trisha Stern — was I remember-
ing their names from this week or last?

Besides, there was no way to know
whether Marjorie's address book had been
put under my stove tonight. It might have

been there for days.

If Castro's deputies had looked under the stove when they'd searched the house, then it would be obvious that someone had planted the book after they left. If they hadn't and it had been there all along, would they admit to a less than thorough search?

B. H. Hovanian answered his phone on the first ring. He listened as I told him what I'd found and how it had been discovered. "And yes I touched it, before I knew what it was. I'm not used to thinking like a criminal."

"Well, don't touch it again. You call Castro and I'll be right over."

He clicked off before I could say anything. Michele Castro, too, answered on the first ring, as though she'd been waiting for my call.

"I found an address book that belongs to Marjorie Mellon. It was under my stove. Actually, Scooter Johnson found it," I told her, sticking to Hovanian's advice that the information I shared be all that was necessary to tell the truth without going beyond what was sufficient to make my point.

"I'll be right over," she said, as though she'd been listening in on my call to my lawyer and was echoing his words.

196

While I waited for them to arrive, I helped Neil, groggy and unsteady on his feet, into his bed, and then sat at the kitchen counter and stared at the book. Secrets lurked inside, even if I might not understand what they meant. My prints were already on a couple of pages. Would a forensics lab really check every single page? What was the difference between three sets of Lili Marino prints and five?

I jammed my hands against my sides and marched myself into the living room, but the book's siren call drew me back to the kitchen.

Either Hovanian or Castro would arrive in the next five or six minutes, I judged when I looked at the clock. I reached for a dish towel, covered my hand and then flipped open the book and riffled through the pages. Names, addresses, phone numbers, email addresses were neatly printed on the tiny pages. Bartle, Conklin, Evans, Paul, Selinsky, Trent — the names of people I knew jumped out at me, while the others blurred into a parade of syllables, businesses, relatives, maybe even lovers for all I knew.

Many of the names were marked with an asterisk, and when I studied them I realized that they were probably clients. So many asterisks — maybe I should go into the cleaning business instead of scrambling for freelance writing jobs.

The thought of someone taking advantage of Marjorie's death that way gave me the shivers. Could she have been killed by a potential business rival?

I was about to close the book when I noticed that the back inside cover was filled with doodles and scribbles. Marjorie wasn't much of an artist, favoring crosshatched shading on irregular shaped boxes and six-petaled flowers that grew in nobody's garden. Several letters and numbers were sprinkled among the squiggles.

blue 85 Kyt

Meaningless? Maybe. Or maybe one of those jottings was a key. Or not. I copied the letters and numbers onto the back of an envelope and stuck it in a drawer, under the flatware divider. When I looked at the page more closely, I realized that some of the doodles were attempts to cover up other words or numbers. I squinted, was about to get my magnifying glass from the gourd studio when a car pulled into the driveway. B.H. stepped into the moonlit night from a tan Honda with its fair share of dents and dings. He looked up at the stars, then headed for the back porch. I answered his knock and let him in.

"That's it?" he said, staring at the worn red book on the butcher block.

So much for social graces. I nodded, folded my arms across my chest, waited for him to say or do something. He glanced around the kitchen and took the dish towel I'd just replaced on the ring, opened the book and flipped pages. Every few seconds he stopped and cocked his head and shut his eyes, as though he were listening for something and didn't want his concentration to be affected by his other senses. When he closed the book, he hung the towel back on the hook.

"So, she's got a lot of clients, and knows a lot of other people. All I'm getting is that it was time for Marjorie Mellon to get a bigger address book."

"You missed something," I said. I took the towel, turned to the page filled with doodles and scribbles.

My timing was perfect. Lights flashing, a car pulled up beside Hovanian's Honda. At least Michele Castro didn't use the siren to alert all the sleeping inhabitants of Walden Corners that she was on her way to nab a criminal. I let her in and nodded in the direction of the book. B.H. was leaning against the counter, hands thrust in pockets, looking for all the world like a model for Gap chinos.

A very appealing model, I caught myself thinking.

"Scooter Johnson found this under the stove," I said, "and I called you right away."

"So you were here on a social visit?" She looked at B.H. and then circled the butcher block island, knelt, and peered under the stove.

"She called me too." His eyes followed her as she stood and faced us again. "This is getting almost comical. Whoever is trying to make it look like Lili Marino is responsible for Marjorie Mellon's death is only making herself or himself look like a fool."

Despite my vulnerable position, I couldn't help smiling at his pronouns. He hadn't used the masculine default. B. H. Hovanian was more thoughtful than I realized.

Castro pulled on a pair of surgical gloves, slipped the book into a large plastic bag, and zipped it closed. "Nothing about this is funny. You said you never heard anyone come in, but it might have happened while you were asleep. Or it might have happened tonight. While you were at the meeting."

I shook my head. "Could be. But my brother and Scooter and Armel Noonan were here the whole time. I don't remember who searched the kitchen when you came with those warrants, but that person didn't find it. Either time you went through my house. And I didn't see it the last time I washed the floor."

Not exactly what I'd meant to say — we all looked down and saw the spot where I'd spilled coffee, another where the rice had overflowed the pot on the stove before I could turn the flame down, and a small brownish blob that might have been congealed gravy or something much less appetizing.

I thought back to that first search — I was sure that one of the deputies had been assigned to the kitchen while Castro worked the bedroom and my studio. I had no doubt that she remembered the same facts. The second time around, they did only a cursory search, concentrating instead on the computer and the printer. But I wasn't about to gloat, or even point that out to her.

Hovanian broke the silence. "My guess is that it was here one of the times you searched the house. You were meant to find it. Lili or any other sane human being wouldn't steal a murder victim's address book and then leave it for someone else to find so she could call the police. It doesn't make sense. The only thing that works logi-

201

cally is that the person who put it under that stove knew the house would be searched. They didn't want Lili or Scooter to find it. They wanted the police to discover that book."

Her cheeks flaming, Castro didn't argue. Her silence made it clear that it wasn't her job to convince B.H. that his logic didn't matter and the fact of that book showing up in my kitchen did. "We'll check it for prints. I don't need you to do anything right now, but this time I really don't want you to leave town, at least not for a couple of days."

I glanced at B.H., at his raised eyebrow and, strangely, at his hands, which rested on the butcher block. His fingers looked strong, decisive, as though *they* worked out every day, too.

"You can't restrict her movements, Michele." His voice, not loud, was nonetheless emphatic. "Unless you're going to arrest her."

I'd remember that direct gaze and forthright manner when I played poker — and probably at other times when I'd find myself drifting in thought and seeking comfort. But bluffing wasn't in my bag of tricks, and I wasn't sure that it was a good idea that Hovanian had played the challenge card right then. Still, I had to trust him. I gulped back the plea that rose to my lips and clenched my teeth to keep from speaking.

"Not yet," Castro said as she followed every twitch of my face with her eyes. "I'm not going to arrest her yet."

Which left a whole lot open to interpretation. But B. H. Hovanian didn't appear to be interested in the subtleties.

"You'd better have some really solid ground. I can make a better case for police incompetence than you can for Lili Marino's guilt. It's late, and unless there's anything else you want to chat about, I want to go home and I want to let Ms. Marino have the quiet enjoyment of her home returned to her."

They stared at each other, two cool customers. It struck me that they'd forgotten that I was the reason they were both standing in this kitchen at 11:22 on a Monday night. They were inhabiting a professional space, not a personal one, and it annoyed me that they'd both lost of sight of me. Especially B. H. Hovanian.

The words they'd used, their maneuvers, gave each of them a special pleasure, it was clear. But I didn't like being the pawn, the girl-in-the-middle. None of what was happening felt like a game to me.

"I'm going to wash my face and brush my

teeth," I said, already moving to the doorway. "If you need anything else, I'll be out of the bathroom in a few minutes. Otherwise, would you leave the back way and pull the door shut behind you? It should lock if you pull hard."

It took enormous willpower not to wait and check out their expressions, to see whether they were properly shocked or angry or confused or insulted. But the reward of marching off to the bathroom without looking back was much greater than any satisfaction I might have gotten if I'd lost my nerve and waited for approval.

I must have brushed my teeth for ten minutes as my thoughts bumped up against that jumble of words and numbers in the back of Marjorie's address book. They meant something, I knew they did.

CHAPTER 14

Nothing made any sense.

Someone killed Marjorie Mellon and left the murder weapon in my attic. Had the same someone planted the note in Wonderland Toy Town, and slipped Marjorie's address book under my stove?

Could Trisha Stern, cheerful, focused, married to a nice man who owned a gorgeous piece of property adjacent to the proposed casino site, kill someone to protect her hallowed ground? Or might Seth have thought that getting Marjorie Mellon out of the way would open the door to huge personal profits if his retirement community was built on that land? Nathaniel Bartle wanted justice — by some twisted logic might he have justified those ends by the horrible means of using Marjorie's murder to call attention to his cause? Tony Caterra, who had the subtlety of a tarantula, could potentially benefit from anything that was built on that land, so killing Marjorie wouldn't gain him anything. Reluctantly, I moved him to the "unlikely" category.

And then there was Anita Mellon. Who had been, inconveniently for building a case against her, in Tennessee when Marjorie was killed. She could have had help from someone local, but that seemed like long odds. Besides, you didn't go killing your mother just because you didn't like the way she treated you.

Unless there was more to the story than anyone knew.

The thought chilled me. My relationship with my own mother was certainly complicated, but the challenge of trying to understand her was, so far, worth the effort. I could hardly imagine a world without her energy, her strong opinions, her fierce and unwavering love — and I needed a dose of all that soon.

When I returned to the house after my morning walk, a sweet aroma mingled with scent of freshly brewed coffee.

Neil smiled up at me from his perch on the kitchen stool. "Feel better?" he asked.

"I didn't feel bad to start," I said. "Okay, maybe a little confused. And a little harried when I remember that I have to finish my big writing job. Want some scrambled eggs?"

He shook his head, watching as I deposited my muddy shoes on the mat outside the door. "I made us French toast while you were walking. And I started a dark wash."

Which was, I realized, his way of showing me how mobile and independent he'd become. "Mr. Homemaker. Thanks. I'm starved. And then I have to make a call."

I savored each bit of conversation with my brother and every bite of the wonderful, nutmeg-and-vanilla-soaked French toast, putting off my phone call and the return to work for twenty-six delicious minutes. Finally, I walked the handset into the living room, dialed my mother's office, waited while it rang several times. I was just about to give up when I heard her voice.

"Ruth Marino. Can I help you?"

As though that question had a right answer where my mother and I were concerned.

"Hi, Mom. Just wanted to say hello and hear your voice. Neil's doing great. The therapist says that if everything keeps going so well, he'll be able to play by maybe August. How's Dad?"

"Lili, you don't call to hear my voice. You called because you need something."

My throat swelled and my pulse rate went through the roof. Adrenaline — my own mother stimulated my flight-fight response.

I managed to say, "I need a little contact from you. That's really all. It's been a hard week. How's Dad?"

For once, my mother didn't have a snappy comeback. Instead, after a couple of seconds of silence, she said, "I'm sorry. I went into some automatic thing with you there. I don't like doing that and I'm sure you don't either. Let's start again. Hi, Lili. We've been thinking about you and Neil. Do you think you could stand a visit from me and Dad? Just for a day. We wouldn't stay over. I have too much going on with Passover and Easter events the mayor is sponsoring. But we want to see you both."

To my surprise, everything in me relaxed. "That's great. When can you get away?"

My enthusiasm must have caught my mother off guard. "Well, uh . . . I'm not sure exactly. I'll have to call you back," she said. "Your father started a new medication two days ago, and he doesn't like to travel until after the first couple of days have passed. You know, to see if he's going to have any reaction — aside from his anger at how expensive those drugs are. Thank goodness the union covers most of it. I can't tell you how many kids of pharmaceutical executives your father has helped put through college. Is Neil around? I haven't spoken to him in a couple of days."

"I'll put him on in a second, Mom. I want to ask you something first. How does the mayor respond when the press or another person says things about him that aren't true?"

"You don't really want to know about the mayor." The edge was gone from her voice when she said, "You just make sure of two things, baby. That your lawyer knows what he's doing. And you keep in mind that Kris Kristofferson song, okay?"

"Which Kris —"

"It's called "Don't Let the Bastards Get You Down." You have to remember that."

My mother *never* used swear words. But she sure knew her music.

And her daughter.

"Thanks, Mom. Lyrics to live by. Talk to you soon."

"I love you, Lili. Now put Neil on."

When I handed my brother the phone, I felt better than I had in days. I would do this — find a way to prove my innocence and get on with the job of juggling all the bits and pieces of my life. As I washed the breakfast dishes, the sound of running water drowned out Neil's voice. Just as I squeezed out the sponge and set it in its wire basket, I heard him behind me.

"I need more coffee. Want some?"

"Not yet," I said, still full from the juice, bacon, French toast, and coffee we'd just devoured. The brilliant April sunshine and the conversation with my mother had filled me with energy and with hope. "Anyway, Connie will be here any second. Trisha's a little late, isn't she?"

Twenty minutes late, which wasn't like her.

"She'll be here soon. In fact . . ." He smoothed his beard as we looked out the window to see Trisha's car pulling in. She popped out of the car, pulled open the back door, and rummaged in her blue nylon bag.

"I'm going to try to finish that report after Connie leaves. I mixed up some granola and apples to put on the yogurt for lunch in case you get hungry. I'll leave it in the fridge."

"And you said you didn't know how to cook. Seth taught you all that?" Neil grinned and punched my shoulder. "I'm looking forward to dinner tonight, and not only for the falafel. I want to meet his son and get to know the man a little better."

"Ron's a good kid, into sports and motor-cycles and girls." I laughed. "Which makes him the poster teen for normal, I'd say."

Neil swung to the door to answer Trisha's knock.

"Sorry I'm late," she said breathlessly. "I had to pick up some Tintin comics. Last minute birthday gift for my little cousin's party this evening. Four people on line in front of me, and, well, sorry I'm late. I guess I was trying to squeeze too much into too short a time."

"I didn't know Books and Brew carried Tintin," I said. "I tried to get some for my nephew once and they said they'd have to order them."

"Oh, you should have gone across the street to Wonderland. They have every single one. With all my nieces and nephews and cousins, I must spend half my income there. You ready to get going, Neil?"

Wonderland Toy Town — Trisha Stern was a regular customer. One who surely knew where the bathroom was so that she could, oh so casually, deposit a note meant to look like one I'd written. Meant to add to the evidence against me.

Maybe. Until I could prove something, I wouldn't make accusations without proof to back them up.

As Neil settled into the straight-backed chair for his exercises, Connie Lovett's car pulled into my driveway. I watched as she trudged to the front door, her gait slower and more labored than it had been the night before. Maybe she'd had bad news, or was in pain. I hurried to the living room and pulled open the door before she could knock.

"Hey, darlin'." She smiled. "Oops, there goes my Tarheel, still coming out after all these years living with you Yankees. Thanks for switching our class to Wednesday this week. That doctor's appointment . . . Anyway, good to see you."

I brushed her cheek with a kiss and stepped aside for her to enter. "Good to see you, too. Connie, you know Trisha Stern and you've met my brother Neil. Neil, you should see Connie's gourds. She's a natural."

Neil's face brightened with his smile. He raised his right crutch in salute. "I'd love to see them some time. Did I hear you say you're from North Carolina? One of my favorite places."

Beaming with pleasure, Connie said, "Oh, I moved away long before you were born, but there's always a little bit of me that yearns for those beautiful mountains. How's your leg doing? Healing right up, I hope."

"Okay, we all have only one hour," I said over my shoulder as I hustled Connie toward the studio, "so please forgive us if we don't stay around and chat."

Trisha smiled and nodded. Neil said something unintelligible, and I leaned closer to Connie and said, "He'd want you to keep talking to him for an hour. He loves attention. And he loves it even more if it's coming from a woman."

She stopped and frowned up at me. "Don't you go saying things just to make me feel good. That's not a very Brooklyn way to behave. I'll have to revise my opinion of you if you do that. Do I look so bad that you have to tell me lies to make me feel better?"

That was a lot of stuff all at once. Most of it was true, and I didn't know how to respond. But her accusation held the answer. If I was going to be Connie's friend, I needed to be as Brooklyn as I could manage.

"I must be susceptible to your Southern ways, Connie. I did feel protective, because you look tired today. I guess I was trying too hard to make you feel better."

She nodded and lowered herself to the chair. "I *am* tired. I don't understand. Mr. Trent says that it could take a long time for this medicine to kick in and that I should give it another month or even two, but I just don't have any energy. I'm as worn out as a hound dog at the end of hunt day."

My stomach dropped to my toes. I wanted to hug her tight and tell her everything would be all right, but that would have been a lie. "Do you feel like going home?" I asked.

"No!" Her voice was strong, the tone emphatic. "I made it here and I want to learn how to make a pine needle rim for my gourd. Now, how do you do that? And what are all the parts called? I want to be able to order my own materials when I'm done."

She didn't want to be treated like a patient, didn't want to become just an illness. I pressed my hands together. "I'll give you contact information for my vendors. Primitive Originals. The Caning Shop. Turtle Feathers. They're all great to do business with."

A little color crept back into her face, and her smile had more energy in it.

"Nothing about working with gourds is magic, and everything is. It's up to you to find the magic. I'll show you the techniques and explain how to use the materials, and then you'll add your personal Connie-ness, and that's the magic. So, here's how you make a pine needle rim."

I demonstrated how to mark off even intervals using a pencil and a flexible transparent ruler. When the markings were made, I chose a bit for my Dremel, showed Connie how to insert it into the chuck and tighten it so that it wouldn't wobble and injure either the gourd or the gourd artist, and then I made the first hole.

"Even pressure," I said. "And a firm hand. That's the only secret."

When she picked up the tool, it fell out of her hands. I caught it just before it clattered to the floor and put it back in her hand. Tears glistened in her eyes, and defeat slumped her shoulders.

"I should have warned you. It's heavier than you think. I dropped this sucker three, four times before I got the hang of it."

If she could tell that I was lying, she didn't let on. She wiped her eyes with the back of her hand and said, "Okay, let's try this again."

Six minutes later, she had seventeen evenly spaced holes half an inch below the rim of her gourd. She took her time choosing pine needles, lining them up to make sure they were all the same length and laying them out on the work table with care. She was quick to pick up the technique of holding the needles against the rim with one hand and using the upholstery needle to lace the sinew that would hold them in place through the holes. When she came to the end, her eyes were glistening again, but this time a smile of triumph lit her face.

"It's beautiful. Thank you, Lili. Oh thank you so much!" Her small, warm hand squeezed mine, and then she turned the gourd around and around in her palm, stopping to admire the design and how it flowed across the round body, touching the sharp ends of the pine needles where they stuck out and gave the piece some texture.

"It *is* beautiful, Connie. And except for that first hole, you made it all yourself."

She laughed. "Oh no, I remember what you said the first day we sat here. 'Only nature can make a gourd. We just get to listen to its voice.' And I tried to do that here, I really did. Maybe I better wait until next time to start a new one. I want to take this home and just look at it all night."

"Don't tell anyone," I said, "but I've actually done that. So, I'll see you next Tuesday, same time, same place."

I hugged her and carried her bag outside. The sun felt good on my face as I watched her car until it was nothing more than a speck on the road. I might have stood on the walk forever if the peal of the telephone hadn't called me back to the house.

"Hello?" I managed to say as I tried to catch my breath.

"Lili, hi, it's me." Seth sounded harried,

not his usual assured self. "Listen, I hate doing this at the last minute, but I'm afraid I have to cancel dinner tonight. I have a ton of papers that have to be filed tomorrow and Ron has a history test. Can we reschedule? Tomorrow maybe."

"Can't. I have a mediation scheduled in the late afternoon, so I probably won't be great company. Let me check with Neil and I'll get back to you. Good luck with those papers." The depth of my disappointment took me by surprise until I realized that part of it was embarrassment. Now my brother would know that I'd been stood up — in fact, he was being passed over, too, in favor of paperwork.

At least I'd have the chance to put in a couple of hours on the health care booklet. Not exactly my top choice, but it certainly would help the bottom line.

I told Neil about the change in plans with a smile and a matter-of-fact tone. "So I can get some work done and you can finish up that history of Appomatox."

"No problem. We'll do dinner another time. I was kind of looking forward to getting to know him, though. You know, a little chat, see how he behaves around my big sister. And you can tell a lot about a man by the food he cooks and the wine he brings."

"Seth cooks real food in interesting ways," I said, thinking how nearly that described the man himself. "And he doesn't drink. Hasn't in over five years."

I expected my brother to react with surprise, but his eyes crinkled and he nodded.

"That's a new part of the picture. I don't mean . . . Mostly, I like him. He's nice. Maybe a little slick, but nice."

Instead of getting defensive, I shrugged and straightened a stack of *American Craft* magazines and picked two brown leaves from the bamboo plant on the end table.

"You didn't bite," Neil said when I finally did face him. "You must be all grown up. But seriously, be careful with him. I don't know what it is — maybe my brotherly protectiveness. Something's . . . I don't know, he talks to that lady cop in the same tone of voice he talks to you."

I thought back to the time last fall when I'd seen Michele Castro's car in Seth Selinsky's driveway. I'd assumed it was all about business then, but maybe Neil's antennae were picking up something I didn't want to acknowledge, Officer Garrison aside.

"He was trying to do me a favor, so he

was making nice to her."

That sounded good. Or, at least, plausible.

CHAPTER 15

The mediation center was bustling, and I had to scramble and cajole to find a room where we could close the door and not be overheard by half the county. I'd made a bet with myself: Smith, the homeowner, would show up by six, our scheduled time. Caterra, the contractor, would make us wait and drift in at six-thirty with some excuse about having to take care of a problem at a job site.

At six o'clock, though, Mr. Caterra was sitting in the reception area, glancing at his watch every thirty seconds and drumming his fingers on the arm of the office chair.

Was I ever going to stop thinking I knew what these guys would do, how they would behave? I scolded myself, reminded the impartial facilitator in me to be in the moment and respond to the people in the room, not the ones in my head.

From my vantage in the mediators'

lounge, I could see comings and goings, but the door hadn't opened in several minutes. I closed my eyes, tried to picture a broom sweeping away the concerns of my day. Michele Castro kept reappearing, like a stain that was still there after ten washings. This was not a good mental state for a mediator. The next phase was to gather more information and then develop an agenda so we could talk about everything they thought was important. After that would come the fun part — helping them work toward a solution that would be mutually acceptable.

Tony Caterra looked like he was about to either explode or stalk out of the building when Randall Smith strode in, all smiles and apologies about having problems starting his truck. I was looking at a lethal combination: One man caught up in conflict-rage, the other grinning as though the whole thing was a joke.

I strode to the waiting area, offering a gracious smile. "It took me a while, but I managed to snag a room where we can talk privately. Please come this way, gentlemen." I didn't peer over my shoulder to see whether they were following me, or strangling each other, or staring at my receding back. When I reached the room, I stood in the doorway and they clomped in.

Noisily, they took seats. I asked Smith to describe his plumbing problem in detail and he settled down and gave an account of the leak, when it started, what conditions made it worse. He slapped a copy of the estimate on the table and pointed to a couple of items for emphasis.

"See? Replace lead pipes with copper. Stabilize pipes and caulk joints. That's what he said he was gonna do. If he actually did that, then it wouldn't have leaked. But, no, he took my money and did diddly. And then he turned around and gave my money to support the casino because he thought he'd get a piece of the action when the contracts went out for bid."

Caterra sat back, arms folded across his chest, his button-down collar crisp and white against his tan neck, his expression impassive. The man looked as though he spent a lot of time on a golf course.

"What work was actually done?" I asked. "And what materials were used?"

Caterra detailed what his workman did on the four days it took to finish the job. He used words like "S-ring" and "compound this" and "elbow that," the kind of tactic that some men try when they think they'll be able to throw a verbal monkey wrench into the works because the mediator is a woman. I was not impressed.

"So far, what I'm hearing is that the two of you had an agreement. Mr. Smith, you agreed to pay Mr. Caterra his standard hourly rate plus the cost of materials and make the work site accessible at normal working hours. Mr. Caterra, you agreed to fix the leak in Mr. Smith's bathroom, to clean up after each day's work, and to let him know if the cost was going to exceed your estimate. Did I understand that correctly?"

The two men offered grudging acknowledgement that I'd described their arrangement properly.

"Did you ever specify what materials would be used on the job?" If I was right, unspoken assumptions had contributed to the conflict — maybe this would uncover them.

"Never came up." Caterra offered one of his smarmy grins. "What's the difference? I hear he's planning to sell the house anyway if the casino wins, so it won't matter to him."

I wondered whether the man slept at night, what with all those rationalizations dancing in his head.

Smith kept his cool. "We didn't talk about

materials, not exactly. But if the leak never got fixed, it doesn't matter whether he used chewing gum and chicken wire or solid gold pipes. He cheated me. He took my money but he didn't give me what I paid for. Bottom line."

Yes! Smith got it, and he'd said it out loud. Would Tony Caterra think it was important to do the right thing even if no one was looking? I had my doubts — but he was still entitled to help in working out a resolution they could both live with.

"Mr. Caterra, have you ever had to go back to a client and fix a job in which the original problem wasn't solved the first time out?"

His head moved slightly, a barely perceptible nod that I took to be agreement.

"What did you do in that case?" I asked.

Caterra ignored my question. He slid his folded hands along the table and said, "Look, Randy, I did a job for you. You messed up the work by dumping stuff down the sink that I'd just fixed. I don't owe you anything. You need to learn how indoor plumbing works."

The tension level jumped through the roof, until Smith's snort of laughter filled the room. "Great, sounds like you're auditioning as a comedian for a high school talent show. Now if we can get back to business . . . nothing was ever dumped down that sink. You find some oil, I'll pour it on my . . . never mind. I collect all my old oil and junk in large plastic jugs — bleach, laundry soap, that kind of thing. Admit it, Caterra, the guy you sent has messed up two other jobs and you're scrambling just to save your butt and your business. Well, see, I'm not the one gonna eat it because you hired some birdbrain and told him to cheat me blind so you could put extra money in your pocket. So, are you gonna make it good, or am I taking you to court?"

Tony Caterra stared at Randall Smith for what felt like a century. Then, without saying a word, he pushed his chair back, stood, and headed for the door.

I was almost grateful. These clients seemed more interested in having a pissing contest than they did in working things out. I would give them all my energy for as long as they wanted it, but I wouldn't be terribly upset if they decided to take another route to resolution.

"Mr. Caterra." He stopped at the sound of my voice. "Would you like to continue this mediation or would you rather take your chances and let a judge decide how things should be worked out?"

Caterra frowned and stood there, saying nothing.

"Mr. Smith, what would you like to see happen?"

Smith smiled, shook his head, then said, "No kidding, I have a lot of answers to that question that I won't bring up in front of a lady. I'll go to court if I have to. Maybe we should all go home and cool off and try one last time."

Tony Caterra grunted his assent, and I did my best to appear pleased that they were at least willing to try to give mediation one last shot.

The night was warm and clear, but I drove home in a personal fog, my head clouded by worry. I hadn't been arrested, hadn't been charged, but I was a suspect in a murder investigation. I had made a pact with my friends to learn as much as we could about the people on both sides of the casino issue, hoping that we'd come up with a juicy prospect. But the idea of spying on my neighbors left me feeling itchy, as though I would have to take a long, soaking bath to wash away the grit. The only tangible result that had come out of our plan was that my to-do list had grown longer and my sleep shorter.

I still had to finish the writing job that had taken over Neil's borrowed computer and make arrangements for the New Hampshire gallery to ship home my unsold pieces, which made me a little nervous because gourds are fragile things. Still, I couldn't take two days off and go up there myself and leave Neil alone and ignore Michele Castro's warnings not to leave town.

True, some bright spots glimmered — Neil had offered to go online and pay my bills, a chore I hated because it was so tedious and always reminded me of the state of my checking account. And I'd had my roof fixed by a nice young man who had done some work for Nora. He'd been courteous, diligent, thorough — from the evidence so far, the opposite of what I'd seen and heard of Tony Caterra. I hoped he wasn't going to turn out to be a walking cliché, every homeowner's nightmare, the kind of person who probably had to move to a different state every three or four years because he skated a little too close to the edge of the law and community ethics in order to pocket an extra twenty percent.

My gourd studio shimmered like a tantalizing mirage, a promise at the end of a long road marked by obligations. Maybe if I was lucky I'd even get to spend a couple of hours with the gourd seedlings that had been growing in their special trays on the sun porch. They would need transplanting in a month, and I had to find someone with a rototiller to turn the soil. The list of service people that Tom Ford had left was useless — for some reason, he seemed to feel that paying twice the going rate was insurance that a job would be well done.

By the time I got home, I was tempted to throw my hands up, pay homage to my mother's wisdom by downing a couple of shots of Scotch, neat and effective, and then passing out on the sofa in the hope that tomorrow might be a slightly better day. But the sight of Neil, and the sound of his voice chattering about the calls he'd gotten from the infield coach, from our brother Charlie, and from Melissa, distracted me long enough for the impulse to pass.

I wandered out to the sun porch and ran my finger along the tender tops of the green shoots that had poked up through the rich potting soil.

I pictured Tom Ford, medium height, thinning hair, laugh lines radiating from his hazel eyes. He held a glass of sauvignon blanc in one hand and a copy of the *Wall Street Journal* in the other as he lowered himself to the wicker rocker that used to fill the sunniest corner of the porch. He'd kick off his topsiders and smooth the collar of his teal Izod shirt and then gaze out at the expanse of green lawn, thankful for the haven of his three acres on Iron Mill Road. Just for a little contrast, a Johnny Cash song would be playing on the stereo — he'd turn the phone off, so that he could watch the sun set behind the pines.

Or not. The Tom Ford who had called last week was much too caught up in business to relax so completely.

I checked the soil to make sure the seedlings were getting enough water and then went inside to set the dinner table. My cooking skills did extend to pasta, and my automatic pilot took over as I boiled water for the linguini, chopped shallots and red peppers and asparagus for the primavera, sliced cucumbers and celery to go in the salad, and set a hunk of Parmesan on a plate. I was about to carry the salad bowl out to the table when Neil came into the kitchen.

"Lili, I need to talk to you." Concern clouded my brother's eyes. "I hear you when you get up and wander around in the middle of the night. I see the light from under your door at three in the morning. I can't tell exactly, but it seems like you get maybe four hours of sleep a night. And not all at once, either. So maybe I should go home so that you can —"

"Whoa, Neil. You know that has nothing to do with you. This bout of insomnia started before you came. The pharmacist gave me this herbal thing and suggested that I drink warm milk. It's not really working. Yet. Maybe I need to take more of it." I hugged him, hard enough to make him reach out for the wall for support. "You actually make it better, not worse. Having you here is . . . I don't know, it's good for me. Less lonely."

He backed away and leaned against the stool. "But you don't talk to me. You listen to my woes, you make dinner and do the laundry, you joke about how I should take up tap dancing, but you never tell me what's bothering you."

He was right, of course. Despite the heart-to-heart with my friends, I'd kept myself pretty closed off, even from people I loved and trusted.

That didn't mean I had to continue to behave that way.

"So many sad things — Marjorie's murder, Connie's health. Every time someone mentions Melissa's Aunt Bernie, I think about Dad. And so many things to do for my freelance work and to promote the gourds, never mind try to get in some real time in the studio. I haven't spoken to Anne in ages, so I better call her before she decides I'm the worst sister in the world. My life is made of a million little details and I've lost sight of the real shape of it. There's a big picture somewhere but, I don't know, it's like it's one of those pointillist paintings, you know the ones made of little dots of color. You really have to stand pretty far back to understand what the image is. If you're too close, all you see is spots."

"You left out two things," he said quietly. "Me. My long spring and summer off while I sweat out whether the Mets will keep me or sell me on the cheap to get rid of me."

As though he were damaged goods, ready to go to the first bidder at a fire-sale price. But I wouldn't lie to him and pretend that he wasn't on my mind. "Yes, sure, that's one of the things I think about."

"But the big thing, and you're not really facing it, is that being a suspect in a murder investigation is a pretty amazing source of stress. I think that's why you're not sleeping."

I'd hoped he hadn't noticed how much it bothered me, because I didn't want my brother to feel that he had to take care of me when the situation was supposed to be the other way around.

"I know, I didn't do it, right? The truth should be enough. That's what I started thinking. But then I heard about the Innocence Project. People wrongly convicted because the local police were eager to put more notches on their belts." Suddenly, a new possibility popped into my head. "Do you think . . . Could Michele Castro have planted that notebook? She and her crew were here just a couple of days earlier. Do you think they're the ones who —"

"Good! There you go, your brain is in gear. You're cranking. Even though I happen to think it's a pretty lame idea. That cop didn't strike me as desperate. She looks like a pretty straight shooter . . . well, you know what I mean. But you had an idea, at least."

I poured dressing over the salad and tossed it, ignoring the stray pieces of romaine that dropped onto the counter. Maybe he was right — I'd been too worried to think clearly.

"Okay, fine, talk this out with me. Someone's trying to frame me for murder. They leave the murder weapon in my house and they drop a note in the toy store bathroom, and then they slip an address book under my stove. All meant to point to me. To give Castro credit, she seemed pretty skeptical. But nobody's coming up with any good ideas about who might have done those things." I paced, my brain and my body buzzing with energy.

"So my friends decide we'll check out the neighbors, and we each try to listen more carefully, with a focus on a couple of people who might have wanted to keep Marjorie Mellon quiet. We're supposed to look for odd behavior, maybe even prod people into saying things. And one of the things that keeps coming back to me is that Trisha Stern appears to have quite a lot to lose if the casino is built. Sometimes she really does sound as though she'd do anything to stop it."

A grimace of disbelief replaced Neil's smile before he looked away. "You can't really believe that. Trisha may have strong feelings about her house and the land, but murder? She's a healer."

"Right. But I can't count anyone out. So I have to look under rocks to see what's hidden." Getting Trisha Stern to open up to me would take a bit of doing. I hadn't gotten very much past civil pleasantries with her. "You can do it more easily than I can.

Talk to her. Find out what she thinks about Marjorie, where she was the afternoon Marjorie was murdered."

He tossed the oily lettuce leaves into the bowl and then looked up and met my gaze. "Nope. Won't do it. I heard you guys the other night. You made it perfectly clear that you wouldn't go poking around into Seth's dark corners. For the very same reason, I will not try to trick Trisha Stern into saying things I don't want to hear. The woman is helping me, for Pete's sake. I need her to trust me, and I need to trust her. Find out another way. You know that you're asking me to choose between you and Trisha? Not a good thing, Lili."

He was right, of course. It would have been easier for him to get information from her that she might not reveal to me . . . but he wasn't willing to taint his relationship with her. He needed to believe in her. As I wanted to believe in Seth.

"Okay, okay, you're right, sorry. Forget it. If I find out anything I won't tell you. You can be surprised when Michele Castro stops by to arrest Trisha in the middle of a leg lift."

"And you," he said with a smile, "can be surprised when you find out that Trisha Stern was teaching a class in anatomy at

Walden High School when the murder was committed."

"She was?" I couldn't decide whether I was relieved or disappointed.

Neil arranged two slices of red pepper on top of the salad. "I don't know. I made that up. But it's a little more plausible than her being a murderer, isn't it?"

I didn't say that I'd come to the point where I believed anything was possible. Even things I wished weren't true.

CHAPTER 16

I bit into my toast, but it tasted like cardboard. Nora's homemade fig jam didn't interest me. And it certainly didn't make up for my lack of sleep. The valerian and warm milk weren't working. After that semi-argument with my brother, my sleep had been even more disturbed. The dark circles under my eyes made me look like a magazine ad for hangover chic.

Neil looked up from his oatmeal. "Mom and Dad want to come up on Monday. I forgot to tell you last night. She reminded me that they've been pretty good, staying away all this time. They'd just be here for the day."

"Huh. When I spoke to Mom yesterday she said something about waiting until Dad got adjusted to his new meds. I think they want to make sure I'm taking good care of you."

My brother smiled placidly and traced

circles in his oatmeal with his spoon. "And that I'm taking care of you. Mom suggested that while they're here you might want to take some time off, maybe go somewhere with your pal Seth, let yourself off the hook for a couple of hours. Dad has a new chess strategy he wants to try on me, and you know Mom. She'll sit here and stare at me as though that will keep me safe."

"Mom said I should leave? She can't stand to spend a whole afternoon with me? And you went along with the plan. That's just great." I tossed the last bit of toast toward the plate and watched it land, jam-side down, on the floor. "I do not appreciate sneak attacks, Neil. You shouldn't have done this."

He reached across the table and touched my hand. "It's not a sneak attack, Lili. Mom called to find out if Monday was okay for a visit, we got to talking, and the next thing she was saying that she was worried about you, but that you'd probably object if she said so. She's just trying to do something to give you a little space. She was being nice. Is that so terrible?"

"No. But someone could have asked me if that's what I wanted." I started slamming the breakfast dishes into the sink, realizing that my anger put me in danger of breaking something, maybe even something I'd regret for the rest of my life. "Listen, I need to pick up a few things in town, and this seems like a good time to do that. Can I get you anything?"

He started to say something, looked down into his bowl, then lifted his head. "I need a refill on my Vicodin. I'll call it in so you don't have to wait."

I nodded, pulled on my sweater and marched out into the bright sunshine. I didn't need this, my own family sneaking around behind my back. I had enough on my mind without having to worry about consoling my parents and assuring them that I was fine, thank you very much.

By the time I'd driven a mile down Iron Mill Road, my anger had turned to confusion. What was so bad about what Neil and my parents had done? Only the way they went about it . . . Why couldn't they just have said that they were concerned about me and left it at that?

Because I would have put them off.

Because I might have felt that they didn't trust me to take care of Neil properly and that they were coming to check up on me.

Because they had anticipated my reaction and had tried to get around it so that they could make sure things were all right with me. The only way they could do that was to slip in under the false pretense of seeing Neil.

Which I hated.

And that was exactly why I was having trouble getting started talking to people I hardly knew about Marjorie Mellon, about where they were the day she was murdered, about how they felt about her. My distaste for dishonest behavior was keeping me from checking out a couple of things that would be useful to know. For instance, if I could find out what Sue Evans knew about the note that was found in the bathroom of her store, that would be really helpful. Probably the best way to do that was through indirection, which I'd always considered to be a polite term for lying. Maybe I was being a tad too absolute about not telling truth — and had been all my life.

Wait just a minute, Miss Honesty, a small voice piped up. *What did you think you were doing when you told Ed Thorsen that you needed time alone and that's why you were moving to the country? You could have said that you knew you didn't want to marry him right then.*

And there were other times, lots of them. I dialed Neil's cell phone from mine, and was glad, in a chicken-hearted way, when his message came on. "Sorry I was so stupid just now. I overreacted. See? Even your elders can be jerks. But at least I can admit it. Which is what I'm doing, along with apologizing. I'll see you later. Love you."

When I parked in front of Wonderland Toy Town, a new and more devious me emerged into the bright morning sunshine. I would find out as much as I could about Sue Evans and the note and any other secrets she might be hiding.

The bell above the door tinkled happily, but except for the Barney theme song playing in the background, the store felt deserted. I poked around among the electric train accessories for a while, then headed for the book section to see if I could find any Tintin comics that my nephew Cameron didn't yet have.

After several minutes, Sue Evans appeared, her patchwork vest bright against a navy silk blouse. "Lili, hi. Is there something I can help you with?"

"I should carry a list," I said, "but I'm looking for a Tintin for my ten-year-old nephew. Are these all you have?"

She laughed. "We carry every single one we can get. They don't sell fast but there's a steady demand. We're missing two of the more recent ones, but I'd bet he already has them. What about this one?" She handed me "Tintin in America," with its picture of a tomahawk-wielding Indian on the cover.

I flipped a couple of pages. "Great, I don't think he has this one."

As she slipped the book into a plastic bag, she said, "Sorry, I didn't hear the bell right away. I was in the back and I sat down for a second and must have dozed off."

"Wish I could do that. I've been having so much trouble sleeping lately." Before I plunged into full snooping mode, I needed to make sure her guard was down. "Joseph Trent gave me some herbal thing a couple of weeks ago but it doesn't work for me."

"That's odd," she said with a bright smile. "He gave me something two months ago and it did the trick. I don't even know what it is. I just took those little tan pills twice and they worked. Maybe if I'd remembered about them last night I wouldn't have fallen asleep at eleven this morning."

Tan pills? Not white capsules? I'd have to ask Mr. Trent for whatever he'd given her. But I wasn't here to find out about sleeping remedies. "You know, if I could make the tension in my life disappear I think I'd sleep better."

Sue's rueful smile never quite reached her green eyes. "Good trick. Let me know if you figure out how to do that. God, there's always something."

"Right. I don't know about you, but I'm always going a little crazy trying to keep up with my family." I waited for a response, but her expression didn't change. "Or all the contradictory advice you hear about how to stay healthy. Now, there's something good for a load of stress."

Again, nothing. She was listening politely, but I hadn't yet found a sore spot. "And work. Boy, if it's not too much work, it's too little."

Bingo. Her eyes widened and she nodded vigorously. "I know what you mean. Except for weekends when my nephew comes in to help, I'm it around here, and it drives me nuts. I do the ordering, I stock the shelves, I help the customers. When business is good, I'm exhausted. When it's slow, I think I'm going to have to turn the key in the door and walk away."

"So, you really have to put up with extremes in the toy business." Would my mediator tactic encourage her to talk? Reflecting what someone said without either judging or advising usually helped them to open up. Giving a person an opening might even help her to fall into the trap without too much pushing. "Sometimes I think I should just buy up a ton of lottery tickets or invest in a casino or something."

"What do you mean? I thought —" Her confused frown turned into a smile. "I get it. You're joking. Well, you never know what it's going to take to stay afloat. You do what you have to, right?"

This fishing expedition wasn't even landing me a soggy breadcrumb. "I guess I should have been clever enough to have rich parents."

"Anita Mellon's not going to have to worry, if she takes care of that money."

My kahuna tuna might just have nibbled at the bait. I willed my face not to show my excitement as I looked at Sue. Her expression changed in a blink, as though she'd erased her frown and drawn a smile onto her face.

I matched her smile and said, "You really think Anita had anything to do with it?"

All I needed was a little more line so that I could reel in what might turn out to be the Big One. Maybe she knew who Anita trusted, someone she might have taken into her confidence and promised a piece of the modest little pie that Marjorie had left behind. But Sue Evans stiffened, visibly shutting out the question. "I have no way to know. I don't mean to rush you but —"

"I'm sorry, really." Time to switch tactics. Maybe a little self-disclosure would open her up. "Listen, we both know that someone found that note in your bathroom. I don't know what you believe, but I didn't write it. I just want to know what it said. You can understand how hard this is for me, I'm sure. I don't know who's trying to point a finger at me, but I had nothing to do with Marjorie's murder. I'm trying to put the pieces together so I can help defend myself."

That felt so much better.

She seemed to get it right away. Her body unclenched and her face softened. She still didn't look at me when she said, "I'm not supposed to talk about what was in that note. I wish I could help you, but Michele Castro made a huge point of telling me that I was to say absolutely nothing. To anyone. Not just you."

"Of course, I understand." I wouldn't put her on the spot, but that didn't mean I couldn't find out more. "Would you answer one thing for me? Marjorie was killed on a Thursday. Yet the note wasn't found until the following Monday. Did you use the store bathroom between those two times?"

"Every day. Several times a day. Customers use that bathroom too, kids, parents. Salespeople. The UPS man. It's almost as busy as K-Mart's toy department," she said ruefully, as she fingered her seed necklace, rubbing one as though it were a protective talisman.

"But if Marjorie dropped it when she was cleaning, that means that nobody noticed it until nearly ten days later." That was difficult for me to believe, given the traffic that had been in and out of that small room daily. Unless Sue made it a practice to snooze in her back room . . .

"All I can tell you is that it must have been under something and then it got moved by maybe a curious four-year-old and then —" She paled and clapped a hand across her mouth.

"What is it?"

She shook her head, silver earrings swinging wildly. "Look, I know you're concerned, but I can't talk about this anymore. I almost said what was in the note. I really am sorry but I can't talk to you any more."

She handed me the plastic bag containing the Tintin comic and walked to the back of the store. I heard a door click shut — she'd taken her secret and disappeared into the back room.

I stepped onto the street into an afternoon that had turned blustery. Thick clouds piled up on the western horizon. The air had a yellowish tint that I'd never seen before, and it made me uneasy. No need to linger in town when I had so much to work do. Best to get Neil's medicine and go straight home.

I ran across the street, dodging the sparse traffic and skirting half a bale of hay that must have dropped off the back of someone's truck. The fluorescent lights inside the pharmacy flickered and blinked a silent warning. The hole in the rug seemed to have gotten larger since the last time I was here, and the whole place had an air of weariness about it that made me understand why some Walden Corners residents had taken to driving the extra six miles to go to the Walgreens.

"Mr. Trent," I called into the void. This seemed to be the day shopkeepers had decided to hide in the back of their stores. That wasn't much of an incentive for doing business here. Maybe they were all caught up in a community depression and needed some community Prozac.

I picked up a jar of vitamins, then set it down on the counter a little harder than might have been necessary. In a few seconds, Joseph Trent's nose and his granny glasses appeared, followed by the rest of him.

"Hi, Mr. Trent. Seems like a quiet day around town." I'd learned that getting right to business felt rude to some long-time residents. My Brooklyn-bred habit of saying what I wanted had taken conscious effort to change.

Joseph Trent's tight lips spread into a smile. "Everyone's getting ready for the storm, so they're out buying batteries and stocking up on bottled water and candles. They never catch on that television stations need to make everything a big deal to keep people watching the commercials. Usually, it's just an ordinary thunderstorm that they blow all out of proportion. What can I do for you, Miss Marino?"

Nobody had called me that since I went to a Park Avenue doctor to see if I'd torn any ligaments or tendons in my knee playing Frisbee in Central Park when I was twenty.

"My brother called in a renewal for his prescriptions. He gets the generic, not the brand name, right?" Making conversation might not get me quicker service today, but it had become something of a personal challenge to see if I could get this dour man to like me. "Should I be worried about that? I mean, you never know what you're getting when you buy pills, but the generics are fine, aren't they?"

Trent pushed his glasses up on his nose, then took them off and set them on the counter. His brown eyes squinted at me and his upper lip twitched. "The government thinks so, most doctors think so."

Somehow, I had managed to insult him. I was definitely not cut out to play at being something I wasn't. I wondered whether Nora or Melissa or Susan were having as hard a time as I was when they poked around to try to help me. Elizabeth was probably accustomed to questioning by indirection. But if I tried too hard, I only ended up with both feet in my mouth.

"Sorry, I was just wondering. You know, you read so much in the papers, it's hard to know what to believe." I watched his face for signs that he was no longer offended, but saw only same stoic expression. I was zero for two with Walden Corners merchants today. "Oh, and I was wondering. You know that sleep-inducing herbal thing you gave me? They don't seem to be working. I wanted to check with you before I took two instead of one. What do you think? Would that be all right? Or should I try whatever you gave Sue Evans?"

Finally, his frown turned to a bright smile. People love to be recognized for their expertise, and I'd pushed the right button.

"I have a stronger version in the back," he said. "If you take two of the old ones, they might upset your stomach. This formula is stronger and it's mixed with something to counteract the digestive problems. I'll get your brother's meds and give you a couple of capsules to try. Take two or even three. If they work, then you can buy a bottle."

"That's great." Relieved that we seemed to be back on friendly footing, I mentally reviewed my conversation in the toy store while he disappeared into his stockroom. Sue had been understandably defensive, not at all happy when I brought up the note. Her mention of Anita was surprising, though. Maybe there was bad blood between them. They were about the same age, might have been classmates. Nora would know.

"You better get on home," Joseph Trent said as he plunked the two pill bottles on the counter and pointed to the windows at the front of the store. "I just looked outside, and right now that sky looks real threatening. See how green that air is? That means there could be a strong thunderstorm or even a tornado on the way. You need to get home before driving gets dangerous."

Beyond the window, scraps of paper and

swirls of dust eddied and danced around the lone figure crossing the street. Her hair was blown first straight out behind her and then as the wind direction changed, whipped straight up, like a cartoon character who had stuck her finger in a live socket. Even when she tried to shake her long brown hair out of her eyes, the wind seemed intent on plastering it to her face.

"You're right. Thanks, Mr. Trent. I guess I won't stop at the Agway this trip. It does look wicked out there." I grabbed the white paper bag and headed for the front of the store. When I pulled the door open, a gust nearly grabbed the knob out of my hand. I tugged it closed and pushed against what felt like a wall of pulsing air as I walked the half block to my Subaru.

CHAPTER 17

The sky, no longer green, had turned evening dark. The wind changed direction as often as a diva changes costumes. The eight mile drive home usually took about fifteen minutes, and I crossed my mental fingers that I'd make it to my driveway before the skies opened up. The streets were deserted. Even the supermarket parking lot held fewer than a dozen cars. I thought I saw B. H. Hovanian make a dash from the diner to his office, but my hands felt glued to the steering wheel and I didn't wave.

As I passed the Agway, a tractor towing an empty hay wagon pulled out in front of me. I gritted my teeth and inched to the center line, but a car was coming toward me and I couldn't pass. The tractor chugged along at ten miles an hour, and as I looked around for a side road to peel off onto, the driver's peaked cap blew off. It sailed onto my windshield, then bounced to the road.

In my rearview mirror, I watched as the wind picked it up and sent it flying again, like a skipping stone on a clear lake — except nothing outside my rolling fortress looked placid and still.

Trees, some with new green leaves that looked tender and tentative, bent and whipped toward the ground. A willow's branches flapped and twisted like a double jointed dancer. I pulled to the left again, crept closer to the tail of the wagon, clung to the steering wheel. Up ahead, no oncoming traffic. Good — but less than a quarter mile away, a hill rose above the fields. If I could clear the tractor and the wagon before a car came over that hill, I could be home in ten minutes. The sky was even darker, the wind more punishing as I pulled out, pressed the accelerator, and cleared the back end of the hay wagon.

I was almost up to the front of the wagon when a pickup truck crested the hill, traveling fast and heading right for me. On my left, the shoulder of the road butted up against a wide green swath that could have been solid or swamp for all I knew. But it was my only choice. I cut the wheel, felt my left front tire hit soft dirt, pulled my foot off the gas pedal and blinked as the truck sped past me in a blur.

Thrumming with adrenaline, my hands shaking, I pressed the brake until the car came to a stop. Was that truck silver?

Seth Selinsky was the only person I knew who drove a silver pickup.

Could he have been behind the wheel . . . and could he have deliberately tried to run me off the road? No matter how hard I tried, I couldn't get a clear mental picture of the driver. Couldn't have been Seth.

Couldn't.

Why would someone want to run me off the road? It didn't make sense. I tried to convince myself that I was as much a surprise to him as he'd been to me, that he hadn't had sufficient time to react. The adrenaline coursing through my veins wouldn't allow me to accept this rational argument. Besides, it had been a pickup truck, that much I knew for sure. Silver — maybe the color had been distorted by the strange storm light. The wind had died a little, and up ahead, the tractor and the hay wagon were pulling off onto a dirt road. Nothing coming in either direction. I felt as though I could fly home under my own power, but I took a deep breath and then exhaled. Still no traffic, so I pulled onto the road, and sped forward. One more mile to Iron Mill Road.

By the time I reached my left turn, my pulse was almost normal, but the sky definitely was not. Darker still, and with a metallic cast that made me think of weathered bronze, it seemed to be pressing down on the trees and flattening them. Up ahead, a bright flash of lightning blazed along the horizon, illuminating the small stone church at the top of the rise, making it look like a Gothic painting. Fat drops of rain hit the windshield. By the time I reached over to turn my wipers on, the rain was so heavy I couldn't see the edge of the road.

I'll never know whether I heard a warning sound first or simply had the good sense to edge the car to the side of the road, but as I pressed the brake and came to a full stop, another flash of lightning lit up the sky and a huge tree crashed across the road right where I would have been if I hadn't pulled over.

Something fell across the top of my car. Instinctively, I ducked. When I peered at the windshield I could barely make out a heavy branch laden with green leaves. The rain continued to pound at every surface, bouncing up in huge fat splashes.

It was one thing to be inside my house when a snowstorm brought down power lines, or to enjoy the adventure of scooping snow to melt for drinking water after a blizzard. This was entirely different. It wasn't a hurricane and so the fury wouldn't last for days. Probably not even hours.

I was still unnerved.

Think, I commanded, but my brain had not yet recovered enough to engage in any rational activity. A black snakelike figure whipped across the road, and a shower of sparks and crackles snapped around me. The downed power line hit a puddle and sizzled, then was carried by a gust up and onto the grass. What was I supposed to do? Getting out of the car seemed wrong, dangerous. Staying in the car felt nearly as vulnerable.

The rain, which had been so heavy I'd been unable to see just a few minutes earlier, was now only a steady downpour. In my rearview mirror, I saw what appeared to be two headlights, neither coming forward nor receding. Another car, stopped dead in the road. It was probably two hundred feet away.

With the tree blocking the road in front of me, my only option was to turn around and find another route to the other end of Iron Mill Road. I backed up, hoping that my car would slip out from under the branch, half expecting another tree to come crashing down and pin me to the spot forever. I kept looking back to the power line, which continued to sizzle and flail like an agitated sea monster spitting fire. If I could complete the U-turn without being electrocuted, I'd be happy. Amazed, but very happy indeed.

As I pulled forward, I gave a final glance to the black, undulating wire, watched in horror as it landed on the roof of the little shed beside the church. I hoped everything was too wet for a fire to start. Brilliant white sparks crackled for ten seconds and then the wire blew off the roof again. I started down the road with my heart pounding and my mouth dry.

The windshield wipers pushed the rain away fast enough for me to make out the vehicle whose headlights I'd seen, still facing me. If someone was hurt or needed help, what would I do? I was terrified — the thought of stepping out of the safety of the carapace of my car made my palms sweat.

But as I approached, I realized that I was about to pull up alongside a silver pickup truck.

New fears sprang to life like mushrooms after a rain. What was going on? First a silver pickup truck nearly ran me off the road, and now here was another one. Or the same one, maybe. Had he reversed course to follow me? It was tempting to floor it and leave a spray of water as the only reminder that I'd been there, but I had to know who was in that vehicle. I pulled up alongside the truck. My windows and his were fogged, making it impossible to see anything more than a shape. I was about to drive away, when the truck's horn blasted and I nearly jumped out of my skin.

The window rolled down and Seth's face appeared, his expression hard to read under the brim of his blue baseball cap. He motioned for me to roll down my window.

I sat frozen, not sure what to do. This was Seth, for Pete's sake. Even through the curtain of rain that separated us, his face seemed wreathed in concern.

"Lili!" he shouted. "Are you okay?"

Reluctantly, I rolled my window partway down. "Fine. That tree missed me. Just. I have to get home and see how Neil is."

"I'll follow." He rolled up his window and pulled forward enough to turn around.

Not exactly what I had in mind. I wanted to recover from this experience without having to confront whether or not the man I was dating had tried to run me off the road. I tried to call Neil on the cell phone, but all I got was one of those annoying beeps-on-caffeine that meant that the circuits were busy. The rain was no more than a shower now, and I turned onto one of the roads that I knew would eventually lead me back home.

Nowhere else were power lines or trees down. In no other spot was the debris from the wicked storm strewn across the road and the fields like a child's toy chest up-ended by a giant throwing a tantrum.

How had I gotten so lucky? But I wasn't the only one almost to be picked up by what must have been a small tornado. If Dorothy had Toto for company, then I had Seth shadowing me. Maybe a little too close for comfort. By the time I pulled into my driveway, all I cared about was making sure my brother was safe. Then I'd concentrate on getting dry and warm. I wanted to sit still for at least an hour without worrying whether I'd be electrocuted, drowned, crushed by a tree, or accordion-pleated by a truck.

Seth was right behind me. I didn't wait for him as I dodged the raindrops and ran up the back stairs and into the kitchen. Neil stood at the stove pressing buttons and looking totally frustrated.

"You need to be a genius to reset these clocks," he grumbled. But he turned and held out his arms and hugged me to him, holding me tight until I pulled away gently. "I was so worried about you. So was —"

Seth shut the door behind him and shook his head like a shaggy sheepdog that had just retrieved a stick from a pond. "Lili! I was so worried. Neil said you'd gone into town and you didn't answer your cell phone and then the radio said there'd been reports of a tornado headed our way and —"

"I'm fine. I'm a little shaken up and I feel like I only have seven lives left, but I'm fine." Now that I was in the warm house, my soaked shirt and my hair made me cold to the core. If I didn't do something, the shivering shakes would take over. "I'm going to take a hot shower and then put on some dry clothes."

Neither of them said anything. I stripped off my wet clothes in the bathroom and stood under the stream of hot water long enough for my tense muscles to relax just a little. I rubbed my pink skin with a towel until not a drop of moisture remained, pulled on my terrycloth robe, and let the hair dryer blow warm air on my neck, my face, and eventually my hair.

By the time I'd pulled on blue sweatpants, white cotton turtleneck, and my white socks and sneakers, I felt like a different person. One who wanted to find out about the incident on Route 9.

Neil was in the living room, flipping through a magazine. He waved as I padded into the kitchen, where Seth was hovering over a saucepan, putting the finishing touches on a tray that had already been supplied with bowls, spoons, and napkins. The aroma of hot chicken soup, which had been in the back of the refrigerator for a couple of days, was so welcoming I almost melted on the spot. Instead, I turned to Seth and said, "Where were you going in such a hurry on Route Nine?"

He looked at me as though I'd lost my mind. "When?"

Hovanian had advised me to say only what was necessary and sufficient to answer the question, but he'd said nothing about how to respond when someone answered a question with another question. At least this was an easy one.

"About fifteen minutes before the tornado tossed that tree in front of my car." The only way I could do this was to make him maintain eye contact with me, and I watched those long lashes blink a couple of times as though he was trying to calculate a particularly difficult chemistry equation.

"Before that tornado hit the hill I was here, asking Neil if he was sure you'd taken your cell phone with you because you weren't answering. What's this about, Lili? You look . . . I don't know, angry."

Seth Selinsky hadn't seen me angry yet, but he was about to.

"You might be angry with the person who tried to run you off the road, don't you think?" I said it softly, through clenched teeth. When I glanced over at Neil, he was looking down at his cast, as though it was the most interesting thing in the room.

This wasn't fair, not to Neil and maybe not to Seth, although at the moment that concerned me a whole lot less than finding out the truth. That truck . . . Had it been nothing more than coincidence?

"Look, maybe I was hallucinating. Or maybe it wasn't you. But I saw a silver pickup truck barreling down the road toward me without even slowing down. I know I wasn't fantasizing when that truck didn't even stop to see what happened after I skidded into the weeds at the edge of the road."

Can you ever put the toothpaste back in the tube?

As soon as the words were out of my mouth, I regretted them. I sank back against the counter, afraid to look up and see the expressions on Seth's and Neil's faces.

"Are you okay, Lili? It wasn't me. Maybe the driver was too shaken himself. I don't know what happened, but I was here with Neil."

When I did look up, I saw worry brimming in Seth's dark eyes. He took a step toward me, then shook his head and made no further move in my direction, as though he knew I'd have to be the one to decide how close we might get.

"I don't know," I said in a barely audible voice. "I thought I was handling everything — I'm sorry. I didn't mean to be a witch."

Seth came around the counter and put his hands on my shoulders, pressing on my tight muscles with his fingers. "Too much stress, that's all. You've got a million little knots here and here and here."

With each word and each bit of pressure, he touched a sore spot and massaged it until it loosened a little. My eyes fell shut, and I felt myself go limp under his touch. When he got to a spot on the side of my neck, he hit the jackpot — a tiny burst of pain was followed by a sense of release so complete that I almost cried. I don't know how long I stood there, feeling the warmth of his hands as he massaged every little packet of steel and turned it into silk again. His warm breath on my neck stirred a memory of nicer times, and I must have sighed.

"That's good, Lili. Listen, why don't you go lie down now? See if you can nap. I'll call you tomorrow." Seth came around in front of me, kissed my eyes, and then let himself out the back door.

I waved to Neil as I headed to my bedroom. The bed was soft and welcoming, and I was asleep before I could wonder how Seth had found me.

CHAPTER 18

The sun blazed in the sky, cutting a swath of light across my eyes that made me wince even before I opened them. I glanced at the clock. Seven thirty.

Seven thirty? Either I'd just been transported to the Arctic Circle or I'd slept around the clock, nothing I'd ever done before. My mouth felt dry, but otherwise every part of me felt better than I had in weeks, relaxed, rested, and definitely energized. I recognized this — this was my normal, something that had been missing for too long.

Neil was already showered, dressed, and making breakfast. Smatterings of small talk and some decent scrambled eggs filled half an hour, fueling me with enough energy to look forward to finishing up the dreaded co-payment and deductible sections of the health benefits booklet I had to turn in by Monday.

"Gotta get to work." I danced over to my brother and planted a kiss on his forehead. "Beard's looking great. You trim it?"

Grinning, he said, "You didn't even notice. Melissa trimmed it two days ago. She stopped by to see if you wanted to go to the movies and we got to talking and she found your scissors in the bathroom, and voila! A new me. She's got a great touch."

"Oh ho. I'd say TMI, but I really want to hear more." Could an older sister ever have too much information about what was going on between her baby brother and a good friend? "Whenever you want to talk, of course."

"Nothing to tell." He grinned. "At least not yet. Anyway, here's Trisha."

I peered out the window and saw Trisha Stern marching toward the front of the house, her equipment bag slung over her shoulder and her smile as radiant as the bright sunshine.

"Give me a few minutes with her, okay?" I was ready to take on anything today, even a woman who had practically said she'd go to any extreme to protect the sanctity of her land. Of course, it wasn't the only avenue that might lead us to the person who had killed Marjorie. There were other persons of interest, as Dad used to say. I just didn't know who they all were yet.

Neil pushed himself to a standing position and hobbled to the hall on his crutches. "Sounds like my old Lili. Glad to have you back. I'll be in the bathroom, pretending to be engaged in morning ablutions. You're not going to find out anything terrible from Trisha, you know, but give it a try so that you can let it go."

He disappeared as Trisha's light, rapid knock filled the air. When I opened the door, she breezed in, all smiles and good energy. She greeted me cheerily and declined my offer of coffee as she set her bag near the straight back chair where Neil sat for most of their sessions.

"Neil's just washing up. He'll be right out," I said over the sound of the running water from the nearby bathroom. "You make out okay in the storm?"

"Fine." She looked up at me, her eyes clouding. "Except for a huge tree that came down right across the bed of tulips I planted last year. That, and the garage windows that were smashed by flying construction debris. Which also got Jonathan's gazebo, and that's just a pile of sticks now. To say nothing of the flood in our basement because the casino road isn't properly graded so all the runoff goes right to our yard and then into our house."

"That sounds awful. But how could there be construction debris when the casino doesn't have approval? And you called it the casino road." If Ira Jackson was counting enough chickens to start the building process, then not all the news was getting out to the public.

She laughed bitterly. "He says he's putting in basic services for whoever ends up buying the property. Makes it more attractive to potential buyers so they don't have to do the grading and put in the water and electricity and all that. I think he's probably been paid off already by someone. No one does that in advance of sale unless you know where a building is going to be."

I sipped from my lukewarm coffee, trying to make sense of what she'd just told me. Ira Jackson's construction material had damaged Trisha's property in what the local radio reports had called a tornado . . . which, for insurance purposes probably qualified as an act of God. If she wasn't angry before, she certainly had every right to be furious now.

"I didn't know about all that activity on the property. Anything you can do?" I certainly wouldn't be the one to sit at the table, but a mediator might help her get some compensation and, equally important, some sense that the responsible person understood that his negligence had caused her considerable distress.

"Sure, I can take every damn piece of wood and glass and metal and lord knows what that blew over onto my land and move it right back to his property. Right in the middle of the damn road, so that he'd have to take notice that something terrible happened because of his negligence. If he wasn't so greedy, he'd have spent the money to secure those materials properly, but he's too damn cheap."

The more we discussed the damage done to her property during the storm, the more agitated Trisha became. I'd never seen her like this, wouldn't have known that the calm, supportive Trisha who worked with Neil and exuded positive energy was capable of such intensity. With one hand, she swiped at the fringe of hair on her forehead, and with the other she plucked at the seam along the pocket of her workout pants.

"You really don't think much of him, do you?" One more level — I wanted to push her just a little further, so that her defenses would be down and she'd be likely to answer my questions.

"I do think about Ira Jackson a lot. All the

time. I think about how he's so interested in lining his pockets that he doesn't care who or what he ruins." As she spoke, she paced from one end of the living room to the other, hardly aware of my presence. "People like that should have something really awful happen to them so that they can learn compassion. It's not going to happen any other way."

"He never really heard you when you tried to say how you felt about the casino. Some very angry feelings built up in you, didn't they? He kept moving forward, no matter what anyone said. And then Marjorie picked up his ball and started to run with it." I paused but she kept marching back and forth across the room, restless and unfocused.

She stopped, her face crumpling. "What are you saying, Lili? Are you accusing me of something? I don't believe this." Trisha Stern started to toss things back into her bag while I stood speechless, trying to think what I could do to salvage the situation.

I hadn't accused her of anything, not really. Her reaction startled me, and I had to do something to recover. "Trisha, wait. Please, I didn't mean anything. Please don't go. I'm really sorry if I offended you. My brother really —"

"Hey, something wrong?" Neil hobbled back into the living room, stopping in the doorway and glancing first at me and then at Trisha. For the first time since he'd arrived, my brother looked sad. Neil's perplexed frown softened as he turned to Trisha. "What's up?"

I held my breath, praying that Trisha would accept my apology, for my brother's sake. Her face no longer had the serene, open quality that made her so likeable, so easy to talk to. This had escalated beyond anything I'd intended. Now I'd alienated the person who was supposed to help Neil recover from his accident. If she left . . .

"I'm so sorry, Trisha. I've been going nuts trying to find out anything that would clear my name. I hope you can understand. It's been so —"

"Look, I can understand your anxiety but it's not fair to take it out on me."

The ice in her blue eyes melted just enough to give me an opening to try to convince her to stay. "You're right, I wasn't being fair. Gene Murphy and Michele Castro are good cops. They have experience and resources I don't have. It's just . . . I'm not used to sitting still when there's something I can do to help myself. Obviously, I'm not doing a good job of it. And I really am sorry."

"Then maybe you should talk to Anita Mellon," Trisha said, still glaring at me. "I hear she's back in town to sign some papers. She might know more than anyone else about what happened to her mother. But you better figure out how to avoid making her angry and defensive, you know?"

Now that we were speaking calmly, what I heard disturbed me. Trisha's indignation was clear — maybe even a bit too clear. Yet all I'd done was to mention Marjorie's name and she'd reacted as though I'd called her a flag burner.

For the first time since I'd moved to Walden Corners, I wondered whether small town life really was right for me.

"You ready to get to work, Neil?" Trisha's voice was strained, but she smiled as she took the strap and the weights out of her bag. "You're doing great but you can't take a day off yet. Let's start with some aerobic warm up."

I slipped out of the living room and headed for my desk. I had a brochure to finish. Maybe work, even work I wanted to get out of the way as quickly as possible, would focus me long enough to clear my head so that I could think about everything

Trisha had said — especially that deflection of attention away from herself and onto Anita Mellon.

Who really did deserve my attention. Even if nothing came of it, I'd have to figure out a way to meet Marjorie's long-suffering daughter.

The Taconic Inn sparkled in the sun, white columns and the wide plank porch inviting. The rocking chairs would be taken out of storage soon, wicker tables placed between them. The hanging baskets filled with lipstick plants and trailing ivy would form a curtain that would give the illusion that the stately old building was surrounded by nature instead of being on a highway.

I parked in the rear lot and pushed open the screen door to the kitchen. Nora stood, hands on hips, staring down at a mound of asparagus.

"Soup or soufflé?" I asked.

She turned, her face lighting with a smile. "Soufflé — what a great idea! Perfect to go with the lamb. Now all I need is another color family. Beets, maybe, or carrots."

"Definitely carrots. With a mint glaze." I lifted the lid on a huge stockpot and inhaled the comforting aroma of chicken stock. "You have a few minutes?"

Nora nodded and passed me a vegetable peeler. "You peel the carrots, I'll prep the asparagus, and we'll talk."

"I hear that Anita Mellon is back in town to take care of some business. You went to school with her, right? What's she like?"

"Flashy." She smiled and cut off the ends of several stalks of asparagus. "You ever hear Dolly Parton tell the story of how she got her style? She was ten, shopping in town with her Mama, and she pointed to the blonde woman with bright red lips who was wearing a low-cut blouse and tight skirt. 'She's real purty,' she said to her Mama. And her Mama said, 'She's trash.' Dolly said that she knew that was what she wanted to be when she grew up — trash. Well, that's Anita."

I laughed. "Isn't that the way it is? We either want to be our mother or the farthest thing from. Marjorie wasn't unattractive, but she certainly didn't go out of her way with her appearance."

"Anita drove her nuts. I remember her complaining, we must have been in eighth grade, that her mother had thrown away all her lipsticks. She wore the tightest sweaters, the shortest skirts, had the longest hair. The boys stared, the girls couldn't decide whether we envied her or despised her. By the time we hit high school, she was running with older boys." Nora frowned as she chopped asparagus and tossed it into a pot, ladled out some of the stock and then set the pot on a burner. "I always felt a little sorry for her."

"Because she had no friends?"

"Because she had no idea that she was really pretty under all that makeup. Because she wasn't secure enough to be herself. She once told me that her mother made her wash the kitchen floor four times until it was done to her satisfaction. And that Marjorie laughed when Anita told her she wanted to be a nurse. Said that it took brains and that she was better off using the assets she had to make her way in the world."

My mother was starting to sound like a saint.

"So they never got along. And Anita was Marjorie's sole heir. Which would be interesting, except that she was in Tennessee on the day Marjorie was murdered."

"But Seth Selinsky wasn't," Nora said. "In Tennessee that day, I mean."

I know I stopped breathing, but I have no memory of inhaling again. Nora put her knife down and took mine from my hand, led me to a chair and sat down across from me at the same table where the poker group had met several nights earlier.

"I just found out something that I was going to tell you when I finished the dinner prep." She spoke softly, her voice reassuring and warm. "He flew to Nashville day before yesterday. Left from Albany airport at the crack of dawn, came back on the last flight that same day. My cousin works the airline ticket counter. She recognized him. He got all flustered and said something about a real estate deal. I don't know if it means anything or not, Lili, but I thought you should know."

That dinner he'd canceled — he'd gone to Nashville instead. To talk to Anita Mellon?

"I don't get it. Why? What would Seth have to do with Anita, and how does it fit into what happened to Marjorie?"

Nora jumped up from her seat and turned down the flame under the asparagus pot. When she turned to face me again, her eyes had that sorrowful look that made me want to look away. "I don't know the answers to those questions. I do know that he went with Anita through most of tenth grade. He was in his senior year. Then some dropout mechanic from Pine Plains appeared on the scene. Seth was pretty depressed that whole spring. Moped around, nearly failed history. Finally got it together enough to pass the exam. He went off to his grandparents' farm in Wisconsin for the summer and when he came back he was a new boy. Man, really. He left for college, and as far as I know didn't have anything to do with Anita after that."

People grow up. They change. They learn. If someone were to judge me by the person I was in high school, I'd be in trouble. But in all these days, during the entire time I'd been upset and working hard to clear my name, Seth Selinsky had never once mentioned his relationship with Anita. He'd gone all the way to Tennessee. To see her? And now she was back in town.

"Thanks for telling me, Nora. I don't know what any of it means, except that it doesn't look good, does it?"

"You're the one who says to be careful about jumping to conclusions. I can tick off explanations for his behavior that don't have sinister meaning, but we'd both be imagining things. You ever ask him where he was when Marjorie was killed?"

"I couldn't." But it was clear that I'd have to face that now. If Seth and Anita had conspired to murder Marjorie so that Anita could get her inheritance a little early . . . If it had, indeed, been Seth who had tried to run me off the road on the day of the storm . . . The thought made my whole body tight with anger.

"Of course not. I still think you can't put these facts together and condemn the man, though. Maybe you should try talking to Anita, see if you can get anything from her." A bird twittered outside, and Nora looked out the window, then back to me.

"What would I say to Anita? 'Hi, I think maybe you and the guy I've been going out with murdered your mother and now you're trying to frame me so please turn yourself in so my life can get back to normal?' I don't think that would work."

Nora walked over to the door, pushed it shut, and plucked a gray sweatshirt from the hook. "No, probably not. But if you went over there and said that you wanted to return Marjorie's sweatshirt and then just got her talking, that might do it. You can say that Marjorie left it at your house when she stopped by to talk to you about something, I don't know, you'll figure that part out."

I took the well-worn cotton sweatshirt from her, wondering about the person who had worked out in it or just hung around the house wearing it. I'd known Marjorie as a smart, articulate, hardworking woman who had strong feelings about the casino. Her daughter had known another Marjorie, one who had little use for imperfection. How much anger, I wondered, could a child accumulate? And what would happen when it came out?

CHAPTER 19

"Take it however you like, I'm going with you." My brother straightened the collar of his knitted shirt, a creamy beige that went well with his dark hair and fair skin. His cast had acquired a soft, grayish color that looked good next to the faded denim of his jeans. We'd slashed a couple of pairs of pants so that he could get them over the cast. On Neil it just looked like a new style.

"As my protection?" The thought of him wrestling with a woman with false eyelashes and glossy lipstick almost made me laugh. "It's all right, Neil, I can do this on my own."

"Can, sure. But won't because I'm going with you. Who do you think will get Anita Mellon to talk more, you or me?" He flashed one of his boyish grins and held both hands under his chin, the cherub with ulterior motives. "Besides, I'm going stir crazy here. I mean, it's a great place and all, but I've been here for two weeks without seeing a single thing that I didn't know I was going to see. I need something new. I need some stimulation. So I'm going with you."

If Anita still had any of that girl in her that Nora had described, then Neil would surely be the right one to have along. She'd sounded harried when I asked if I could stop by to return the sweatshirt, but agreed to a ten o'clock meeting. I couldn't help wondering whether Seth Selinsky's silver pickup would be parked beside the big maple tree near the grand old house.

Only a dark, nondescript rental car sat under those spreading branches. I pulled up beside it, came around and got Neil's crutches from the back, and helped him out of the car.

"Never did this on gravel before," he said. He planted the rubber tips of his crutches firmly, swung forward, then repeated the motion until he'd made his way to the front steps. I followed behind, ready to catch him, but although he went more slowly than usual, he was steady and strong all the way up the steps to the porch and then to the front door, where he pressed the buzzer.

The grass hadn't yet grown enough to need cutting, but weeds were starting to sprout in the bed of daffodils and tulips that bordered the porch. If Anita planned to sell this place, she needed to hire someone to tend the property. Curb appeal counted, even where there were no curbs.

"You sure she said ten?" Neil leaned forward and peered into the window, then straightened again.

"Yes. That must be her car." I pressed the bell one more time, and finally heard quick, light footsteps on the stairs, then the click of locks, and finally the door was pulled back.

The woman standing before me was nobody's idea of trash.

She had shoulder length brown hair, large green eyes, and a small, perfectly-shaped mouth that smiled a greeting. "Hi, you must be Lili. And you are — ?"

"Neil Marino. I'm Lili's brother. I've been cooped up with this," he said pointing to his cast, "so this is a special treat for me. I'm sorry for your loss, Ms. Mellon."

The woman at the door shook her head. "Oh, no, I'm not Anita. She's upstairs getting dressed. I'm her friend Linda Bannerman. Please, come in. Anita will be down in a few minutes."

She led the way through a center hall into a room that Nora's mother would have called a parlor. A patterned rug covered most of the wide-plank floor, and two red camelback sofas formed an L under the windows. The coffee table and end tables were dark wood, and a hunt scene, complete with trumpet and jodhpurs, filled one wall. Porcelain figurines, an old scrimshaw horn, a graceful clock that had stopped at noon — or midnight — were artfully arranged on the tables and interspersed among the books in a built-in nook. The room didn't look at all like one in which I'd imagined Marjorie. But, then, I hardly knew the woman.

"Get you some coffee? Tea?" Linda spoke directly to Neil, who had settled into a chair with a low ottoman that gave his broken leg support.

"Not for me, thanks. You came with Anita from Tennessee?" Neil's smile was one of his bright, you're-so-interesting ones. His beard made him look almost professorial, kind and wise.

I'd have to compliment him later on his technique and his timing. Linda took a while to come up with an answer to what seemed like a very easy question.

"I live in Rhinebeck. Anita and I have known each other for years. I just stopped by to see how she was doing, bring her some lamb stew I made the other day, you know, offer my support." She sat across from Neil, her hands folded in her lap and her smile looking as if she'd drawn it on when she met us at the door.

So Anita had a good local buddy after all, someone who knew she was coming to town. Someone who had gone out of her way to pay a condolence call. Someone who might have been a good enough friend to help Anita claim her inheritance a little earlier than Marjorie had planned.

"That's really nice of you. I know how important it is to be with people you care about at a time like this. I didn't know Marjorie well, but that's a terrible way to lose your mother."

That seemed neutral enough, but Linda didn't want to talk about Marjorie. She nodded and glanced at her watch uncomfortably.

"So, you've lived in the Hudson Valley all your life?" Neil leaned forward a little.

To my amazement, Linda matched the movement, creating a connection between them that left me as the observer. "Not all my life. I went to college in the city, studied art history at NYU. Two years without any luck finding a job — that was a wake-up call, let me tell you. I went searching for something useful to do. Something that actually let me pay the bills. So I came back here and got a real estate license."

"Sounds like you ended up with the best of all possible worlds. And now you're going to list this house for Anita, I bet. The market's still hot here, so that's great for both of you."

I enjoyed sitting back and watching Neil at work. I might even learn a thing or two that I could use in mediation. But Linda surprised me by jumping up and marching to the doorway.

"Right," she said, her eyes swiveling toward the hall. "Hang on a sec, I'm going to see what's keeping her. Excuse me."

"What was that all about? Seemed like a simple statement about real estate, didn't it?" I looked around the room for anything personal, a photograph, a memento of a family event, but either Marjorie had not a sentimental bone in her body, or Anita had already cleared out anything of personal significance.

Neil grinned and stroked his trim beard. "This is fun. If the Mets don't take me back, maybe I'll just get me a private detective's license."

"Sure, you'd love sitting in a car drinking bad coffee and waiting for the unfaithful wife to open the motel door so you can snap a picture." I lowered my voice to a whisper. "What did you say to her that got her all upset? Why do you think she got so bothered when you mentioned the market being hot? Maybe it was the listing comment, because the state of the market isn't exactly a secret. Maybe she didn't —"

Neil's hand made a patting motion in the air. Quiet, he was telling me, and then he put on an expectant smile. Two seconds later, Linda and a woman who surely was Anita walked into the room. This was more like the person I'd expected. Her perfume enveloped her in a musky cloud. Anita's hair was layered and streaked, her makeup — two colors of eye shadow, contoured cheekbones courtesy of well-applied blush, lips that were outlined in plum and then filled with a shimmery copper — extravagant, and her slacks and V-neck sweater designed to show exactly what kind, if not what brand of, undergarments she wore. She looked like she might have stepped out of a high school graduation photo, if you ignored the squint lines in the corners of her eyes.

"You must be Anita," I said, rising and offering my hand. "I'm Lili Marino and this is my brother Neil. We just wanted to say how sorry we are about your mother's death."

Anita's well-shaped left eyebrow lifted. "Thanks. You're the person who found the rifle, right?"

Okay, so nothing about her was subtle. Which wasn't necessarily a bad thing in this circumstance. "Sort of. It fell out of a ceiling tile. I don't know how it got there."

I didn't ask her if she knew.

"Yeah, well, I guess my mother made some enemies." Anita stood in the middle of the room, her gaze searching the tables for something. She turned to Linda, her smooth forehead twisted into a frown. "Where did you put my orange juice?"

Linda sighed, pivoted, and disappeared into another room. She'd been changed by Anita's presence into a timid creature who bore little resemblance to the attractive woman who had greeted us. Whether Anita had some hold on her from the past or the present, Linda had been transformed into a grudging puppet.

"It's going to take me forever to get rid of this stuff. You know anything about antiques? My mother says she learned a lot, going into people's houses and their offices and cleaning. Learned maybe more than she should have. Anyway, she knew antiques.

Bought stuff that people thought was junk, sold it for a small fortune. I don't know about any of that." Anita flopped onto one of the sofas and drew her legs under her. In the light that filtered through the sheer curtains she almost looked like one of those forties movie stars, reeking of glamour and danger.

Neil pointed to a figurine of a shepherdess, complete with bonnet and staff. "That one looks English to me. Beautiful skin, that long hair. You could have been the model for that one. She looks kind of lonely, though."

I could hardly believe his chutzpah. So blatant, so bold. But he seemed to have struck some tender place in Anita Mellon. She dabbed at the outer corner of her eye with a red-tipped pinky and nodded. "My mother used to tell me that she wouldn't sell that doll because she looked like me. The old bird hardly ever showed a soft spot, but that thing, it made her go all goofy."

Neil nodded and did his leaning forward thing again. "Sounds like you didn't have an easy relationship. That must make this time even harder. I really am sorry."

Anita's eyes narrowed and she sat up straight, her head cocked. A second later, Linda appeared in the doorway bearing a tumbler of orange juice. Even though I couldn't smell the vodka, I was sure it was there. Anita gulped a third of the liquid and then set the glass on an embroidered doily on the table. Linda hung back in the doorway, hands folded in front of her.

How, I wondered, had Anita gotten such power over this woman?

"What did you say?" Anita frowned, peering at Neil as though he were the only person in the room. Then she laughed, a bitter sound that made me cringe. "Oh, right. An easy relationship. The only easy relationship I had in my life was with Connie Lovett. She was the only one who ever cared about what happened to me."

I couldn't help looking over at Linda. Her eyes widened and her mouth opened, but she said nothing.

"I guess my relationship with my mother would have been okay if only I hadn't fought back when she made me clean the bathroom floor with a toothbrush. If I'd accepted that I was destined to amount to nothing, that I'd ruined her life simply by being born. As though I asked to be. Not to her, anyway. And you know, this time isn't harder. It's easier, not having to listen to her pick me apart."

In two strides, Linda appeared in front of

Anita. Startled, Anita glared up at the woman, who smiled more confidently now. "I made some coffee. I'll bring it out. You guys take milk and sugar?"

Anita drank down half the remaining liquid in her glass and said, "Sure. Bring some of those cookies, too."

Her speech had become slurred and her smile lopsided. Linda disappeared and I knew we had only a short time to find out anything more, at least on this visit. We'd gotten nothing by dancing around and pretending. I had nothing to lose by tangoing over to the real question.

"It's so sad, your mother's death. It must be hard, not knowing what happened. Everyone thinks it was because of her stand in favor of the casino, but nobody really knows. I'm sure you're anxious for the police to find the person who killed her."

Anita picked at the scarlet polish on her thumbnail. "Yeah, it's sad. And yeah it's hard. But my mother wasn't killed because of any damn casino. She told me . . ." She cocked her head, listening for footsteps, I presumed. The soft clink of china and silverware were the only sounds from the rear of the house.

This time, I leaned forward, right into her space so that she couldn't pretend I wasn't there. "Your mother told you . . . ?"

"Oh, yeah. She told me she found something that would turn this town upside down. I never heard her sound so angry. I mean, about something besides me. She said it was one of her —"

"Here's the coffee." Linda put the tray on the table, smiling too hard and trying to hide her shaking hands. "These little cookies, someone baked them and brought them over. That's one of the nice things about living in a small town. People are always doing things like that, thoughtful. Things that take only a little time, but that let the other person know you're thinking about them. It's not like that in the city. It's —"

"Will you please stop babbling?" Anita leaned back again and turned to me. "She didn't tell me what it was. Said I'd mess things up if I knew. I mean, that was just like her. Toss out a crumb, then hit the hand that reaches for it with a hammer. Man, she was a piece of work."

My heart pounded and Neil's breath sounded louder in my ear.

"What were you talking about just before she said that?" Neil's voice was soft, soothing, and his dark eyes oozed sympathy.

Linda fussed with the cookies and held the plate out toward Neil but he ignored her. If I could have booted her into the next county I would have done that happily. She was only trying to please, I told myself. Maybe I was imagining too much when I looked at Anita and Linda and saw something more.

"She was telling me what a tramp I am. Well, maybe not in those words, but that was what she meant. And then she laughed and took a breath and said it, just like that. Nothing before and nothing after, except to tell me she'd call me at the regular time. Saturday afternoon at two. Every week, whether she had something to say or not."

"So you have no idea what she found out? Something that would turn this town upside down — that sounds like it might have had to do with the casino. Did you talk about the casino that day?"

Suddenly, Anita looked at me as though I were an alien who had just appeared in her living room. "I'm going upstairs," she said. "I don't mean to be rude, but I'm tired. Thank you for stopping by and for bringing that thing."

Linda steadied her as she negotiated a path around the coffee table. Anita Mellon leaned against her friend and said, "Pull the door shut when you go out."

Neil and I sat in the empty room for a full

minute before either of us could move. "Not exactly your run-of-the-mill condolence call," he said as he lowered his leg to the carpet. "Let's get out of this place. It gives me the creeps."

We drove off in silence, thoughts swimming in my brain like brightly colored fish that caught my attention for fleeting seconds until the next one appeared.

Marjorie might not have delivered her message in the most subtle way, but those weekly calls should have been a clue to Anita that her mother cared, in her own way. A little, at least.

What was going on between Linda and Anita, and did it have anything to do with Marjorie's murder?

And how did Seth fit into this little *pas de deux?* Maybe it was a dance for three. I hated that I couldn't just up and ask him . . . or could I?

"Neil, I need some advice." The sun had warmed the air enough for me to roll my window down, and I enjoyed the feel of the breeze on my skin.

"It's about Seth, right?"

I glanced over at my brother, who for once was not smiling. How had he read my mind? "Well, yeah. I'm not even going to ask how you know that. I used to feel that there was potential for a real relationship with him. You know, we could talk to each other easily, we liked a lot of the same things, we both were okay taking it slow to see how things went. And they went along just fine."

"Until you found that rifle in your ceiling and then got all caught up in suspecting everyone," Neil said.

"Guilty." But that didn't mean that I didn't have good reason to be wary of Seth Selinsky. "Okay, I've pushed him away. I can't tell if I imagined things the day of the storm. He says he was with you when that truck came flying over the hill. The timing still feels like maybe . . . or maybe not. But it was weird that he ended up right behind me. Plus, he has this grand scheme to use the land where the casino was to be built, so getting Marjorie out of the way would help grease the wheels of his venture. And now i hear he flew out to see Anita, which opens up a new universe of motives."

"Fine," my brother said, a hint of exasperation in his voice, "but I can't put it all together to make murder."

I had to admit that he was right. "I know. I'm totally confused, but I'm sure there's a lot that we don't know. Some thing, some reason, some event we haven't heard about yet."

"How clever of you to notice." Neil touched my arm, then moved his hand away. "Maybe you're trying too hard, Lili. Maybe you need to let it go with Seth."

But I didn't want to. I wanted to rescue the possibilities. "Let's say you're Seth and you're completely innocent. What would you be thinking about now?"

"Let's go for the easy answer first. Let's say I'm Seth and I'm guilty. I'm somehow involved in Marjorie's murder and I'm watching you get all suspicious and pull away. I'd be on edge, I'd be wondering just how much you know and what you're going to do about it. I'd be working on a contingency plan right about now."

I didn't even want to think what that might include.

"Okay, that sounds logical. But what about my first question?"

My brother looked out his side window, so I couldn't see his expression. We were passing the Rockefeller farm, with its guest house that had been cunningly designed to look like a very large silo. Every time I drove by the wonderfully well-kept spread, I marveled at what huge sums of money could do. Finally, Neil turned and I glanced over to see an amused smile on his face.

"You know what — the answer is the

same. I'd be wondering what you're thinking and what you're going to do about it. Either way, a little extra friendliness on your part might get you what want. If he's not involved, you'll be putting your relationship back on track. If he is, then you might calm some of his worries by playing nice. I just don't think you should be alone with him, at least not for a while. So I'm not going home yet, and I don't think you should go out with him yet. But invite him over, or cozy up at the next casino meeting or something and see what happens."

What Neil said made a lot of sense to me. It was safe. It was prudent. It just wasn't very satisfying.

CHAPTER 20

She told me she found out something that would turn this town upside down.

I repeated the words aloud, trying to match Anita's inflection, the tone of voice. It didn't scan right, didn't match the sound of what she'd said. If I could get it right, I'd have a pointer, a direction to follow.

When I sat down at the computer to work on the brochure, the refrain got louder. The more Anita Mellon's words pattered around in my brain, the more I knew they would lead to the key to this puzzling situation. I couldn't switch off the song and finish my writing job, not until I understood what Anita — and more important, Marjorie — meant. In my skittering, fitful state, I wasn't likely to get there on my own. I needed help — the kind of help I trusted, the kind that knew the fabric of Walden Corners so well they could see the tiniest moth hole begin.

"We'll convene a meeting this evening,"

Nora said when I phoned her. "Can't do it here because I promised Scooter that he and Armel could have quiet to finish up their term papers. Maybe Elizabeth's, I'll check. Anyway, I just tried out a new chocolate mousse pie recipe and I need some tasters to let me know if it works. But when we're all gathered, you have to tell us about Anita. I'm a little hurt she didn't ask about us."

"Anita Mellon is the definition of self-absorbed," I said. "Was she always like that?"

Nora didn't answer right away. "I suppose. But when we were young, I remember thinking that she had to be. Nobody else thought about her."

I arrived at Elizabeth's and parked behind the four cars already in the drive. The night was soft, the air warmer than it had been, and the fragrance of the lilacs in bloom was like nectar that I wanted to drink in until I was so full I couldn't move. But I had to move, and it had to be forward. Waiting around while the meter on B. H. Hovanian's time ticked up a bill would only lead to years of servitude — indentured or not, that wasn't the future I envisioned.

I knocked, pushed the door open, and

passed through the cherrywood and granite kitchen, following the sound of voices to the living room. Melissa and Elizabeth sat on opposite ends of the white leather sofa, Nora sprawled in one of the white wing-back chairs flanking the fireplace, and Susan sat cross-legged in front of the glass-topped coffee table. Susan pointed to a plate with the most amazingly rich-looking slice of chocolate mousse pie topped with swirls of whipped cream. Out of habit and in respect for the ten pounds I wanted to lose, I resisted for two seconds, then carried it over to the matching chair on the other side of the fireplace.

"We have a lot to talk about," Nora announced. "Let's get right to it. Lili, why don't you tell us about your meeting with Anita?"

"I have to say, I probably would have recognized her from your descriptions. Except for the wrinkles near her eyes, she probably looks about the same as the last time you all saw her. Frozen in time. Except for her companion. You never mentioned her."

Melissa frowned enough for everyone. "Companion?"

My eyes drifted to the plate balanced on my lap. "Linda Bannerman. From

Rhinebeck. They seemed very . . . close." It wasn't the ambiguity of their relationship that intrigued me, really. It was the fact that Anita appeared to have some kind of power over the other woman. "As though Anita knew something about Linda and had totally cowed the woman into a kind of emotional slavery."

Nora's sigh broke the silence. "She lived in Rhinebeck, went to high school there, so I didn't know her, really. I've met her a couple of times in the past ten years, you know, local business events. She always struck me as smart enough but not a leader. It was Anita who held court with the kids, even the ones from other schools — they'd probably be goths today — you know, the outsiders who dressed to attract attention. Like Linda, back then."

"Big change," Melissa said, "once Linda went away to school. It was like she came back normal."

Nora sighed. "Sheesh, high school is such drama. Sorting people out by how they look . . . how weird is that? But Anita's clothes and her makeup were things that made it hard for me to warm to her. I mean, I wanted to. I wanted to be a big person and not let appearances put me off. But it felt like she decided I wasn't cool or something

and so she ignored me whenever I tried to
. . ."

"You were *too* cool." Susan sniffed and tossed her red curls. "She knew that if she was seen with you, the outsiders would reject her and find a new leader and she'd be left where she started. My mom and dad once dragged me to a barbecue at the Bannerman's, some kind of business obligation. Linda was an only child, grew up with rich parents in a huge house that required outdoor and indoor help. Servants, right? It was a rumor, but I remember hearing that Linda got pregnant in junior year."

"Not a rumor."

All eyes turned to Nora.

"I can't remember how I know this, maybe something Connie told my husband when they worked together at Walden High. They were putting together a program on teen pregnancy and telling stories about local kids, saying how nothing much had changed since our day. Anyway, Anita was the one who went with Linda to get it taken care of. Out in Pennsylvania somewhere, so that Linda's parents wouldn't know. I wish I had listened more carefully when Coach told me."

I stared at the red, orange, and gray painting above the sofa, thoughts exploding in my head like those colors against the backdrop of this snowy room. That might explain what I'd seen in the house. The real question was how long a period of servitude Anita would demand to repay that long ago favor, and to what lengths Linda would go in order to satisfy her.

Elizabeth cleared her throat noisily. "So what did Anita say this morning?"

Heads swiveled in my direction, as though the ball had just been hit over the net and now it was up to me to make the perfect return volley.

"She said one very interesting thing. She was talking about a conversation with her mother and she said, 'She told me she found out something that would turn this town upside down.' But Marjorie never told her what it — oh no!"

Time stopped then.

My heart ticked and I was aware of each tiny muscle in my face as a smile formed. My laugh was a release of tension that started in my chest and made its way to my throat, where it bubbled out in a rain of sound. Finally, I inhaled deeply and looked into the confused and expectant eyes of my friends.

"This has been driving me nuts all day. Those words kept going around in my brain but they weren't right, they didn't scan correctly. I was so frustrated I thought I'd spit. What Anita really said was 'She told me she *found* something that would turn this town upside down.' Not found out. Just plain found. As in discover. Come upon. Find. A thing."

"While she was working," Melissa said softly. "She must have made her discovery when she was cleaning."

"That's it! How could we have missed something so obvious?" I jumped out of my chair and marched around the room, stopping only long enough to put my pie plate back on the serving tray. "Marjorie ran a commercial cleaning business. So maybe whoever murdered her wasn't trying to stop the casino. Maybe they were trying to keep her from revealing some secret she discovered when she was vacuuming and dusting."

Blood pounded in my ears, and I watched the stunned faces of the others as this new idea sank in.

"What?" Melissa pointed her fork at Elizabeth, whose narrowed eyes blinked once. "It's possible, right?"

"Of course it's possible." Elizabeth's lawyer voice was a half-tone louder than her normal conversational speech, and her eyes brightened with excitement. "You have any idea how many people Marjorie Mellon might have had the goods on? Anyone who comes into a business after hours has access to whatever's lying around. She knows secrets that no one else does."

"Doesn't that make *you* a better suspect than me?" My brain was busy sweeping out old assumptions to make room for new possibilities. Elizabeth had said two or three times that she looked forward to going to work on Thursdays because Marjorie put things right in her office every Wednesday evening at eight.

"Believe it or not, we're not the only ones thinking this way. Michele Castro stopped by to see me this morning. And it wasn't a social visit, either. She asked a lot of questions about Marjorie. When she'd been at the office, what our relationship was, whether I left my computer on when she came, whether the file cabinets were locked. Pretty easy to read between those lines. What she was really asking was whether Marjorie had access to information that I might want to hide from the rest of the world."

"So, what might she have discovered? Who are her clients?" Susan pushed out of her chair and stacked empty dessert plates on the serving tray, her red hair flying out behind her. "What would be damaging enough that it would be worth killing for?"

We sat in silence with our own secrets for a few long seconds. There were lots of things I'd done in my life that I wouldn't want to broadcast to the entire world — shoplifting an Annie Lennox CD when I was thirteen; having a one week secret fling with a college friend's newly discarded boyfriend; telling my sister Anne that I had the flu on her twenty-fifth birthday and then spending my precious Saturday in my gourd studio. None of these were offenses I couldn't get over.

"Good question," I said. "First of all, it would have to be something that would change your life if other people knew."

"Make you lose your spouse or your business or your reputation, you mean?" Nora looked skeptical. "Why wouldn't you just pick up and start over somewhere else?"

Elizabeth laughed. "There you go, thinking like a normal person. Someone who can take a life for any reason except self-defense doesn't think like a normal person. I guess I'm the one with the most experience in dealing with the criminal mind. Uh uh, don't you go there, Melissa Paul. I see that twinkle in your eye."

We all saw it. Melissa looked down into

her tea cup, the knowing smile still lifting the corners of her mouth. Finally, as though she could hold it back no longer, she said, "I was just thinking that you're very good at what you do. Which means you have to out-think the other side. Which means that you've had some practice trying to come up with bizarre and illegal schemes. Right?"

"Now my secret's out." Elizabeth laughed with the rest of us. "But I don't have any big ideas, not yet. So, let's look at what we have so far. Marjorie found something, possibly that belonged to someone she worked for. That someone's life would have been ruined if Marjorie revealed that something. We need to start with a list of her clients. Normally, that would be difficult to obtain, given that we have no power to impound her files or her computers."

Her smile gave me a shiver. She was going to suggest something that would have us skating on the edge of legal. Elizabeth Conklin drew out the moment for the sake of heightening the drama until Nora tapped her fingernail against the rim of the pie plate.

"But you're going to tell us why it's not going to be so hard this time, right?"

"Who knows as much about people's business as a cleaning person?" One raised eyebrow nearly touched Elizabeth's hairline.

"Marjorie probably didn't have her nails done, so it isn't her manicurist." Who else? "Her hairdresser?"

Elizabeth shook her head slowly. "Marjorie went to the barber shop, had him cut her curls the same length all over, and then she left. No gossip."

"No, it's not who she would tell about her clients, but who would already know them." Melissa's eyes narrowed. "An accountant. That's the only . . . I'm right, aren't I? You know Marjorie's accountant."

Elizabeth's grin was answer enough. "I don't want to get him in trouble by asking him outright for that list. So maybe I'll visit his office, and while I'm there he might just happen to leave her client list out on his desk while he visits the men's room. If I can figure out how to tell him what I need without actually saying it."

Nobody expressed a shred of doubt that Elizabeth would find a way make her intentions known to the accountant.

"Meanwhile, though, we know enough about Marjorie's clients to get started." Assuming her role as unofficial recording secretary, Nora started listing names. "Elizabeth Conklin, Seth Selinsky, Joseph Trent, Holly Herman, Luney Toons."

"B. H. Hovanian," Elizabeth said, avoiding my eyes. "Walden Savings and Loan."

"Taconic Inn," Melissa said, grinning. "Four times a year, you know, when we do big seasonal changes. I think she also does that — *did* that — for Maria's Italian Restaurant and for that new, expensive French bistro in Rhinebeck."

"Seems like enough to start. I vote that we save Elizabeth Conklin and Melissa Paul for last." Everyone giggled nervously, and I laughed with them. The next part was what was making me nervous. "I'm not going to be the one to talk to Seth. If one of you finds out something, fine, I'll live with that. But I don't want to go sneaking around in the dusty corners of his life."

"I'll do it," Nora offered. "He's always been nice to me, helped me take a second mortgage after Coach died. I'll see what I can find out."

"I'll talk to Rick Luney," Elizabeth said. "We bump into each other at the diner at least once a week, and he likes to gossip much more than he likes to work. I think I can get him to open up."

"Holly Herman," Susan declared, as though she were bidding on a fine antique at an auction. "I must spend half my salary at the bookstore, so we're on pretty friendly terms."

The list was narrowing; only Melissa and I hadn't made our choice. "I can't very well be impartial about B. H. Hovanian since he's my lawyer. So that leaves Joseph Trent. I go there for Neil's meds, and he's even given me some herbal sleeping remedy, so I can check him out."

"Which leaves me to find out what's beneath the very virile surface of our Armenian lawyer friend. I don't mind doing that, not one bit." Melissa smiled.

Unexpectedly, I felt a pang of jealousy. He was an attractive man, but we were on a strictly business basis. Weren't we . . . ?

Melissa made designs in the chocolate mousse with her fork and said, "Sounds good, our plan. But I still don't know what to say. I can't go up to someone and say, 'Would you please tell me if you have a secret that Marjorie threatened to expose?' and then wait for the truth to come spilling out."

Elizabeth pressed her elegant fingers together. "We've been limited because we don't have access to what the sheriff's department knows, haven't seen the note that was found in Wonderland, haven't had a chance to examine that address book, weren't present when Marjorie's house and office were searched. So we have to do what we can by creative thinking, observation, and a little canny interrogation."

I laughed. Despite being the one in need of saving, the situation suddenly struck me as amusing. Maybe it was the surreality of it all — my quiet country existence turned into the most challenging contest of my life. And here was a friend talking about "canny interrogation." Before I could say anything, Susan stopped in front of the fireplace and clasped her hands in front of her.

"You know what? I feel dis-canny. Without a single can. I don't know how to get my neighbors to tell me stuff without making them think I've lost my mind." She shook her head and smiled ruefully. "Not that it matters. But I really can't figure out what I'd ask."

"Just keep opening doors," I said, thinking about how mediators are trained to ask questions that get people talking. "Be interested in what they're interested in. Don't put words in anyone's mouth, and don't judge what they say. I guarantee that you'll hear more than you expect."

Elizabeth's mild surprise shifted to a nod of approval. "Lili's right. It's different when I'm in a courtroom or taking a deposition.

When I'm fishing for information, I just try to set things up so that the person can ramble. People love talking about themselves. That's how I found out about Marjorie's will."

She also knew how to get our attention. Everyone froze, mid movement.

"Aha, I knew you'd perk up. I just want to make sure we don't think ourselves into a corner, that we keep all the possibilities alive. Long story short, Marjorie's attorney's clerk was sitting next to me at The Creamery this morning. I engaged her in a little chit chat about her son, who's graduating from Walden High this June. One thing led to another and suddenly we were talking about Anita Mellon, about how she'd never finished school, and how hard things are for her." Elizabeth licked a curl of whipped cream from her fork and smiled.

"Stop playing, Elizabeth, and tell us!" Melissa's smile was real but so was the annoyance in her voice.

"Okay. Anita inherits the house. Plus investments — are you ready? — worth nearly a million dollars." Now, Elizabeth sat back and took a long gulp of now cool tea. "If that's not a good reason to make sure Mommy Dearest bites the dust I don't know what is. The fact that Anita was in

Tennessee at the time isn't really important."

"She could have hired someone," Nora said, sitting on the edge of her chair. "Someone local she could pay off. Or even someone not local."

Melissa frowned and said, "Or even someone she didn't have to pay off."

Linda Bannerman's pleasant face wafted in front of me like a smoke ring that curled through the air and then disappeared.

"But then why would they try to make it look as though I was the one responsible?" My thoughts wouldn't line up, wouldn't stop long enough to be sorted out and evaluated. "So, does this mean we drop the casino idea? What about the people whose property is directly adjacent to the site? People whose lives would be most directly affected, aside from Ira Jackson, who owns the land."

"Only two people abut that parcel directly. Nathaniel Bartle owns the big field that forms the north and the west borders, so I guess his pro-casino ethics trump his privacy concerns. Jonathan Kirschbaum and Trisha Stern own the plot on the east side of the site. The road is the south border." Melissa's voice dropped off at the end of her sentence, and she seemed to drift away into thought.

"What *about* Jonathan and Trisha? She's said more times than I can count on both hands and feet how much she loves her house. Sometimes I think she married him for that piece of land." I wished I didn't like Trisha as much as I did, wished I'd have a more objective view of her passion for her home and where that might lead her. "You think your principal might have taught her how to shoot a rifle? She didn't grow up in the country like the rest of you. Watching your fathers and the neighbors and all."

"Trisha's too smart to think she might actually get away with murder," Susan said. "And too nice to do it. I don't see it. But given the mysteries of human nature and how much we don't know about the people in our lives we can't rule her out."

Now it was Elizabeth's turn to jump out of her chair and pace the floor in her stockinged feet. Her long dark hair, freed from its pins and clips, swung like a sheet of silk as she made a sharp turn and came to a stop in the middle of the room. "We're stuck here. We're going around in the same circles. We need a rectangle or a hexagon or some other shape. I hate to say this, but we really do need to think outside the box."

My pulse quickened. She was right, and I

had the feeling that we were about to sail into new waters. "Okay, we've gone down a couple of paths. There's the casino, our poor mistreated Anita, and now the entire roster of Marjorie's clients. Is there something we're not seeing, another category?"

"The part we keep shoving off to the side," Nora said softly, "is that someone is trying very hard to make it look as though you killed Marjorie. We need to look at who had something against Marjorie, sure. But we shouldn't forget that someone wants to pin this on you."

Elizabeth stopped so suddenly she almost knocked over the chunky red vase on the coffee table. "Who would gain from both things — Marjorie's death and Lili being blamed? Anita doesn't have anything to do with Lili. I know Tom Ford wrote a letter to the town council opposing the casino but why would he want to frame Lili? He's not getting the cottage back. It might have been an unorthodox method of payment, but the cottage is hers and it's legal. The real estate attorneys made sure the deed was in Lili's name and she's been paying taxes. What about Seth? Maybe he opposes the casino because he thinks it will dry up his business and also because he has another use for the land. Framing Lili would be an extreme way to tell her that he doesn't think the relationship is going anywhere."

"What?" I felt gut-punched. "Are you saying . . . did he tell you he doesn't want to see me any more?"

All eyes turned toward the fireplace. Elizabeth frowned, took her time, finally said, "I don't know anything about how Seth feels about you. We're exploring possibilities. Talking hypotheticals. Trying things on to see if they fit all the circumstances."

Of course that's what we were doing. So, why had it felt as though she'd said the very thing I didn't want to hear? I wanted to be the one to call it off, to say it wasn't working. When the time came. *If* the time came . . .

"Sorry. Touchy subject. Let's go on," I said evenly, hoping my smile convinced everyone that all was fine with me.

"That reminds me," Nora said, her generous mouth spreading in a smile. "You get your computer back, Lili?"

"Not yet. They said they'd let me know when the tests are finished. Listen, instead of going around in circles, let's go in one direction at a time. Maybe we'll keep coming back to the same place, but that's all we can do. Let's concentrate on Marjorie's clients. Start with the ones we know and then when Elizabeth gets the complete list we can expand."

Everyone agreed that the plan was sound.

"And," I said as I finally lifted my fork and scooped up a piece of Nora's beautiful pie, "I'm going to tell Michele Castro about my conversation with Anita."

Elizabeth had returned to the sofa and sat, feet planted straight in front of her, like a schoolgirl trying for a behavior commendation. She quirked an eyebrow and nodded. "We do need to let the police know when we find anything significant. And Anita's little bombshell definitely qualifies."

That phone call wouldn't be the most fun I ever had, but it had to be done.

CHAPTER 21

Michele Castro asked a couple of questions about Anita and our conversation, and then thanked me for my time. The phone call lasted about seven minutes, and when it was over, I felt deflated. The relief I'd expected lasted only long enough for me to replace the receiver.

"You have to talk to Seth and find out what's going on. That's why you're so wired. I know you think it's because you're falling behind on your writing deadlines. But that's not why. That's just another result of all the other stuff. The stuff that you can't just push into a drawer until later." My brother pointed his grilled cheese sandwich at me accusingly. "You need to get it over with, Lili. Have the talk. Ask the questions. But do it smart. Safe, I mean."

"I'm not sure I want to hear the answers." That was it. As soon as the words left my mouth, I knew that Neil was right and I'd have to do it. Otherwise, I'd have only fear, and that was a sack of stones I didn't want to drag around with me. "Okay, I'm going to do it. We'll take a walk or something and get things straight."

Neil laughed. "You don't want to do this somewhere that's isolated, right? No meeting the bad guy in a dark alley."

"Not exactly what I had in mind," I said, smiling. "I'll let you know how it goes."

I love that Rhinebeck is fifteen miles from Walden Corners. That makes it close enough for me to enjoy the movies at Downstate, the great selection of books at Oblong, and the lovely luxury items that the exclusive shops sell for prices way out of my range. It's also far enough so that I can avoid the weekenders with attitude that they fling over their shoulders with all the casual self-consciousness of their cashmere sweaters.

"I need to buy my brother a special birthday gift," I'd told Seth. "Would you meet me at Ponte Vecchio and help me pick out just the right thing?"

That part was true.

And it was also true that when I saw Seth get out of his truck, a pang of regret stabbed at my heart. His son Ron climbed down from the passenger side and the two stood talking and laughing for a minute, until Seth grabbed the six-foot tall boy in a hug and then watched as Ron headed for the movie theater. Even from across the street, his face glowed with satisfaction. At least he didn't seem to be conflicted about fatherhood.

I waved, and Seth headed toward me. His jeans showed his long legs off, and his broad shoulders filled out the teal blue sweater nicely. He looked pretty fine, and I almost forgot the plan.

He kissed my cheek and then stood back and looked at me. "So, should we go walk around the store and pretend that we're looking at cashmere sweaters or do you want to tell me what this is really about?"

I'm sure I turned the color of the tulips in the window box of the antique shop down the street.

"Okay, so I'm not good at prevarication. I do have other talents." I collected my wits and grabbed Seth's elbow. "Let's walk a little and then we'll go sit down someplace where we can see each others' eyes."

"Always a good idea. I mean, if you're going to say what I think, then making eye contact is going to make it harder and maybe you won't say it."

As we approached the town parking lot, the meaning of his words hit me. He thought

I was going to tell him that I didn't want to see him any more. This had gotten way out of hand. All because I'd let my imagination get carried away. And I was still doing it.

"There's a bench," I said. "Look casual and maybe no one will know we're going to grab it."

He laughed and sat down on the bench. His eyes scanned my face as I unzipped my sweatshirt and then sat beside him.

"I'm confused, and we need to talk about a couple of things." Well, that certainly sounded like the intro to a brush-off. "It's all about Marjorie's murder. I've been under the microscope, which has me in knots. I no longer trust people I thought I could depend on. I keep seeing things through a dark lens. Some of it has affected how I think about you. Two things especially."

Before I could find the words to start the hard part he said, "I bet I know what one of them is. Your gang has connections to everyone in four surroundings counties, so I have to assume that you've heard about my little trip to see Anita. I see now that I should have just told you where I was going and why, instead of making up that lame excuse about canceling dinner to do paperwork. I should have let you know *who*. It was pure business — the house, a possible mortgage customer. I was trying to keep things simple at a time when you had so much on your plate. I'm sure by now your friends have told you that I dated Anita in high school. That was more than twenty years ago, Lili. There's nothing between us now except a potential business deal. I'm sorry I wasn't completely honest."

Either he was a very good actor, or I wanted to believe him, or he was telling the truth.

I nodded. "Makes sense, what you're saying. I can understand that it's a little tricky, trying to protect me. That's another conversation, though. Plus, we're seeing each other, we care about each other, but we don't owe each other explanations for every move. God, I hope I *never* get into a relationship where that's a requirement."

"See? I knew you were more than just a pretty face." His smile softened. "So we're okay about me going to Tennessee?"

"I am. You too? Poor Anita — she seemed so angry when I saw her. Is that a permanent state, do you think?" I was stalling and I knew it, avoiding the next question.

"If she wasn't born angry, then Marjorie did a fine job of making her that way. When we were young, Anita used to get into so

320

much trouble. Kid stuff, really, when I look back on it. You know — shoplifting, spray-painting graffiti on public buildings, breaking into the school. Even then, I knew that she wanted to get some kind of reaction from her mother, but all she got was grounded. Once we —" His face reddened and he looked away, eyes downcast and head shaking.

"What? You started to say something. What was it?" I kept my voice soft, neutral.

He looked up, directly into my eyes. I tried to remove any trace of judgment from my mind. Whatever they did all those years ago, they were only kids.

"We doped Marjorie's drink. It was Homecoming Week, my senior year. She begged me to take her to the dance. She'd been grounded for one thing or another. The plan was for me to get some of my father's sleeping pills and then she'd put them in her mother's Scotch, and she'd slip out so we could go to the dance."

So Marjorie and my mother had at least one thing in common.

"And you did it?" This time, a note of surprise crept into my voice, but I smiled as though to say "Oh, those wacky kids."

He nodded. "She emptied two of those capsules into her mother's glass, waited until Marjorie passed out on the sofa, and then ran out the back door. We had it all planned. Her dress and shoes and stuff were in my car. I waited for her about fifty yards from her house on the side of the road. She walked off into the woods, and voila! Out stepped a party girl."

From someone else, in some other situation, the story might have made me smile indulgently. No harm, no foul, and youthful ingenuity had saved the day. But today, all I could think was that Seth Selinsky and Anita Mellon had conspired against Marjorie once. Or was it only once?

"I guess, looking back, it was really bad judgment on my part. Who knows what could have happened to her mother. But I wasn't so smart then." He frowned, examining his palms as carefully as a fortuneteller. "Marjorie had this way of making everyone feel either hurt or angry. You know how the kids say it — she was harsh, man. Definitely not the dispenser of warm fuzzies. Made the rest of us appreciate our parents in a whole new way. I realized pretty early on that one of the reasons I had a hard time when we broke up was that I felt sorry for Anita."

Had Anita told Seth about her mother's discovery? If I believed him about the trip, that it was simply business and not an opportunity to conspire to kill Marjorie, then I should ask him.

"You know I stopped by at Anita's to return a sweatshirt of Marjorie's, right?"

Seth answered with a frown.

"Well, I did. And she told me something that made me think twice." My forehead scrunched together. I meant to keep my feelings out of the telling, but my face had other ideas. A compact little bird with glistening brown feathers and a cheerful white face lit on the sidewalk in front of us and pecked energetically at things I couldn't see.

"Aren't you going to tell me what she said?"

When I looked up finally, Seth was turned toward me with a puzzled, expectant expression on his face. "Didn't she tell you when you saw her? I assume she came back to Walden Corners after the funeral to follow up on what she told me. She could have just let you and Linda handle all the real estate transactions."

A hiss of exasperation escaped with Seth's breath. "Lili, you're not being clear. And you're definitely not being straight with me. This feels really crappy. I feel like I'm being accused of something without ever knowing

323

what the charges are. Okay, maybe I'm being dramatic but I still don't like this."

Who could blame him? He was right on all counts.

"Sorry. Let me try again. Did Anita tell you anything about Marjorie knowing a secret?" I was still holding back, but it was the only way to get a real answer.

Seth laughed. "If Anita knew Marjorie's secret, she'd have used it by now. She's not much for long-term planning. No, she didn't say anything like that. I hope it isn't about me."

I must have paled, because he took my hand and said, "I was kidding. I don't have any secrets. Well, maybe my business strategies, but that's not something that Marjorie would have bothered about. I'm afraid I'm as clueless as anyone about Marjorie's secret."

"If you were about to call me clueless . . ."

He laughed. "Okay, I answered one question. What's the other?"

"Remember the day of the tornado?"

Seth's face turned white. "Of course. That was one of the scariest hours of my life. Why? What does —"

"Lili, Seth, hi."

I looked up into Connie Lovett's clouded eyes. Her bright blue Yankees cap shadowed the top part of her face but it couldn't hide her gray pallor and the downturned corners of her mouth. She hung onto Mel's arm as though she might sink to the ground if not for his support. Seth jumped up and motioned for Connie to sit.

"Thanks for warming it for me," she said, her voice shaky and her smile weak as Mel helped her lower herself to the hard slats of the bench. "I just wanted to say hello. I thought the sunshine and a little activity would make me feel better. I just saw poor Anita, and that certainly didn't help anything."

"A bad day?" I asked gently.

"I'm not sure I'll make it to your place on Tuesday." Her eyes darted from the bird to her husband, and then, briefly, to my face. "I guess modern medicine has its miracles, but I'm not one of them."

"Oh, Connie, I'm sorry you feel so bad. Is there anything I can do? Have you let the doctor know? Maybe he can change the dosage or something. Want me to bring the gourds to you? I can do that, no problem." I was throwing a lot at her in an attempt to solve a problem that I was powerless to change. I finally willed myself to shut up.

"Thanks but I don't think so. Maybe I'll feel better next week," she said. "I should go fill that prescription. The doctor said this is the last week I'll take them."

"The last week?" I heard the alarm in my voice and wished I could take it back. "And then what?"

"Then he'll try something else," Mel said gently.

"Which probably won't be any better than this. This was the one I was counting on." Connie pushed herself to a standing position, accepting Mel's hand to help her steady herself. "Sorry for being the bearer of gloom. You enjoy this day, you hear?"

I watched as Connie shuffled beside her husband toward the parking lot, wishing with all my might that I had something to break or stomp or throw. It wasn't fair, and there was nothing I could do about it.

"It's hard to see her like that. She's trying, though." Seth's voice cracked with emotion. "That's not always enough, is it?"

I had no answer. Not to his question, not to Connie's situation. And definitely not to what I should do next.

"You said you had two questions for me. You started to say something about the day of the storm."

I almost got up, walked away, and took his original explanation as gospel. Nearly threw the whole thing over in favor of getting in my car and going back to my house, where I could cry as loud and as long as I wanted to at the prospect of losing Connie. Instead I said, "Did you try to run me off the road?"

Seth stared at me, his eyes flickering over parts of my face with such intense concentration that I felt as though he could see through my skin to the bones beneath.

"Lili, I already told you. I was looking for you. I was so relieved when I saw your car ahead of me. I didn't try to run you off the road. I don't know how you can think that." His voice had grown softer with each word, so that by the time he finished his sentence I was practically reading his lips. "And if you really do think I did something so awful, then . . . I don't know. What about trust? I mean, isn't it sort of a requirement?"

"Let's back up." I took a deep breath and glanced up into the face of a man strolling past. His frankly curious gaze made me want to pull the shades down, but there were no shades here. "That truck was silver. There I was, driving along Route Nine, kind of in a hurry because the sky was so, you know, *yellow.* I knew there was going to be a storm, but I was stuck behind a hay wagon going about zero miles an hour. So I pulled out, right near Walden Lane, and all of a sudden this pickup truck crested the hill. I thought I could speed up and get around the wagon, but the truck kept coming right at me. I had to pull onto the shoulder to keep from getting creamed. By someone driving a silver pickup truck just like yours."

Even telling the story set me thrumming. My jaw clenched and my breath quickened, and my arms vibrated like plucked guitar strings.

"Not so much of a stretch to believe that there could be two people around with silver trucks. Anyway, I wasn't anywhere near Route Nine. I was on Iron Mill Road, going from your house toward town." He sat further back, away from me, squeezing himself into a corner of the bench. "You carried this around all this time? Even after we talked about it? No wonder I've been picking up weird signals."

"I'm sorry. It just . . . I couldn't stop thinking about it. I guess it *was* only a coincidence." If making a royal mess of things was a contest, I'd win in a walk.

If he was telling the truth.

"Can we go have coffee down the street and see what the pie special is? And talk about something that's not loaded, you know, movies or books or politics or religion?"

Seth's smile was worth waiting for. "How about something light, like fixing the health care system or the Middle East crisis? Come on, I think it's your turn to buy."

Maybe this had been the right thing to do after all. A sliver of light had entered the cave of my heart's secrets, and that felt very good indeed.

CHAPTER 22

The final casino meeting was to start at seven o'clock in the high school auditorium, the largest gathering place in town. The buzz was that people would be turned away when the fire marshall thought the maximum head count had been reached, and Nora suggested that we arrive no later than six.

At five forty-five, the parking lot was full.

"Good thing we drove together. If everyone came four to a car, we might not even get in. Elizabeth and Melissa might not have been able to save us seats, so be prepared to stand." Nora deftly maneuvered the car into a space behind the open shed that served as an animal barn for 4-H members. "Coach would have said this is stretching the rules. These spots are supposed to be for feed deliveries, but no one's going to be dropping off mash or bran tonight."

"Your name on the auto registration," I

shrugged, happy that she'd mentioned her husband. In the seven months since his death, she'd seldom referred to him in casual conversation.

"If the car gets towed, I'm not the only one who'll be walking home." She waited until I shut my door and locked the car with a chirp. We marched toward the bright lights of the open double doors behind two couples who walked side by side, holding hands. The night air was damp, stars obscured behind thick clouds. It had rained only twice, the day of the big storm and one other, since I'd found the rifle in my attic.

Could four weeks have passed already?

According to my work schedule, I'd delivered the spa flyer and the health benefits booklet, was ten days late delivering the Boite Blanc brochure, and hadn't even started proposals for two more jobs that I'd promised for last week. If I had another month like that, I'd be in trouble.

Neil was already making plans to go back to his apartment. Mom and Dad had postponed their planned visit to me, waiting until after they helped my brother get settled at home. Michele Castro and Gene Murphy seemed no closer to finding Marjorie Mellon's killer than they were when Neil first drove up in that long black limo.

Connie Lovett's health had declined, and I'd been through a series of surprises that I never would have predicted when I took Tom Ford up on his offer and moved into the cottage.

"Earth to Lili, they saved us seats." Nora nodded in the direction of Melissa, Elizabeth, and Susan, who sat several seats in from the center aisle. Jackets draped over the backs of two seats on either side of the group marked them as taken.

"I'll take the far seat," Nora said. "Exercise will do me good."

I squeezed her hand and then let go as a large woman with an oversize handbag pressed past us, headed for the only empty seat at the far end of the row.

"She could have used the other aisle," Melissa stage whispered.

"That would have required a little thinking." Susan scowled, then leaned toward me and said, "I hear Anita's got a buyer for the house, Seth's working on a mortgage for the buyer, and the will makes it all legal. Marjorie finally did something nice for her daughter."

"But it took her dying to make it happen." A wave of sadness settled in my chest, for Anita and even for Marjorie, who must have been one very unhappy person. I needed to shake off their feelings and experience some of my own.

"I've thought about it a lot lately." Nora sighed and shrugged. "Marjorie did the best she could. I don't think she was trying to hurt her daughter. Just . . . I don't know, it's hard to be a single parent."

With Susan, Melissa, and Elizabeth seated between us, I couldn't make out Nora's expression. Was she saying that she was having a hard time with her son?

She lifted her head, leaned forward and sought out my eyes. "I'm fine. Scooter's fine. But for a while there, I heard myself getting sharp with him over nothing. Funny thing was, it wasn't about him, it was all about me. About how hard it is to decide things alone, to know the guy things. As soon as I figured that out, I stopped. He's a good boy."

"Nora, he's a great kid," I said, aware that the din around us had swelled so that no one else seemed to hear that we were saying some pretty private things. "It's new to both of you, still. No husband, no father. I wish Neil were going to be around more. He loved hanging out with Scooter."

"But Neil's leaving day after tomorrow, right? That's what Scooter told me he said the other day."

"Yes, that's the plan," I said. "I've loved having him around, but I think both of us are ready for a little separate space. So next time you all come to my house, there won't be four women pretending that they're not flirting with a man nearly a decade younger. Neil already thinks it's only natural that women melt in his presence. I'm trying to retrain him so that his wife — whoever she is — doesn't have so much work to do."

When I smiled down the row, I saw that Melissa had looked away from me and was staring off at the stage, where three men and four women, members of the town council, stood in animated conversation. If I'd thought about it a little, I might not have been so surprised at the sadness I saw in her eyes. My friend had a crush on my brother, and over the past few weeks I'd allowed the realization to flit right out of my head as though it were a butterfly and not a real person's real feelings.

Nora laughed. "Wouldn't it be great if every guy had a little bit of Neil in him?"

A man dressed in worn jeans and a faded denim shirt walked by, his thin lips pressed together and his eyebrows furrowing above his nose. His head seemed too big for his thin body, bobbing like a bulbous onion on a stalk that might give way at any second.

He looked from Melissa to Elizabeth to me, stared and lifted his chin to peer further down his nose. Then he sniffed and went on his way.

Until that moment, I hadn't seriously considered that being seen with me might have negative consequences for my friends. Everyone knew about the rifle and most people had heard about the note and the address book. As long-time members of this small community, they were putting a lot on the line.

Until the person who killed Marjorie Mellon was arrested, my own personal dark cloud would remain in position, fixed overhead. According to B. H. Hovanian, I could help myself by being watchful, and this was certainly a good place to do that. The room was crammed with suspects. I could eliminate the four women sitting next to me, and probably let Michele Castro off the hook . . . but everyone else? Seth waved to me from the front of the auditorium, and I scanned the rows between us.

I knew precious little about even the people I recognized. Ira Jackson, handyman, bigot, stepfather of Michele Castro, and owner of the land on which the proposed casino would be built. Joseph Trent, pharmacist and father of two college age students. Trisha Stern, married to the high school principal, who gloried in her new home adjacent to the proposed casino site. Connie Lovett and her husband Mel, holding hands as though that contact would keep them both safe from the disease that would eventually get her.

Any one of them could have put the rifle in my attic, made sure a crumpled note was found in the bathroom of Wonderland Toy Town, crept into my house and slipped Marjorie's address book under the stove. But why? What had I done to any of these people, besides move into Tom's house and start to carve out a life for myself here?

Elizabeth's voice penetrated my self-pitying fog. "I almost forgot. I heard that B. H. has some news."

Her news fanned the embers of my unease. "And he didn't think he needed to tell me? What an arrogant —"

"He's verifying it. That's probably why he hasn't told you. It's halls-of-justice information, you know, passed on in the corridor in between cases. But he says he believes his source." She tapped the purse in her lap, sounding a tattoo to announce what she'd heard. "The paper came back with several decent prints, and none of them matches yours. Plus your printer has some weird idiosyncrasies that don't coincide with the note. So, maybe you've moved down from number one suspect."

"Good — now I can give my brother back his computer. And think about whether it's time to get a new lawyer. Or at least ask this one why he's withholding things that I should know." I glanced around the room again and spotted B. H. Hovanian, leaning against the back wall, his legs crossed at the ankles and his arms folded across his chest. Without saying a word he was delivering a message: "I'm relaxed and I'm in control," he told anyone who glanced his way, and "I don't believe a word you're saying."

The seat folded with a slap as I stood up. He needed to tell me what he knew right now. I wriggled my way past loafers and work boots and sneakers to the aisle, where I practically bumped into Joseph Trent. His sharp features seemed to soften as I approached.

"Hi, Lili. How's the sleep problem? Any better?"

Anxious to move on but pleased that he'd remembered, I said, "Not much. At least I have some good books to read. Thanks for asking, Mr. Trent."

"Stop by and I'll give you something else. Or next time try taking three." He nodded and turned so that I could pass, but the aisle was so crowded I could hardly get by without having to change course or crab-walk through clusters of people.

"You know how you're voting yet?" Ira Jackson asked, his ferret-face a grimace of hostility.

I smiled and shrugged and kept going, until Connie Lovett's husband Mel tugged at my sleeve. "Listen, I just wanted to thank you for giving my wife something to look forward to."

My throat lumped up, but I managed to say, "I love working with Connie. She's got enough enthusiasm to light up all of Walden Corners."

As I maneuvered through the crowd, I realized that B.H. wasn't holding up his piece of the wall any more, and I wondered whether he'd seen me heading in his direction and made a quick escape. I kept walking, all the way through the open doors to the large entry foyer filled with glass display cases and shiny marble floors.

"You looking for someone else who needs a breath of fresh air?"

The deep voice was unmistakable, and when I turned there he was, peering at the display of trophies surrounded by photographs of Nora's husband, who had served

338

as coach of the football team. In the glare of the fluorescent lights my attorney looked tired, maybe even a decade older than the forty years I'd assigned to him when we first met. I couldn't help but notice the butterflies in my stomach, even as I pushed them off into a dark corner.

"Why didn't you tell me about the reports on the note and the printer? And I want to know what the note said." I knew I sounded accusatory, the second time in a single day that I'd pinned an interesting, available man to the wall with questions that revealed my suspicions. My mediation experience had taught me that in every negotiation there's a difference between a position and an interest. One was all about posturing, the other focused on the ultimate goal you wanted to achieve. Berating him for not telling me about the note wouldn't get me what I really wanted. It *did* send a signal he couldn't miss.

"I didn't think it would be news to you, but I did tell you. Your cell phone was turned off. Try voice mail. And you'll find a message on your answering machine when you get home. You weren't there at five-twenty. That's when I called. Castro said you can stop by and get your computer and printer any time tomorrow." He had the good grace not to gloat, or even to smile in triumph. "I'm not going to tell you about the note because I don't want those words in your head. I don't want those ideas to be floating around and maybe come out in some tangled way that might make things look bad for you. It'll all become public knowledge eventually, but for now just do without."

I had nothing left to protest. He'd protected my interests in both things, had treated me with respect. Almost. Respect without trust didn't really count in this situation. "You think I'm so impressionable? I can tell the difference between real life and fiction, and I can separate what I know from the words someone wants to put in my mouth."

"Nope. You're not impressionable. You're just not familiar with this particular aspect of the human mind. You know about the advice Spanish senoritas are given when they're looking for their true love? Their *abuela* tells them to walk around the square on Friday night dressed in their finery, and as they walk they are not to think about marriage. An impossible task. If you can admit to being human, then maybe you can just let it go for now. I'll be in touch if anything comes up. I want to hear the presentations," he said glancing at his watch. "Trent starts exactly on the dot."

"You think the casino is a good idea for Walden Corners?"

Berge Hartounian Hovanian folded his arms across his chest and smiled. "I'll tell you what I think is bad for this town, and that's people taking advantage of a murder to try to intimidate others into shutting up about what they believe. Let's go back inside. We might hear something interesting."

At that moment, I wouldn't have minded standing right there in the high school foyer and talking to B. H. Hovanian about almost anything, but he patted my shoulder and pushed open the doors to the noise and heat of the auditorium.

Joseph Trent, gavel firmly in hand, banged once on the podium and peered over the top of his glasses. "Settle down. We have to clear out of here by ten tonight and there's a lot of people want to have their say. But before that, the first thing tonight is a presentation from Connecticut, where they've had a casino for the past twelve years. The mayor will speak for ten minutes and then we'll have twenty minutes for you to ask her questions."

The voices that droned on for the next hour barely reached my consciousness. I

341

knew how I felt about the casino. I'd heard all the arguments on both sides, and, bad attitude though it was, I doubted that my feelings would change no matter what was said.

Which left me mucking about in the swamp of feelings I wasn't so sure about. Seth and B.H. and Tom Ford tromped around, vague figures I couldn't quite bring into focus. Connie Lovett made an appearance, with Anita and her shadow, Linda, hovering in the background. Neil paced uneasily at the edge of the mist.

At least I was getting my computer back. Maybe that would be a step toward things returning to semi-normal. If you could call being a murder suspect normal . . .

CHAPTER 23

My mother found something.

I awoke on the day Neil was to leave with the words playing like country music lyrics in my brain. Reba or Faith would smile sweetly, knowingly, and then go ahead and do whatever she needed to do. What I needed to do today was make a celebration breakfast to send my brother home feeling good about the progress he'd made. I wanted to assuage any guilt he might feel about leaving Walden Corners. He needed to put all his energies into getting better.

But from the delicious aroma of coffee, of onions and butter sizzling in a pan, it was clear that Neil had beaten me to it. I showered in record time, jumped into jeans and a bright yellow T-shirt, and reached the kitchen just as he was garnishing the plates with red grapes and bright green parsley.

"How elegant." I admired his handiwork as I poured myself a cup of coffee. "You sure were the early bird this morning. Didn't you sleep well last night?"

"Too well. As though someone hit me over the head. I took one of your herbal sleep things and it knocked me out in about thirty minutes and that was that. Never heard you come home, never heard the train whistle. The birds woke me at about five. I haven't felt so rested in years."

Why a twenty-four year old man who worked out hard every day should wake up feeling tired was a puzzle, but if Neil said it, then it was true.

"Good, because those pills don't do a thing for me. Take them. I have to find something else. Hey, look at you!"

My hand slid over his baby-smooth cheeks. The Mets were keeping him on the roster. He believed he was going to play. I hugged him tight.

"Thought you'd never notice," he said, grinning. He exuded a healthy glow that gave me great satisfaction — I might not have knit his broken bones together, but at least his time in Walden Corners had been well spent. "They called last night but I wanted to tell you my own way. And Trisha's sure the docs will clear me."

"Well, you nearly distracted me with all this food stuff." I peered into the small glass

344

bowls, each one filled with a different, bright ingredient. If variety of color and texture were the measure of an omelet, the one my brother was about to make would score a nine, at least.

He stopped in front of me and put his hands on my shoulders. "I promised myself not to get sappy so here goes. Thanks, Lili. You were a lifesaver. You gave me a quiet, beautiful place to just be for a while. You found Trisha. You didn't noodge me to death about how I felt about maybe not playing for my Amazin's. You gave me . . ."

My eyes welled up when I saw his tears. We both swallowed hard. I was about to pull him into a hug, but he shook his head and stepped back.

"I have to finish," he said, reaching for a paper towel and noisily blowing his nose. "You gave me space to find out that I believed I could come back from this and play again. You gave me hope. Thanks."

Unlike most guys, Neil had always been able to talk about his feelings. It certainly wasn't because he was following Dad as a role model. Maybe he watched a lot of Oprah and Dr. Phil when I wasn't around. Whatever its source, Neil's openness had never been quite so eloquent. I was touched.

"I'm glad I could do it. Sheesh, I'm going

to miss you." I waved my words away. "That is *not* to be construed as guilt-tripping. It's been great seeing you in a new way, having you here so we could talk things through. I'm thrilled that it's working out for you to play."

This time, I did grab him in a hug, making sure to let go before his muscles tightened into withdrawal. He grinned, then turned on the flame under the cast iron fry pan. He moved the little glass dishes to the counter beside the stove, tossed another chunk of butter into the pan and then emptied the herbs, spices, and vegetables into the sizzling butter. He dumped in the beaten eggs, stirred the whole thing with a wooden spoon, then dropped the bits of bacon and shredded cheddar into the eggs.

"Pour us coffee, would you?" he said as he tipped the pan to move some runny egg to the hot surface. "That driver's going to be here in ninety minutes, and I want everything to be perfect for our farewell meal."

Glad to have the distraction of the final session of the Smith-Caterra mediation, I drove into Hudson relaxed enough to notice the changes in the landscape. The lumpy brown soil of the newly turned hay fields stood in contrast to the glossy green leaves adorning the trees. Wildflowers, yellow and white and lavender, brightened patches of weeds, and the birds trilled happy songs. It was hard to stay sad about my brother's departure with all the glories of spring around me.

In town, I picked up my computer and printer, stowed them in my car, and arrived at the mediation center fifteen minutes early. Both men arrived exactly at four. Randall Smith sat down and started working on something in a small notebook and Tony Caterra began reading *The Hudson Register* sports section.

"Afternoon, gentlemen. Ready to get started?"

I led the way to the room, and they settled themselves at the table. Caterra picked up a pencil and doodled swirls and hatch marks and zigzaggy lines that started at the top left of the paper and marched across the page in rows. Smith tapped the eraser end of his pencil on the table in a rhythmic beat.

"Thanks for coming in for our third session. So, anything happen this week that you'd like to discuss here?" I turned to Randall Smith.

He finished the third row of doodles and then looked up. "Yes. Something happened.

That something is that I got two quotes for redoing the work and they're ten percent below Caterra's original estimate." He shoved papers across the table to me.

I left them there and made a point of not looking at them. As in court proceedings, mediators lived by a document-sharing rule. If one person saw it, then everyone could see it.

"We can look at those in a bit. Why did you get those estimates, Mr. Smith, and what do they mean to you?"

Caterra had a glint in his eye, a Gotcha look that I'd learned to ignore during the sessions, although it made me grit my teeth whenever that smirk appeared.

Smith snorted and reached for the papers. "They mean that for the exact same work, using the same materials Caterra promised but didn't deliver, these two guys would charge me several hundred dollars less. So I paid extra for the privilege of being ripped off."

"So, this week you got two separate estimates for the work Mr. Caterra did, using the same materials, and the quoted prices were less than Mr. Caterra charged. Did I understand that right?" Could it be that Smith had finally gotten past the emotional issues, the anger he felt when he thought he was being ripped off? If that had happened, coming to an agreement was a real possibility — if Tony Caterra didn't try to glib his way out of accepting any responsibility.

Smith grunted and nodded. I turned to Caterra. "Anything come up for you this week, Mr. Caterra?"

Instead of the bluff and bluster I expected, Caterra set the pencil on the table and looked directly into my eyes. "I've had some time to go over my records, to check out what happened on the Smith job, and I saw some things I want to share with you."

Share. This wasn't a word I'd expect to hear from the man to my left. Even Randall Smith sat forward on his chair, the posture of a man eager to hear what was about to be said.

Caterra turned his gaze to Smith. "Come to find out, the materials I ordered for your job, one of my foremen thought they were for another job and took them. Then when Arnie was putting things together to go to your house, he saw these other things, assumed that's what he was supposed to use and went ahead and loaded the truck with them. Not until last week did I know about this."

My breath quickened. An apology would have been nice, but an admission of a mistake was certainly a step in the right direction. This was a good time to get them talking about the future.

First, I summarized Caterra's statements. Then I said, "So, now that you've heard each other talk about new information you found out this week, do you have any thoughts about how you want to proceed?"

Smith squinted across the table at Tony Caterra. "You're telling me that you didn't know those materials were being used? You didn't tell Arnie to go ahead and take the cheap stuff? So that you could make an even bigger profit by pulling a fast one on some redneck moron who would never know the difference. Are you saying this was a mistake and not plain bald greed?"

Greed — had it driven someone to kill Marjorie Mellon? Who would benefit? — that was the question we'd been asking for a month. The list seemed endless: Anita, and by extension Linda, anyone who would gain something if the casino was defeated, a client whose secret Marjorie had discovered.

I was brought back to the present by the sound of voices. While my mind drifted to my own problems, it had happened. The moment mediators live for. The parties had begun to talk to each other as though I wasn't even in the room. I kept out of the way and let them go at it. With an occasional steering question from me, twenty minutes later the foundation for an agreement was in place. Caterra had admitted that his worker had used inappropriate materials, was less than competent, and had been fired. After only a little back-and-forthing, Caterra agreed to come out himself and fix the leak without charge, and to use a high grade of materials without additional charge. He'd pay for three-quarters of the restoration of the furniture and damage to the dining room. Smith agreed to stop trashing Caterra to the entire county, and even said that if the problem was taken care of, he'd figure out a way to recommend Caterra to his friends and neighbors.

The greed Smith saw everywhere wasn't really at the heart of the matter. Caterra's disdain for Smith's style had nothing to do with it. They'd been careless, defensive, each had dismissed the other's concerns. Neither of them said that, though, and since mediators don't lecture, at least not out loud, I didn't either.

I typed up the agreement, we reviewed it, both men signed it, and I watched them walk out looking years younger than they had in that first session, when anger and resentment had filled both of them. Now, if only I could figure out how to achieve the same kind of outcome for myself.

Coming home to an empty house was stranger than I'd anticipated. I'd left the light on in the kitchen, but the rooms felt empty when I walked in. My brother had been good company, and we'd learned a lot about each other in the weeks he'd lived with me. Now we were back in our separate lives. Soon, having this space to myself again would be a relief. I'd lived by my own rhythms and impulses long enough for the pleasures of solitude to take root.

So I thought.

With the right person, and Neil apparently was a right person in many ways — well, definitely not the moonlight-and-champagne part — I could have company and also solitude. I had to admit it — I missed his company. I rummaged in the refrigerator for leftovers and found only a small bowl of cole slaw and half a sweet potato. Seth could probably whip up something brilliant with the contents of my kitchen, but I'd make do with the sweet potato and the cole slaw. Shopping would have to wait until tomorrow.

I sliced the sweet potato and heated it in the small cast iron skillet, topped it with yogurt, and carried my meager repast into the living room, where I plopped onto the sofa and clicked on the television. I should have felt good about the agreement in the Caterra-Smith case, but I kept thinking that my biggest contribution had been to be distracted enough to give them the space to work it out for themselves.

That's not true, I reminded myself. I'd created a safe environment for them to talk. And talk they did, so much over the course of three sessions that I feared their voices would stay in my head forever. When it was all over, it came down to familiar issues. Respect. Reputation. Honesty. Compassion. But nobody could see that until they got some other things out of the way. Defensiveness. A tendency to blame others. Accusations of greed and a bad attitude.

As I was about to stab a slice of sweet potato with my fork, the phone rang.

"I have too much lasagna here." Nora's playful voice was a happy surprise.

"I know exactly how to fix that. Fifteen minutes?"

My friend laughed. "I was sure you'd be able to solve my problem."

"Yo, Lili, wachoo dune?" Scooter Johnson wriggled his shoulders and hitched his jeans with his elbows. His eyes twinkled with delight in the game he'd started months earlier.

"Wassup, gansta? You shouldn't take this MTV stuff too seriously. Rots your brain and other body parts, you know. Anyway, I just happened to smell the lasagna and —"

"Lili!" Nora's smile as she came into the kitchen registered delight. "Between your brother and our work schedules and the casino meetings and all, it feels like we haven't really *seen* each other in weeks."

I set my bottle of Chianti Classico on the butcher block. "I know. I've missed you guys. I'm so glad to be here that I'll even help make the salad."

"You're always welcome in our home. Especially if you offer to chop vegetables." She pulled open the refrigerator and knelt in front of the crisper, handing out lettuce, celery, a bag of carrots, a gleaming red pepper.

"Yo, Lili, thanks. I hate all that peeling. The only fun thing about making salads is . . . ta da!" Scooter held up the lettuce spinner and grinned.

Already, the warmth of their company was making me feel human again, and we laughed and joked our way through the salad preparation. Except for one moment, when Scooter asked about my gourds, and Connie Lovett's wan face flashed into my mind, the charm held fast.

"We shall dine by candlelight tonight," Nora said as she set three kente cloth placemats on the dining room table. The ebony candlesticks took the place of honor, and when she leaned forward to light the ivory-colored tapers, her face glowed with pleasure in the flickering light. I pictured Nora's great-grandmother sitting down to a meal before a fire in the veldt, my mother's grandmother lighting Sabbath candles in the Kiev shtetl, my father's grandmother pushing kindling into her Venetian clay oven.

"Thank you," I said softly. "I needed this."

She squeezed my shoulder and handed me the silverware and three blue cotton napkins. "And I need this to get to the table. Everything's ready."

When we finished setting the table, Scooter presented the lasagna as though it were the crown jewels. "Esteemed ladies, dinner is served."

"Yo, Scooter, thanks." I sat to Nora's left, leaving Coach's seat unoccupied. His presence still filled the house. By some way of measuring, seven months wasn't a very long time at all.

"You know anything about economics?"

Scooter asked.

"Yeah, that you shouldn't spend more than you earn." I finished chewing, swallowed, wiped my mouth with the napkin. "God, Nora, this is amazing. You mean as in school subject economics?"

Scooter nodded, his mouth pursed together as though he were working on a knotty problem. "I have to write a paper on the effects of capitalism on an emerging nation. How it's going to change the society, things like that."

Nora paid very close attention to the intricacies of spearing a lettuce leaf. Only the tiniest of smiles at the corners of her mouth betrayed her amusement.

"You're in, what, junior year? Man, that sounds like a college question." I'd learned to respect the quality of the schools in Walden Corners. Maybe it did take a village and not some huge bureaucracy to make some things work properly.

"It's an AP course. At least I'll get college credit for it. Ms. Savin says we need to learn to think around the corners of things." He rolled his eyes. "All I can come up with is that capitalism will create a middle class. And get some infrastructure built. You know, roads, bridges, maybe new cities. Communications."

"That's great. So, those are pretty big changes." I scooped up another forkful of lasagna, and let the rich flavors fill my mouth. I had never thought of myself as a teacher, but my time with Connie and now this conversation with Scooter hinted that it might not be the harsh sentence I'd always imagined. "What about social changes, personal ones, families and stuff? You think about that?"

Nora put her fork down and watched our exchange with great interest.

"Infrastructure, that's probably a good thing. Hospitals, schools, contact with the rest of the world. I got that far. But, damn, if it's gonna end up like it is here . . . That casino, I think it's just the idea of greedy people who want somebody else to pay for the schools and all that. Some social changes feel like we're going backwards." He shook his head.

"What do you mean?" I had an idea of his concerns, but I didn't want to assume anything. Different generation, different combination of cynicism and idealism.

"You're gonna take these tribal places where everyone leads a simple life and make it complicated? Like, who needs to worry about SATs, right? And the families, every-one working together in the fields or something, they're gonna change. They'll get into this weird head of me first and to hell with you. You know, like that greed thing again. I don't know if it's worth it."

"That's a huge question. Powerful motivator, that greed. More is never enough for some folks." At least now I understood the balance a little better — the idealism was about the same as it had been when I was sixteen.

"What about living a more fulfilling life? Having time to enjoy things like the arts — books, music, theater? Which you get by working toward a decent job, so that you're not scrambling all the time. And what's so great about a tribe making your rules, instead of a local government you can vote out of office?" Nora shrugged and smiled. "I'm pretty sure no system is perfect."

Scooter frowned and said, "Well, duh. Okay, you're saying maybe the price we pay for what we get is high but it's worth it. Huh."

"That's one possible conclusion. But here's the thing. You've almost got enough material for your paper. Sounds like Ms. Savin will be looking for what you think will be positives and negatives. Just keep asking yourself those questions."

Scooter's laugh tumbled out, and I was

glad to hear that it was a boy's laugh. "If I keep asking those questions, I'll never get to basketball practice. Thanks for the help, Lili. Bye, Mom. I'll be back by nine."

He cleared the table in a blur of motion, then grabbed his car keys from the kitchen counter and slammed the back door.

Nora stood, hands on hips, an indulgent mother smile brightening her face. "He's a good boy but he sure is noisy. Thanks for talking to him about school stuff. When he asks me, it feels like a challenge and I get all teacherish. You just had a conversation with him, and it got him pointed in the right direction."

Greed.

Me first and to hell with you, a very bad attitude indeed, one that might have played a part in Marjorie's murder. Anita's inheritance. People afraid that the casino would ruin their lives and depress real estate values. Lots of possibilities for self-interest to lead to desperate measures.

"Nora, do you think whoever killed Marjorie had any idea how many lives would be affected? Anita's, of course. Marjorie's clients and the people supporting the casino. And anyone who ends up being a suspect." I sighed, trying to shake the image of a huge, hungry mouth being stuffed with lasagna, salad, cars, houses, jewelry, greedy for more of everything. Not caring about anyone or anything else except filling itself with more, more. "Of course not. That would make her . . . or him . . . normal, like Elizabeth said."

Nora turned from the sink and hugged me, then stood back and wiped her hands on an orange dish towel. "I have something to tell you," she said. "Again. It's probably not a big deal, but it was one of those odd moments and I feel like I have to pass it along."

I sat on a stool beside the butcher block counter. Nora perched next to me, her eyes avoiding mine until she got settled. Then she fixed me with a look that contained a world of confusion in it.

"You remember I was the one supposed to check out Seth from Marjorie's client list? Well, I stopped by at his office with a pie and an excuse. Told him it was a belated thank you for his help after Coach died. Which it was, but I might have forgotten a while longer if not for your being a suspect. Anyway, we chatted for about ten minutes. Easy talk, you know."

I did know. Seth could have a conversation with nearly anyone about nearly anything. I wasn't sure I wanted to hear the rest.

"I brought up Anita and he told me about his visit to Tennessee. Seemed a little embarrassed but he didn't try to hide it or anything. And after he finished, he said the oddest thing." She stared out the window, where darkness had fallen. "He said, 'I'm so tired of the game.' Just like that, nothing else. After that he made some show of having an appointment and practically hustled me out of there."

Odd moment, indeed. His comment could mean anything, an off-hand remark about the mortgage business or playing at social niceties. He'd let his guard down with Nora for a second. That didn't mean he was calling our relationship a sham. Or that he was protecting himself against the discovery that he had been part of some complicated scheme to murder Marjorie.

"Well, people who are tired of playing end up making mistakes." I hopped down from the stool and bent to pick up an olive from the floor. "You still have that DVD of *Shaun of the Dead*? I'm in the mood for a good laugh."

CHAPTER 24

I fell asleep hard and awoke thinking about Connie Lovett. Maybe I'd be told to mind my own business, but I had to give it one last try — if Connie couldn't come to the gourd lesson, my mountain of gourd equipment could be winnowed to a few essentials so it could go to her house. My writing jobs would wait — Connie might not.

Mel Lovett answered on the first ring.

"Hi, this is Lili Marino. I know Connie said she wasn't up to coming out here, but I'd very much like to bring some equipment and do a lesson at your house. Would you ask her if that's all right?"

After a brief silence, Mel said, "She's in the shower. She might say no if I ask her, but I think she'd be pleased if you just showed up."

I couldn't do that, wouldn't pretend to know better than she did what Connie wanted. "I'm just not comfortable with that,

Mel. Please ask her. I don't mind holding on."

He didn't say a word, but the phone clunked against a hard surface and his footsteps sounded, fading as he crossed the floor. I didn't envy him, juggling his own emotions and Connie's, never able to put the inevitable far from his mind. I heard voices, then footsteps again.

"She said yes." His voice was lighter, a note of surprise lifting it out of the sadness. "Thanks, Lili. Is eleven okay? She needs to eat and get dressed and all."

I glanced at the clock on the wall. Eight forty-five. "Sure, I'll see you then."

He hung up without saying good-bye.

In two hours, I could finish the proposal for the hotel employees manual. I sat down at the computer, stared at the screen, played a game of Spider, stared at the screen some more. I couldn't dredge up ideas or even words. I wouldn't impose this restlessness on my gourds. Maybe I just didn't want to be alone. The Taconic Inn was just down the road from the Lovetts. Nobody would mind if I popped in unannounced for a quick visit.

Melissa Paul whacked at the braided rug hanging on the clothesline and then shielded her face from the rain of dust that exploded toward her. "You believe this? I vacuum twice a week, and when I do spring cleaning I still manage to nearly choke myself on what's caught in these loops of fiber. Watch out." The rug beater, a curlicue of metal on a long wooden handle, slammed against the rug again.

"You do this for every rug every spring?" Running a ten-bedroom inn that also housed a respected restaurant took a lot of work, I knew, but I'd never envisioned this Colonial activity. "Do you wash all the butter churns too?"

Melissa wrinkled her nose and grinned. "Fun*ny*. You might not believe it but I like doing this. I get a good rhythm going and it's very satisfying."

She really meant it, I could tell. Which was why she was the innkeeper and I was the woman who had stitched together a life that didn't let me focus on only one thing so that I could call myself a gourd artist or a mediator or a writer. I shook the ruminations away and said, "You have time for a coffee break? I'm on my way to the Lovett's, and I have forty-five minutes to kill."

She set the beater on the ground and hooked her arm through mine. "I thought you'd never ask. I like doing that, but I like sitting around with a friend even better."

Laughing and chattering about her spring cleaning, Melissa led me into the cool of the inn kitchen. I got down white porcelain mugs, the china sugar bowl, spoons while she put croissants on plates.

"How do you stay a size six with all this great food around?" Whenever I stopped at the inn, Melissa was always bringing out some rich temptation. And she never just watched, either.

"So now you understand about the rugs?" She slathered her croissant with raspberry jam and took a huge bite. "And the vacuuming and chopping vegetables and hauling out garbage and making beds and doing laundry and cleaning gutters and —"

"Okay, I'm impressed." I knew she had help, but she worked right along with them, every day. "And now you're adding another restaurant. Soon you'll be a size four."

She laughed. "Nora's in charge of that one. Our partnership is really working out better than I expected. Oh, did I tell you I spoke to B.H.? You know, my assignment, so to speak."

At the mention of my attorney's name, my stomach did a little flip. I managed to smile and shake my head and hold my breath, all at the same time.

"He made it easy for me. Came to the restaurant for dinner night before last. All by himself. So after he ordered a drink I went over and chatted. You know, innkeeper greeting customer stuff."

That was another aspect of her business I'd never be good at. Small talk was definitely not my strong suit. "And?" I said, as nonchalantly as I could.

"And he flirted with me. For five minutes. Told me how wonderful the place looked, how wonderful I looked, how he felt he could count on the experience of being well cared for here." A blush crept into her cheeks and her hand went to her hair. "But I didn't bite. I remembered what you and Elizabeth said about asking questions that would get someone talking, so I chatted him up about Marjorie."

I ripped off a piece of croissant and popped it in my mouth to keep from saying "And?" again.

"He definitely didn't want to go there. Seemed bored by the whole thing but I'm sure it was just that he knows he can't talk about a case he's involved with. Then he slipped in a really interesting bit of business." Melissa sipped her coffee, a frown gathering across her forehead. "He asked me if I was interested in having a business partner. To develop more inns and restaurants in the Hudson Valley and the Berkshires. He said he wanted to have a minority interest, in return for a fair share of profits. I couldn't believe it. I sort of stammered my way through some questions. How much did he want to put into the venture? Why did he think this was a good investment? Would he want to have a say in things, you know, the feel of a place, the menu, that kind of thing."

"And?"

"And he said he was interested in making a change in his life. That he saw it as a way to stop pushing papers and making speeches in front of people who would rather be doing the laundry than sitting on a jury. But, you know, then he just shook his head and slugged down his drink — good Scotch, the kind he usually nurses for half an hour — and said that I should forgive him for being so impulsive, that he needed to think things through. Like magic, his appetizer appeared right then, so I left him to his dinner. We got busy and I didn't even see him leave."

Thoughts clanged against each other. In my mind, there arose a great clatter . . . What was I doing, thinking in children's rhymes?

I was avoiding thinking clearly about Melissa's conversation with Hovanian. I really needed to take a deep breath and apply a little sane logic to the question of whether their discussion shed any light on the murder of Marjorie Mellon.

"First thing that strikes me is that he's got a lot of money. What if Marjorie discovered that it wasn't kosher?" It was much easier to deal with that notion than the almost-proffered partnership offer that he'd set in front of Melissa.

"Mmmmph," she said through a mouthful of flaky pastry. She chewed and swallowed and started again. "Exactly. That's one of the things I thought. I have the perfect opening to ask him more about it. You know, his offer and all."

"You'd really consider taking on another partner? What about Nora? Don't you have to consult her about that?"

Melissa nodded and wiped the dollop of jam from the corner of her mouth. "Absolutely. If I were serious about having a *business* partner. That's not in the cards. I don't want to become HoJo's East or anything. I'm having fun, making enough money to put some away, and I have no desire to get all corporate and greedy."

There was the G word again. Maybe I was just paying attention differently, but it seemed to be on everyone's lips these days.

"That sounds right. Let's back up. You said that the idea of Marjorie discovering something weird about how Hovanian got his money was *one* of the things you thought. What was another?"

"Mmmm," she said. This time, her mouth wasn't full of food and a dreamy smile spread across her face. "The other thing I thought was that now that your brother is gone, probably never to return except for brief fly-overs between games, B.H. suddenly struck me as a very attractive man."

Coffee sloshed onto the table as I set my cup down. I dabbed at it with a paper towel, got up and searched for the garbage.

"What's the matter, Lili? Don't you think he's, well . . . intriguing?"

My back to her, I nodded and mumbled assent, and didn't say that intriguing was exactly how I would describe Berge Hartounian Hovanian.

If I were to imagine the perfect family and then conjure up the perfect house for them to live in, it would pretty much be a replica of Mel and Connie Lovett's center hall colonial. Set on a knoll with a pond at the bottom of the gentle hill, the yellow clapboards and white trim sparkled in the late morning sun. The kitchen, spacious and sunny, flowed into a brick-floored breakfast area, and Connie sat in the window seat, working on a crossword puzzle. She got up when Mel led me into the room.

"Lili, I couldn't resist your offer." Her voice was weak and she appeared to have lost even more weight. Her jeans and sweatshirt hung from her body. "We should get started. I don't know how long I'll last."

Mel blanched at her remark, then helped her to her feet. "She's all set up in the mud room. Took over an entire wall with her gourd equipment." His voice didn't quite match the nonchalance of his words.

I followed behind, wondering whether this had been such a good idea after all. I didn't want to be responsible for wearing her out — but maybe our time would have the opposite effect. Even if the only outcome was that Connie would have twenty pleasant minutes in which she forgot about her troubles, then I'd be happy. I exhaled, and then tried to breathe in some positive thoughts.

"I thought we'd try some pyrography today," I said. "You know, it's woodburning. Like the Boy Scouts used to do."

Mel smiled as he helped Connie into her chair. "Still do. My grandson made me a box for my wallet and keys and such. Exactly like the one I made my grandpa when I was nine. I'll be in the kitchen if you need anything."

Connie tugged at his sleeve until he leaned down and kissed her cheek and then he left. "Okay," she said smiling, "let's burn some gourds."

I set up the transformer, connected a stylus with a tiny round tip, turned the dial so that the heat was set at six, a good setting for general pyrography on a gourd with a medium thick shell. "See this cork protector?" I said, pointing to the two-inch cylinder that encircled the stylus. "It's like those cardboard sleeves for coffee cups. Keeps you from getting burned. So that's where you hold the stylus. Some folks call it a pen, but that's confusing to me, even though it looks like one. No ink. Not a pen."

Connie reached for her gourd.

"Respirators first," I reminded her. I reached into my box, pulled out my mask, waited until she fixed hers firmly across her nose and mouth.

I showed her how to hold the stylus. "Lightly, that's it. The hot point is going to do the work, not the pressure. And if you want to do curved lines, I find it's easier to turn the gourd and keep the stylus still."

Smoke curled up from the gourd, and the peculiar and satisfying smell of gourdburning wafted through the air. Connie's expression was familiar, a combination of transfixed wonder and utter concentration that I'd seen on the faces of most gourders when they learn a new skill. Her lips pressed together and the stylus glided over the surface of the gourd until a deep brown line nearly encircled the rim. As she was about to complete the circle, her hand jerked and a small gouge blossomed at the end of the line.

She exhaled between clenched teeth and turned to me with tears in her eyes. "I can't do this. I'm not strong enough to hold this damn thing. I don't know why I even try."

I replaced the stylus in its holder and squeezed Connie's arm. "You try because it's who you are. You're not one to give up. Even when things are hard."

Her eyes, when she met my gaze, glittered with anger. "You can't know. You just can't know how it is. It takes so much energy just to . . ." She shook her head, covered my hand with hers. "I'm sorry. I guess I'm too tired to do this after all. I didn't mean to snap at you. But I'm glad you're here. I want to ask you a favor."

I flipped off the transformer and said,

"Anything, Connie. You know that. Whatever you need."

She turned the gourd in her hands, then looked up at me. "I can't tell anyone else. Not Mel, certainly, and not my doctor. Not until I know. I mean, I'm pretty sure, but I need proof." She sank back in her chair, breathing hard from the exertion of her speech.

Her words were confusing, but knowing Connie, she'd get to the point in a minute. I wanted to wrap her in a soft pink cloud and pour sunshine on her head. Instead of asking questions, I waited.

"I think the pills I've been taking are fakes."

"What?" I felt as though someone had punched me in the stomach. My head spun and a million thoughts clamored for attention. "Why?"

"Everything I read on the Internet, I should have had problems with my hands and feet. It's pretty universal. Burning, itching. By the second month, I should have had some sign of that. But there's nothing." Her voice was stronger and her eyes glittered with anger. "I mentioned it to my doc. He said maybe I was just an exception. But I don't think so."

My brain calmed down enough so that I

began to understand some of the implications. If she was right about the pills being fakes, then someone had given her placebos instead of the chemotherapy she was supposed to get. If it was accidental, a mistake at the drug manufacturing plant or a labeling error, then incompetence might kill her. If it was intentional, then either someone was trying to get rid of Connie or . . .

"Connie, how much do those pills cost?"

She nodded. "A lot. Eighty dollars each. And I take forty-two a month. The insurance covers most of it, but I see the bills."

I was still trying to catch my breath. That was a lot of money to me, to anyone who didn't have millions stashed away somewhere. Who would benefit from giving Connie pills that wouldn't help her?

The drug manufacturer wouldn't do it. Doctors wouldn't keep ordering pills that didn't work. A drug distributor? Were there such things — companies that shipped drugs from various manufacturers to . . .

"Oh, you're saying that . . . Joseph Trent?" My voice was barely a whisper.

Connie exhaled hard. "I know. I didn't let myself even consider it at first. But the more I looked for another answer, the more he seemed to be the only real possibility. And then I started thinking about it. His store is so shabby. He hasn't taken a vacation in six years."

"Since the Walgreens opened up down the road, right?"

She nodded. "His shoes have holes in the soles. His wife looks so sad all the time. I need to know, Lili, I really need to know. Can you help me?"

"Of course." I grabbed her hand. "I'm not sure how, but I'll figure it out. I'll get my network going and I'll find someone who can test one of those pills to see what's in it. You have a couple extra?"

She reached into her pocket and handed me a pill bottle. "I need these like Bill Gates need another million."

"Billion," I said. "I'll call you as soon as I know anything."

CHAPTER 25

"I've got a pharmacist friend. We'll go see him together," Karen had said after I told her Connie's story over the phone. "Come down. Right now."

With no traffic and a sense of urgency turning me into Leadfoot, the drive from Walden Corners to Brooklyn had taken less than two hours. We'd walked to Smith Street hissing and stomping out our anger. Mr. Kim, a man with a sweet smile and bottle-thick glasses, understood what Karen was asking right away, and agreed to help.

"Two hours," he said, his mouth crinkling into a display of disapproval. He'd turned and disappeared through a doorway, leaving Mrs. Kim to continue smiling at us. Karen had leaned across the counter, kissed the startled woman on the cheek, and then grabbed my elbow and led me back out onto the street.

We spent the next half hour drinking coffee and pretending to catch up on the lives of mutual friends, but our hearts weren't in it.

"Nothing's worse than cold coffee and boring gossip." Karen screwed her face into a frown and glared at her reflection in the mirror on the wall across from our small table. The café was practically empty, and so were our latte cups. She signaled for another round and fingerbrushed a stray turquoise hair back into place. "Tell me about your murder."

"God, Karen, it's not *my* murder! Although the sheriff's office keeps coming up with things that somebody's doing to make it look that way." My friend never asked a simple question when something shocking would do — I'd forgotten that. "Sorry. I don't know if there's a single new bit of information. The cops seem to be earnest about doing the right thing, but they have to wade through a townful of suspects. If I had to put my money on someone right now it would be Anita Mellon, Marjorie's daughter."

"Matricide. Usually it's an Oedipal thing. Wouldn't it be great if Anita turned out to be a cross-dresser and was really a guy? Then he'd be able to sell his story to *The Enquirer* for even more money." She shook her head. "I've been reading too many graphic novels lately."

"As in graphic sex and violence? I thought you hated that."

She shook her head with an I-don't-know-what-to-do-with-you smile. "Comics. That's the latest thing. Although I suspect Jane Austen would turn up her sensibilities at the thought of calling them novels. And what about your guy, the one with the football player son? Last time we spoke he was on your short list."

I glanced at my watch. Mr. Kim would be another hour. I might as well keep myself in this conversation or I'd go nuts waiting. Not that my impulse to delay answering was a form of denial or anything. Not that it meant I didn't really want to face Karen's question.

"He's such a nice guy. He loves to cook, he's interested in all kinds of music and books and stuff. He's solvent and a good parent. Not to mention good-looking, with a great body. But he's been acting weird since Marjorie's murder. He says he's worried about me but then he turns around and cancels a dinner because he has to do paperwork and later he admits that he went to see Anita in Nashville about a business deal. And then he apologizes for not telling the truth. Dunno, Karen. I just don't know about this guy."

She grinned. "You sound the way you did when you were getting ready to break up with Ed Thorsen. Remember? You used to trot out all his good qualities. He was stable and compassionate and ambitious — for someone in the education field. He liked snorkeling. I can't remember but you might have even said he had good taste in ties."

"Oh, man, was I that transparent?" I laughed uncomfortably. "Took me months to get smart enough to see that I admired him, I respected him, but I did not, no way, shape, or form, love him. Breaking that engagement was so hard."

"But you're not engaged to Seth, right. And you never said you love him. He's an attractive, available man you have a good time with, that's all. Why do you need him to be more than that?"

"Maybe I want something I can count on." I smiled and shook my head. "And also at the same time something that's going to surprise me. So can I have it both ways, do you think?"

Karen studied my face and then broke out into a grin. "You know when I hear a different buzz in your words, that excitement you're looking for? When you talk about your lawyer."

A heart reader, that's what she was. Karen always knew, even before I did, what I felt. I thought understanding my secrets was my brother Charlie's province, but Karen could read my heart with a precision that spooked me. Once again, she'd gotten it right.

"Okay, all right. I haven't said it out loud to myself but you're right. He's not like anyone I've ever met. He's . . . I don't know, he's . . ."

"Old?" She toyed with her coffee cup. "And also new. Listen, you need to make sure you're not turning into one of the girls who likes a guy for three, six, nine months and then when the novelty wears off you get restless and move on to something else."

"Me? Not a chance. But it takes that long to get to know a person beyond the surface, right? Anyway, I don't really have the energy for a relationship until a couple of other things are cleared up. Like the possibility of someone intentionally giving my friend phony pills instead of the expensive drug that's supposed to keep her alive." I looked at my watch. Another twelve minutes had passed.

"Then let's go back to the drugstore. Mr. Kim's going to know in ten minutes, I can feel it. He said it would take two hours, but he's going to know sooner."

Relieved, I grabbed my purse, threw a five and two ones on the table, and followed her out into the gray and chilly drizzle. I'd learned not to question Karen when she *knew* something.

"You know, the sidewalks have that smell. Dampness and dust. When I lived here, that's what rain smelled like."

Karen frowned. "Well? That's what rain does smell like. Oh, wait, I forgot. You're a country girl now."

"Earth and grass, right? I can tell you what ugly smells like."

She practically growled her agreement as she pushed open the door to Kim's Pharmacy.

I followed her inside.

"You back too soon." Mrs. Kim shook her head. "He say three o'clock."

I pivoted and grabbed the door handle, but Karen tugged at my sleeve.

"I know, but I had this feeling that —"

Like magic, Mr. Kim appeared from the back of the store. I felt like a defendant when the head juror first files back into the courtroom. His face gave away nothing at all, and I couldn't find my voice to ask what he'd found.

"So, Mr. Kim, what did you find?" Karen

asked sweetly.

Mr. Kim pushed his glasses up so that they rested on his shiny bald spot and he thrust his clenched fist forward. "Phony," he declared.

Even after the room stopped spinning, I was dizzy. Dizzy with anger and disbelief. Dizzy with questions. I was only vaguely aware of Mrs. Kim's warm hands on my arm, leading me to a chair beside the counter.

"Here," she said as she handed me a cup that was warm to the touch. "Drink this. Go ahead, won't hurt you. Tea. Green tea. Good for you."

Karen knelt beside me. "You okay?"

I nodded and sipped the tea, then took a long swig and swallowed. "He's killing her," I whispered. "I have to do something. I have to get back there. Mr. Kim, do you know what it is?"

"Baking soda and something to make it hold. That's all." Splotches of red dotted his cheeks and he shook his head. "What I can do — what else? That's so bad, bad. I can't believe. A pharmacist to do such a thing? I can't believe."

"If it's the guy I think it is, then you'd never guess. Mr. Perfect Upright Pharmacist. Head of the town council. Used to be on the school board. His wife volunteers at the local nursing home, reading to the old folks. A pharmacist, for crying out loud." It was still hard to wrap my mind around the possibility.

I held onto the counter to keep from zigzagging all over the store. Slow down, I warned myself. There was nothing to be gained from driving back into town in my blue charger with sixshooters blazing unless I could prove my theory.

What if Connie wasn't the only one Joseph Trent was tricking?

Other people might be in danger. I had to go slow in order to do this right. If I rushed, I'd make mistakes. Besides, I couldn't go accusing Trent of anything to anyone until I knew more. I didn't want to forever be snickered at — there's the crazy woman who made up a story about the head of the town council being a murderer, they'd whisper to their children.

"You can write a note on your stationery saying what you found. I'll need the rest of these, so that I can turn them over to the police." Of course I had to call the police. I couldn't, shouldn't wait until I got home to keep Trent from poisoning another victim. The first step would be to call B. H. Hovanian. As soon as I could stop my hands from shaking.

Joseph Trent's mild features swam before me, a little disapproving, a little tense with annoyance when the crowd wouldn't quiet down in response to the pounding of his gavel. How could he possibly have done such a hideous, unthinkable thing?

"Here, take another sip." Mrs. Kim guided my hand, and I drank the tea. "You are smart girl to figure this out. You maybe save some people. But you have to have your head screwed on right to do right thing."

I laughed, at her knowledge of street slang and at the sentiments she'd expressed. I did have to be thinking clearly, or I could still blow this.

"Thanks, Mrs. Kim. You're right. I don't even know if it was the pharmacist, for sure. Maybe someone at the drug company switched pills." I thought about Tony Caterra's worker, inadvertently using materials intended for the Smith job, creating a kind of havoc that nearly resulted in a court case. This switch, intentional or not, had consequences that bore so much more weight, that changed the basic foundations of so many assumptions about the world.

"Drug companies probably have all sorts of safeguards against tampering, wouldn't you think?" Karen frowned and shook her head. "Maybe it wasn't your Mr. Trent, but it sure seems that way from here."

"At least two other people that I know about died recently. People who probably were getting their drugs from Trent. I wonder if he . . . I have to make a quick phone call." I punched out B.H.'s number and got only a recorded message. Annoyed, I said, "This is Lili Marino. I've got information that Mr. Hovanian needs to know. It really is life and death stuff. Please have him call me right away."

As soon as I clicked off, Mr. Kim handed me a note reporting that he'd tested the pills I gave him and had found them to contain no Xeloda. Baking soda, he'd written and underlined the words with three slashing lines. The note would do. I folded it and slipped it into my wallet just as my cell phone rang.

"Life and death?" B.H. sounded impatient. "What's up?"

I told him the whole story, from Connie's suspicion to my confirmation with Mr. Kim. "I didn't want to have the pills checked locally because if they were legitimate, then I'd be damaging Mr. Trent's reputation — and my own — for nothing. Look, I don't know who else might be getting bad medicine, that's one of the things I'm really worried about. Can you do anything to stop him?"

I heard his breathing, slow and deep, and finally he said, "You get back here with the rest of those pills. Come right to my office. I'll call you if there's anything else I need from you. And don't say anything to anyone."

I crossed my fingers and yesed him. Mel and Connie Lovett had every right to know what was going on.

"This is a small token of my appreciation for taking the time to help me," I said as I pulled a small gourd ornament from my pack and set it on the counter. "I really do thank you."

Mr. Kim's delighted smile confirmed that I'd done the right thing. Mrs. Kim picked up the gourd and cooed over it, then grabbed me in a hug.

"You be careful," she said. "Lotta bastids out there."

Karen hooked her arm through mine and we headed toward the door, then paused. "I told you he'd know. You have to drive back right away. Want company?"

"I have to make another phone call first. And, yes, I'd love company. You have anyone in mind?"

She laughed. From Mr. Kim's window, I

watched the traffic roll down the wet street and pressed the Lovetts' number. Connie answered on the second ring.

"You were right. The pills are baking soda. I'm so sorry, Connie. You have to go see your doctor. But don't say anything to anyone else. I called B. H. Hovanian and he made me promise not to tell anyone. I'm sure he's going to contact the sheriff's office. We don't know for sure that it's Joseph Trent yet, but if it is, it would be a shame to have him walk away from this because he got an early warning. So keep it quiet, all right?"

She didn't answer immediately. Finally she said, "I'm not going to tell Mel. I'm afraid of what he'd do to the man. I'll wait until afternoon to call Doctor Axelrod and see what he wants me to do. Thanks, Lili. I . . ."

I waited while she blew her nose. "Connie, listen, you just take care of yourself. I'll talk to you later."

Karen looked at me, then shook her head. "I can understand a kid from the ghetto thinking it's okay to mug some suit who's making more money than he can spend in this lifetime. I can even get it why some of these corporate jerks thought it was okay to cook books so that they could have pretty cashmere throw pillows for their personal jets or something. But why would a supposedly nice guy play with the lives of people he knows this way? How could he sleep at night?"

"Valerian," I said. "Or Ambien or something. I wonder if the pills he gave me were the real stuff. Not the same thing, of course, not nearly the profit involved."

"Whoo boy, when the town finds out about Mr. Model Citizen, there'll be —"

"That's it!" I shouted. "That was the secret that Marjorie found out. Oh, man, of course it is. She found some papers, something, that showed Trent was making the switch. I don't know what or how, but that's what she found."

We were both silent as the meaning of it all sank in.

Joseph Trent had murdered Marjorie Mellon. He'd nearly killed Connie, probably been responsible for the deaths of Aunt Bernie, Rod Phillips, and who knew how many others.

But the fact that the pills were phonies didn't prove anything yet.

"This doesn't do it, Karen. I wish I could figure out a way to prove what Trent was up to. Without more proof, he can just throw up his hands and say that this was what the drug company sent him. I don't want that miserable excuse for a human being to walk away on this. The cops will do their thing, and I'm sure they'll get what they need. But jeez it would feel good to nail him to the ground myself."

Karen's thumbs up was permission enough to go ahead.

"Mr. Kim, I need the name and the telephone number of the company that makes the drug. The billing department if you can get it for me. I'm going to tell them that I need to straighten out a bill for Xeloda."

"Tell them they didn't charge enough," Karen said. "That'll get their attention."

He smiled, bowed his head, and then went into the back of the store. The bell above the door tinkled and two women in their seventies walked in, chattering away about their aches and pains and complaining about the rain. Mrs. Kim smiled, a different expression than when Karen and I walked in. A good businesswoman, she sweetied one and honeyed the other, asked about their grandchildren, got their prescriptions, and handed them over with a cheery thank you.

I scanned the vitamin shelves, pretending not to be impatient, pretending not to be ready to burst into laughter when the taller woman said, "She speaks a very good English for a Chinese."

Korean, I wanted to say.

But Mr. Kim appeared just as the two women left and he handed me a slip of paper. "You ask for Mary. You tell her you do my books and you do Trent books. She will take care of you," he said. "When you talk to her, you ask about an order for a box of fifty units of your drug. That's how they sell it."

"You're the best." I squeezed his hand, kissed Mrs. Kim on the cheek, and grabbed Karen's hand.

"You call, tell us what happens." The furrow between Mrs. Kim's eyes deepened as she frowned. "You get the bastid."

CHAPTER 26

It took a couple of minutes of sitting quietly in my car, eyes closed and breathing into my diaphragm, for me to get it together to make the call. Karen sat beside me, hands in her lap, head bobbing slightly as she went deeper into her meditation. My voice would disturb her, but I could wait no longer.

I punched in the numbers from Mr. Kim's note and tapped my finger on the dashboard as the phone rang. Two, three, four rings. My anxiety level rose with each ring. Five, six. Where was the answering machine? On the seventh ring, an impatient voice said, "This is Mary."

"Hi, Mary. My name is . . ." Not Lili Marino. I couldn't chance Castro finding out. I fished around in my brain and grabbed the first thing that floated by. "Rhonda Fleming. I'm a bookkeeper. I do some work for Mr. Kim in Brooklyn and also for Joseph Trent up in Walden Corners."

"Rhonda Fleming? You're kidding me." Her giggle segued into a booming laugh. "Tell me you have red hair and a cute nose and —"

"I know." Let me get out of this one without blowing it, I prayed. "My mother was a fan of movies from the forties. Most people don't even get the reference. You like those old movies?"

"Are you kidding?" Mary sounded as though she was getting ready to list every black-and-white movie she'd ever seen. Then I heard the telltale click of another call coming through on her line. Sighing, she said, "Would you hold on for a minute?"

"Sure, no problem."

Karen quirked an eyebrow. "Tell her your boss is shouting at you. Something. Anything to cut to the chase."

Just then, Mary returned.

"Sorry about that. So anyway I was gonna say —"

"Okay, Mr. Garner. As soon as I finish this call." I waited a beat and then said, "Sorry, my boss needs to see me in his office two minutes ago. Listen, I'm trying to get some billing stuff straightened out. I'm looking at Trent Pharmacy's purchase order from back in March. You know, the one for a box of fifty capsules of Xeloda? Mr. Trent thinks you undercharged him. I know that would mess up your books so I wanted to clear it up."

Mary's laugh boomed across the line. "Goddamned pharmacists. They're the most honest people I ever met. Hold on, let me check the computer."

Honest. Not the word I'd use to describe our Mr. T. A burly man passed by, tugged along the sidewalk by a corgi whose short legs windmilled forward. Two kids on scooters whooped as they flew past the car. Karen had resumed her meditation. Through the outside noise, I listened as Mary tapped away on the keys. I thought I heard a muttered "Huh" and then more tapping, following by a loud exhale.

"March? I don't see anything on my computer from March. Or February. Or January. Are you sure you didn't get it from one of the — oh, wait, none of the distributors carries this. Are you sure about the name of the drug?"

As sure as I was that my name was Lili Marino.

"You know, maybe he wrote down something else and I didn't read it right. He's almost as bad as some of those doctors. Wait a minute, that's probably what happened." I was winging it here, and I had to keep her from worrying over this after we'd hung up. "He makes his l's look like d's and his o's and a's are hard to tell apart. Of course, how dumb of me. Listen, I'm sorry to take up your time. He'd kill me if he knew I was bothering you about something I should have read correctly in the first place."

"Oh, honey, don't worry about that. I like having an excuse not to have to call people and tell them that they're late paying their bills. You gave me a little break. So you're all set now?"

"Yes, all taken care of. Thanks, Mary. You're the best. Talk to you later."

So Joseph Trent had never ordered a single dose of Xeloda. And Connie had paid him eighty dollars for each of those pills pressed out of baking soda. Two a day for three weeks. That was over three thousand dollars in his pocket each month. Two months for Connie, and who knew how many more for other unsuspecting customers. I felt sick to my stomach and at the same time filled with a rage I'd never known before.

"You look green." Karen's voice was soft, and when she touched my arm I nearly jumped out of my seat.

"I'll feel much better when this is all over and Joseph Trent is in prison where he can't hurt anyone else. God, I couldn't stand it if he managed to get away. Strap yourself in, baby, this bucket is about to take off."

We were sailing past the Poughkeepsie turnoff when I nearly ran us off onto the side of the road.

"I know what it is!" And this time, it really was the key that would make everything fit together. It would be part of the proof, one of the bricks that would seal Mr. Joseph Trent's fate so that he could never hurt anyone ever again. "We have to make a detour before we hit the lawyer's office. And if I'm right, then Marjorie Mellon will have been instrumental in nailing her own murderer."

Linda answered the bell, a frown wreathing her face. "She's resting," she said.

Karen stood beside me as I leaned against the door so that Linda couldn't close it on my foot. I pushed my way into the house. "I only need a second of her time. This is critical. Someone's life may be at stake. And Marjorie's murderer might be the guilty one. Two minutes. If she can put this whole episode to rest, maybe she'll be able to sleep without drowning her pain in a gallon of vodka every day."

"Maybe she doesn't want to put it to rest." Linda glared at me. "Our Anita loves drama, and this one can last the rest of her life, if we're careful."

"But not the rest of mine. I'm going up there." I was ready to get physical, if that's what it took, but with perfect dramatic timing, Anita Mellon appeared at the top of the stairs.

She tugged at the sash of her peach satin robe and then wobbled to the first step. "What's all the noise? Linda, I thought — oh, it's you."

Great. Now I'd have to convince a drunk that something she'd packed away — or maybe even thrown away — was of critical importance to me.

"Hi, Anita. Listen, I just found out something that I think is the key to catching the person who killed your mother. If I'm right, you'll play a huge role in this."

Karen ran a hand over her spiked hair. "Who knows, maybe it would even be something you could sell to a movie company. You know, daughter helps catch mother's killer. Great movie of the week stuff."

Linda *tsk*ed and started up the stairs. "You think you're going to get a piece of that? No way, honey. This is Anita's. I'll make sure her interests are protected."

The guard dog needed a bone.

"My main interest is making sure that I'm

no longer a suspect. And there's something else, too. The person who I think killed Marjorie might be responsible for the deaths of at least three other people. That would make it even a bigger story. But I need something, proof of what was going on. I believe your mother found papers or a notebook or something that we need to turn over to the police.

Karen trailed behind as I followed Linda to the second step below the landing. Anita had her hands on the rail, and Linda stood in front of her, ready to snarl if I came any closer. I looked up at the two women, gauging what my next move should be. They needed to be gentled. They needed to be convinced.

"You remember what you said last week? About Marjorie telling you that she found something that would blow the town wide open. Well, I think she was murdered to keep that from happening. And I think I know what it was. If you can produce this thing and turn it over to the police, you'll be a hero. An honest to goodness hero, Anita. The people in this town will not only respect you for what you did, they'll honor you. I don't know, an Anita Mellon park, or the Anita Mellon school. I'm not kidding, it's that big."

Even Linda was paying attention now. "So, what is this magical thing and what do we do with it if we find it?"

Anita stepped around her friend and loomed above me. She could reach out and, with not much of a tap, send me tumbling down the stairs, knocking Karen over like a bowling pin as I went. My heart pounded as I watched her eyes. Then she grinned.

"You trust me?" she asked. Her sly smile changed into a mask of resolve. "Well, you're going to have to. You're going to have to tell me the whole story. And then you're going to have to go away while I figure out what I'm going to do."

"Can we sit down somewhere? I'm getting a stiff neck looking up this way." I started down the stairs after Karen without waiting for an answer, and was pleased to hear footsteps behind me. When I reached the bottom landing, I turned and waited for Anita to take the lead.

She walked into the sunny kitchen and pointed to the ladderback chairs cushioned with red and gold pillows. Linda took up the rear. Without waiting for a visible signal, she hung back, leaning against the counter watchful and silent.

"I think your mother uncovered a second set of books that Joseph Trent kept." I

398

watched Anita's face.

Her mouth pursed into a skeptical moue and she shrugged. "So? Every retail business I ever heard of keeps two sets of books. One for the IRS and the other to show the real profit and loss. Joseph Trent wouldn't think that was a good reason to kill someone."

"I agree. But Trent had something more to hide than cash income from chewing gum and razor blades. He was telling people he was giving them very expensive drugs — I mean, eighty, ninety dollars a pill — but really they were just baking soda. So I'm thinking his official books showed those drugs as expenses. But his personal books would show his real income. Without ever having paid for the drugs."

It took a while for the full impact of what I was saying to sink in. Anita got there before Linda did.

"So people could have gotten really sick? Maybe even died? And all the time he was putting the money in his pocket? What kind of monster could . . ." Color drained from her face and a huge tear rolled out of each eye. She swallowed hard, shook her head. "Connie. That bastard did that to Connie, didn't he?"

I took her hand in mine. "Connie's the

one who figured it out in the first place. I checked out the drugs he gave her and they were completely fake. And now we need the proof. It must be in some kind of ledger or a notebook or a computer disk or something. Some place where Joseph Trent kept his own records."

"Probably not computer disks. My mother wouldn't go near those things. I think I know where it might be." She jumped up and practically ran to the back door.

If anyone was watching, the scene would have had a comical aspect to it — Anita in her high heels and peach bathrobe in the lead, followed by me in my jeans and white blouse and Karen with her blue hair sticking up in spiky tufts. A confused and angry Linda brought up the rear once again. We flew out the door and headed for the garden gate, where Anita stopped short.

"Another hour and these things would be history." She knelt beside the metal barrel, a fifty-five gallon drum that had been turned into an incinerator, and poked through the stack of papers and books awaiting the match. Wordlessly, she handed a blue notebook to Karen, then a black-and-white composition book to me, and a green leather journal to Linda. I paged through mine. Scribblings about a garden and a catalog of bird sightings. No columns of numbers, no references to drugs. I was about to toss it back onto the burn pile when Karen's gasp stopped me cold.

I'd never seen her speechless, but all she could do was point.

The page was filled with dates, names, and numbers. Not names of people, though. Each drug was printed neatly, with its price beside it.

Xeloda	42 units	$3,360
Temodar	20 units	$3,700
Anzemet	50 units	$4,000

Those three drugs, repeated over several months. Over eleven thousand dollars a month.

"For this, Connie Lovett and probably Aunt Bernie and Rod Phillips were allowed to sicken and die," I said. "It takes a particular kind of twisted mind to come up with a scheme like this."

"Unbelievable." Anita's voice was only a whisper. "But how did my mother know what this meant?"

I'd been wondering that myself. "She must have found something else when —"

Karen, who had continued to flip pages, shouted. "Here. It's right here. He recorded everything. Cost of Drugs, $11.18. Total Profit, $122,006.82. Wow, even I can see that would make up for lost revenues from competition from the chains."

A cloud passed in front of the sun just then, as though in deference to the people whose lives Joseph Trent had traded for a little profit. None of us spoke. We walked single file back to the kitchen, where Anita sat down and stared at her hands. Linda handed Karen a plastic bag, and Karen slipped the ledger inside.

"I need to take this to Michele Castro," I said finally.

Anita nodded. "I'm glad my mother found it. I'm really glad it didn't get burned up. I hope Trent gets life in prison. Because then I'd come and visit him every week and tell him stories. About what my mother would be doing, and Connie and Rod and Bernice, if they were still alive. I'd make sure he understands exactly what he did, how many people he hurt when he murdered them."

"Connie's still alive," I said softly. "Maybe her doctor can save her, maybe not. But I'm not counting her among the dead just yet."

Without another word, Anita turned and

disappeared through the doorway. I imagined her plodding steps as she climbed to the second floor. Then I picked up the notebook, and Karen and I walked to my car through the warm sunshine.

CHAPTER 27

We landed at the center of town exactly seventeen minutes later.

Karen adjusted her T-shirt and slammed the car door shut. "So what's this lawyer like? The guy from *Law and Order*? Or maybe he's more like the guy from *To Kill a Mockingbird*."

"One of a kind," I said. How would I describe Berge Hartounian Hovanian? Who could I compare him to? Nobody I'd ever met. He really was an original. "You'll see. He was almost as angry as I was when I told him. I guess he's known Joseph Trent forever. It's going to be even more of a betrayal for all the long time residents of town."

We climbed the stairs to the second floor office, knocked on B.H.'s door, and let ourselves in. When David saw Karen, the secretary's eyes widened with alarm, then relaxed as he realized she was with me. He smoothed his blond pompadour and rose, pressing his hand against his braided leather belt.

"He's expecting you. Go on in. You can have a seat here, Miss . . ."

"No, call me Karen. Karen Gerber." She stuck out her hand, and I knew they'd be chatting about clothes and movies for as long as my interview with Hovanian lasted.

I pushed open the door, closed it behind me, and waited. B. H. Hovanian sat with his back to me. His hands were clasped behind his head and he appeared to be looking out the window at the street scene below. I came up to his desk, my leather heels tapping on the wood floor, and waited. Outside, vehicles drifted across the intersection as the light changed, two women got out of their cars and headed for the wine shop, and an orange sherbet–colored dog trotted along the side of the road at a comfortable pace.

"Sleepy," he said. "Isn't that what they say about towns like Walden Corners?" He swiveled around to face me, his dark eyes sad and the corners of his mouth turned down. Without his glasses, he squinted, and the crease above his nose deepened. "Well, this ought to wake everyone up. Who's your friend with the interesting hair? Where is she?"

"She's in the reception area." As he reached for his glasses I told him about Karen. "She put me in touch with Mr. Kim. The pharmacist in Brooklyn. Karen and I have known each for —"

"Don't tell me," he said. "What you consider a long time is probably just a blink for an old guy like me. I'm going to send David and Karen out on some errands, treat them to dinner, make them feel useful and appreciated. And keep them out from underfoot. We don't know how this thing is going to unfold. He can bring her to your house later."

Impatient to get on with business, I didn't want to prolong things by arguing. Karen would let everyone know if the plan didn't suit her. His instructions delivered to David, B.H. turned to me and said, "That's done. Now we can concentrate. I've spoken to Sheriff Murphy and Michele Castro. They're taking this seriously, but if you're wrong . . . if your Mr. Kim made a mistake . . ."

"I'm not wrong and my Mr. Kim doesn't make mistakes. Let's skip all this stuff and get right to the part where you tell me what they're doing to catch Joseph Trent and make sure he never hurts anyone else ever again in his miserable life."

Hovanian nodded. "Right. Castro wants you to call him and pretend you're in Brooklyn and that you just found out about his little switcheroo. You're furious, how could you, blah blah blah. She's already got a camera set up in the back of his store, where he keeps his records and his computer. She thinks he'll make a move, something that will show he's covering up or deleting files or whatever. As we speak a deputy is out at the house, flashing his search warrant and talking to Mrs. Trent about hunting rifles."

"At least one rifle won't be there. Michele Castro already has custody of it." The plan wasn't right — not complete. Something about it nagged at me.

The lawyer's eyes bore into mine and he shifted his weight forward. "You're uneasy about something."

It was a declaration, not a question. Some part of me was pleased that he'd read me so well, but I shoved that away.

"I want to see his face. I want to make him look into my eyes when I tell him I know that he's been cheating Connie and the others of their lives. Actually, what I really want is for Connie to stand in front of him and in her own way tell him she knows what he's done."

"You really want to put Connie through that now? It's going to be hard enough on her when she has to testify in court."

He was right. It was my need, not Connie's, to have Trent feel the pain that his actions had caused.

"No, Connie doesn't need to be part of this. I know Trent will have plenty of time to suffer in jail, but I want him to really, really understand." My chest was constricted from suppressing the scream of rage that had been building for hours. I had a hard time catching my breath.

"There's time for that," he said, his voice barely audible. "As satisfying as that might seem, it would be a hollow victory if your actions interfered with the police getting enough proof to put the man away. What you don't want is to be responsible for Joseph Trent walking."

I pushed out of the chair and paced the length of the worn oriental rug. Of course I didn't want to screw things up. But Joseph Trent needed to know, in the deepest place in his soul, what he'd done. My stride grew longer and the room suddenly felt too small for all the things I was feeling. When I reached one wall and pivoted, I nearly ran into B. H. Hovanian.

He put his arms around me and held me close to him. I squirmed, and then felt my body sag as his strong arms encircled me. Tears of anger rolled down my cheeks and my breathing slowed gradually. When I finally exhaled and then took in a shuddering gulp of air, he loosened his grip and stepped back.

"Call Trent," he said softly. "I'll ask Castro to phone my cell when they've got him cuffed. We'll go over to the store before they take him away. You're right. He needs to know."

I threw my arms around his neck and hugged him, glad that he understood so thoroughly. "Thank you. For being human."

"That's a first — I'll have to parse that compliment later. You make that call." He handed me a tissue. "Be indignant and don't forget to say that you're in Brooklyn. And make sure you tell him that you haven't told anyone else, that you want to hear his explanation before you call the police."

"Which is probably what Marjorie did, poor thing. Gave him the benefit of the doubt and ended up dead." I needed to do it before I dissolved in the muddle of emotions that raged through me. I dug my cell phone from my purse and dialed the pharmacy number.

With each ring, my calm, still center grew. By the time Joseph Trent answered, the resolve I needed to do this job right had filled all my empty spaces.

"Mr. Trent, this is Lili Marino. I need to talk to you. It's critical. I'm just leaving Brooklyn now. I should be back in about two hours. I really need to talk to you."

His breath rattled across the line. "What's this about?"

"It's, uh . . ." Let him know you're angry, I reminded myself, or at least upset. "It's about Connie Lovett. There's a problem with her meds. Before I go to the police I want to hear what you have to say."

"The police? Can't you tell me what this is about?" His voice was higher now, quavery.

Good. He was afraid. Now I needed to convince him that I was vulnerable, so that his murderous, cheating brain would start spinning out a plan to deal with me, the way he'd dealt with Marjorie.

"I already told you. It's about Connie and her prescription. Now, will you talk to me or should I go right to Sheriff Murphy? I'm really upset. I'm not going to wait forever. What are you going to do? Are you going to talk me, Mr. Trent?" The edge of impatience in my voice might have been too much, but I doubted he was listening for nuances at this point.

Joseph Trent sighed. "I don't know what you're talking about. But you sound very upset. I'll see you, but only to put your mind at rest about whatever it is that you're worried about. The store is closing in an hour, so why don't you come to my house straight from the city? Is that all right?"

So that you can destroy any evidence you might have overlooked, and then when I get there you'll tell me that you want to take a walk — and find a way to kill me?

"Sure, that's fine. I'll see you in —" I stopped myself before I blew the whole thing. I was supposed to be in Brooklyn. "— in two hours, maybe more, depending on traffic."

He clicked off without saying good-bye.

B.H. nodded. "Now we sit. He thinks he has two hours. Castro's watching him. I don't think we'll have a long wait. He's scared. He'll try to cover his tracks."

From the office window, I could see people coming and going from Trent's. Only, nobody had left the store since a young woman and her toddler had gone skipping down the steps, and nobody had entered, nobody in uniform, nobody carrying a drawn gun, nobody with a reason to arrest Joseph Trent. Yet.

"It's twenty minutes already. What do you think he's doing?" I slapped my hand on the windowsill with a thud. Hovanian shot an annoyed glance in my direction. I was about to apologize when a blur of motion below caught my attention. "Wait. There she is!"

Michele Castro's ponytail swung like a pendulum as she raced across the street and up the steps of the pharmacy. Three other officers followed behind her. Two cruisers, lights spinning but sirens off, pulled up into the alley behind the store.

"Okay," B.H. said, "I knew it couldn't be much longer. Are you sure you want to do this? You don't have to, you know. You can just go home and get on with living the rest of your life. Let the system do its job. Start thinking about other things."

That was probably the wise course of action, but I was angrier than I was wise. I'd put the situation behind me after I let Trent know how I felt. All the mediation talk about forgiveness seemed like nothing more than Girl Scout ideas. Maybe I could forgive eventually. But not until I'd confronted my demons. Including Joseph Trent.

I pushed my chair back and headed for the door. He was right behind me, then right beside me. The pace quickened as I followed Hovanian's long stride. Down the stairs, out onto the street. He stopped traffic as though he were parting the Red Sea. We arrived at the entrance to the pharmacy at the same time. A uniformed officer greeted us by blocking our way.

"Officer Castro said we could go inside," I told him. "Lili Marino and B. H. Hovanian."

He nodded, pressed a button on his walkie talkie, said our names. The phone crackled, and I heard Michele Castro's voice, telling him that it was all right for us to go inside.

I almost backed away and ran down the porch stairs to the street. But when I looked through the glass and saw the back of Joseph Trent's head, my anger returned, and with it my courage. The officer pushed open the door and stood aside to allow us to enter.

The pharmacy was a beehive of activity, deputies swarming over the cash register, carrying computer equipment out to the van that was parked in the alley behind the stores, dusting for fingerprints. Michele Castro nodded at us, and we walked to the prescription counter.

"Mr. Trent won't talk until he's got a lawyer. He called your office, Mr. Hovanian, but you weren't there. He already knows I'll be taping anything he might say."

The store lights seemed to brighten and then dim. I never even considered that Joseph Trent might hire B.H. to defend him. But that was foolish. Given his reputation, his would be the first name that would pop into a local resident's mind. I blinked back my disbelief and pressed my lips together.

"Well, I'm here now." B.H. stepped around the chair and looked down at Joseph Trent. I stood frozen, unable to see Trent's face, struggling to breathe.

"I need an attorney." The pharmacist's voice was barely a squeak, but he'd managed to get the words out.

B.H.'s eyes smoldered as he looked down at the man in the chair. "It looks that way. Tell me why. Why do you need a lawyer?"

The bustle of activity continued around us, but it felt as though all that motion was happening in another dimension. All that existed for me was a nine square foot space containing Michele Castro, Joseph Trent, and B. H. Hovanian.

"I'm being accused of murder," Trent whispered. He hung his head, avoiding Hovanian's gaze.

Michele Castro reached down and touched something on her utility belt. A tape recorder. She'd turned it on.

"Whose murder?" Hovanian asked. When Trent mumbled something, Hovanian said, "I didn't hear you. Please pick your head up and tell me who you're being accused of murdering."

Trent's head lifted but his shoulders sagged. "Marjorie Mellon. They're saying I killed Marjorie."

"Anything else?" Hovanian folded his arms across his chest.

"They say that I . . ." Joseph Trent pushed his glasses to the top of his head and rubbed at his eyes. A sob caught in his throat. "They were going to die anyway. Those people were very sick. I was going to lose the store if I didn't do something. They were going to die anyway."

When I caught my breath, I started to move forward but something in B.H.'s eyes stopped me.

"We're all going to die, Mr. Trent. Those people might have had months or years to be with the people they loved. If they'd gotten the right medicine. I'm sorry, but you'll have to find someone else to represent you." He peered down at Trent, his craggy face impassive, and then he stepped out of the

415

circle. When he looked at me he raised his eyebrows in a question.

Trent's hunched back was wracked with sobs.

I shook my head and waited for B.H. to step from behind the counter. Michele Castro pulled a still-sobbing Trent to a standing position, her face emotionless. I wondered how she could keep from being a little rougher, a little harsher with someone like Joseph Trent, but her control kept her movements firm, as though a television camera were recording her actions for the six o'clock news.

With a hand on my elbow, B.H. led me to the door, tapped, waited for the officer to let us out. I inhaled deeply, glad for the sweetness of the air.

"You didn't say anything." B.H. headed for the steps, and I followed.

"But you did. Thank you. You said it clearly. Without the drama." I stopped before we reached the sidewalk. A small crowd had gathered, buzzing and pointing at the store. As we drew closer, they fell silent. "And you declined to represent him. I have to admit, I was a little surprised."

His generous mouth grew wider as he smiled. "Good. I didn't want things to be too predictable between us."

The crowd parted. As soon as we passed, the buzzing started again, louder this time. "What's happening in there, B.H.?" someone called out.

"You know I can't talk about active cases," he said over his shoulder, and then smiled at me. It wasn't his active case, but nobody knew that yet. His hand rested lightly on my elbow as he steered me toward my car. "You want some company? I don't feel like being alone right now."

Another unpredictable turn of events. "How about a drink? I think there's some Scotch somewhere in my house. I don't want to be where people will stare and come up and ask questions about what happened or offer congratulations or anything. I don't even know what I feel about all this except a great relief that it's over."

"Your place. Fifteen minutes," he said as he held my car door open for me.

When he turned to walk to his car, I felt a pang at the thought that he'd be in a separate space. He'd known me better than I knew myself, and I didn't want to let go of that. Not for a very long time.

Chapter 28

"You came back just for this game? That's great!"

Karen swiveled at the sound of Nora's voice and grabbed her in a hug. "Wow, you've got some kind of glow. Not just the game. David and I are going shopping tomorrow in the Berkshires. Hey, Nora, you think we can get away with convincing them we can play partners again?"

Both Elizabeth's eyebrows rose at the same time. "No way, you two. Fool me once, you know the rest."

Nobody would fool Elizabeth twice, and that was a blessing in my life — another blessing. That Connie was now on the real drugs, and looking stronger and feeling better, was the biggest one. Her doctor, chagrined that he hadn't suspected sooner, was delighted and hopeful, and Connie's gourds showed an exuberance that made me feel lucky to be part of her life. Joseph Trent would never dim another light, would not diminish the glow I felt when I looked around and saw my friends sitting around the table without an undercurrent of dissension, hurt, and anger crackling around the room.

"Joseph Trent thought he was going to fool me twice. You know that those white pills he was calling valerian were really crushed up aspirin. B.H. says that he spilled not only all the beans but some of the rice, too. He was setting me up so that if I caused trouble, he could just give me something stronger and I'd be history." I passed the chips to the center of the table.

"You have to wonder — was he a sociopath? I mean, isn't the definition someone who cannot empathize, who has no sense of how other people will be affected by his action? I see a kid like that every couple of years, and it's so scary." Susan flicked her red hair off her forehead and frowned thoughtfully into her wine glass. "Maybe it was just how he responded to the changes up here. I could see it in his face and hear it in everything he said. He'd gotten more and more bitter in the past two years. You know, the chains driving out Mom and Pop businesses. Lifelong service and what do you get, all that. But I'd never have imagined that he'd be greedy enough to do such a thing."

"Not greed, I don't think, even though that's how it might look." Like the Caterra-Smith mediation, what looked like greed at the start was revealed to be something else by the end. In the case of Joseph Trent, it was more like self-preservation born of desperation. "The man didn't know what to do. Profits down, heating costs and taxes up, those kids in college and all. His poor wife — she kept cutting corners and scrimping but the business was going under."

Melissa's scowl deepened. "He killed Aunt Bernie. And Rod Phillips."

"And he got away with it," Elizabeth said, "which gave him license to keep going. His desperation must have kept growing until it became so consuming that it burned up his sense of right and wrong."

"So consuming he didn't even realize that he was planting evidence that could help convict him. Remember that address book that turned up under my stove? Castro finally admitted that no one in her department had checked under the stove during those searches." I still couldn't believe that mild Joseph Trent had slipped into my kitchen and planted Marjorie's little red book where he hoped the police would find it. "Those notes I saw — they were short-hand for one of the expensive meds. Kytril. It's an anti-nausea drug for people on certain chemos and it costs eighty-five dollars a pill. One single, tiny little pill."

Susan glared in outrage. "I cannot bear to have *that* discussion now. It's one of those things that drives me crazy. I know big pharma has to spend money to develop new drugs, but those executives aren't giving up their private planes and four homes and . . ."

"But still. Joseph Trent saw those high prices as an opportunity to help pay his bills." Elizabeth sipped from her wine.

"Now he's going to pay in a different way." I took little satisfaction in the telling. The whole thing left me sad. "B.H. says that Marjorie called him and hinted that she'd found something that she needed to ask him about. He looked around and realized that his books, the ones that almost got burned by Anita, were missing. He got frantic looking for them until he put everything together. So he talked her into a meeting. Smart cookie that she was, she demanded that it be in a public place. He convinced her to drive with him to a diner somewhere."

"Mistake. Big mistake. That one little slip made all the difference." Melissa chewed thoughtfully. "If she'd been a little more careful . . .”

I nodded. “She got in that car with him. Wrong. And he pulled over in the woods, dragged her out of the car and shot her.”

“Blackmail.” Karen nodded and looked around the table. “I bet Marjorie was trying to blackmail him. You think?”

“No. She was just furious.” I was about to start another sentence with “B.H. says” but I caught myself. “I heard that she told Trent she was going to the police. That she told him she couldn’t let him kill anyone else. And that those words were the last she ever said in this world.”

“But why hide the gun in your house? Why not destroy it or take it somewhere far away? If he was smart enough to come up with this scheme, then surely he would have planned out how to get rid of the murder weapon?”

“Plans get interrupted.”

Everyone looked at Karen.

“What?” She swiveled the silver ring on her index finger. “A car was coming or something and he panicked and ran. Saw Lili’s house, saw that no one was home and hid the rifle. Isn’t that what happened?”

I nodded my confirmation.

“At least we had that part right.” Nora laughed. “And like we’ve been saying for a while, once that happened, he started to do as much as he could think of to make it look like Lili was the killer."

"B.H. says Trent's printer is the one that produced that note that was found in Wonderland Toy Town. And he put that address book under my stove the day before he planted the note, hoping the police would do another thorough search of the house. So yes, he was a man on a mission."

Stretching her long legs, Elizabeth made elaborate yawning motions. "Oh dear, I didn't come here to sit through this rerun. What about our so-called game? As I recall, this is poker night."

This rerun, as she called it, had been playing in my mind for days. Hovanian's visit the day after Trent was arrested had been full of interesting details about the case. But most of my mental replay centered around the sizzle of one electric kiss that stopped conversation for what felt like five minutes. I'd pulled away first and had sublimated all my confusion into questions about what would happen next.

Obligingly, B.H. had filled in many of the missing pieces, but no matter how I played it back, I couldn't understand how Joseph Trent had managed to cross the line from healer to murderer. Even before he shot

Marjorie, that was what the man had been doing. Deciding who should live, who didn't deserve the chance that the drugs might produce a miracle, however temporary.

I was startled out of my reflections by a card sliding across the table toward me. Karen was dealing, Susan sitting out the hand. Everyone watched until I picked up my little packet. Then they picked up theirs, each doing the elaborate fan-and-shuffle that would help them play better . . . or fool the rest of us more completely.

Five card stud — what my brother would call real poker — brought out the serious actor in my friends. Which made it harder to read their faces. My strategy for the past several poker nights had been to ignore everyone else and concentrate on my own hand, and my face. Now I wanted to show them consternation. What should I do? Hold 'em or fold 'em?

King of diamonds, king of spades. I looked at two more cards. Queen of clubs, queen of spades. My heart banged wildly as I spread the final card.

King of hearts. A full house.

No question that I was holding 'em this time. But how to bet? Now that became the real dilemma. I didn't want to scare the others out of the pot, which I'd surely do if I didn't exchange any cards and also bet fifty cents. Enough to buy the book on African art that Berge had suggested might interest me — that was my goal for tonight.

"So, what did Seth say when you told him?" Nora smiled and everyone else looked up from their hands and focused on me.

"Told him?" I repeated, stalling for time. "Told him what?"

Wrong maneuver. Now I had everyone's undivided attention.

"That he was no longer . . ." Melissa laughed and reached into the bowl for a handful of peanuts. ". . . on your list of suspects."

Susan's eyes flashed. "Or is it that he's no longer on your list?"

"Wait!" Elizabeth held her hand up, palm out. Her smile crinkled the corners of her eyes. "Don't answer yet. I heard from our esteemed mayor that Tom Ford has some ideas about how to grow Walden Corners now that the referendum is over. The casino's not happening but we still need to figure out how to keep the town going. Patronski says that Tom's coming to town to share some ideas. Maybe get involved in a big way. And maybe, just maybe, there's more to his return than a desire to sustain growth. Well, the growth of the town, anyway. He might be interested in cultivating other things. So, just how long is your list, Lili, my dear?"

My poker face failed me. Tom Ford, back in town? In the flesh? What kind of flesh he inhabited had been such a part of my mental meanderings for so long that the thought of finding out started an internal war. Our connection had been so odd that I'd let him become A Possibility, and now I was caught between conflicting desires. I yearned to know what he looked like. But while the reality might satisfy or it might disappoint, it would surely wipe out the tantalizing fantasies.

And then what would happen to the forward march of my attraction to Berge Hartounian Hovanian?

By the second round, Nora, Elizabeth, and Melissa had folded. Susan stood behind me, then moved to the same position behind Karen's chair, her face revealing nothing.

"Well, let's play poker here," I said, donning my innocent smile. "I'm going to raise fifty cents."

Karen nodded and frowned. "Showdown. But not until I raise you a quarter."

Maybe she had a royal flush, but I wasn't giving up now. We both pushed our chips to the nice little pile in the center of the table.

Win or lose, the idea that I had options was intriguing. I might not be in control of the outcome, but I certainly wouldn't be bored. I was holding three kings, and that was bound to play out in some very interesting ways.